FORTY-SIXTH STREET SMASH

Dennis Petrone

Cover Design by Art Boonklan

ISBN: 1511866950
ISBN 13: 9781511866958
Library of Congress Control Number: 2016900334
Createspace Independent Publishing Platform
North Charleston, South Carolina

Dedicated to everyone who recognizes the importance of having fun in this short life while still doing what they can to make it better.

PREFACE

This book is almost entirely fiction. Almost. Parts of this book are, in a sense, ripped from the headlines. There are a bunch of facts that I incorporated from a real story. But this should in no way be considered a factual retelling of what unfolded. I think of the real facts as trail markers, which I then arranged, filling in the trees.

I returned to my hometown of New York City several years ago, after leaving for college and living overseas for many years. When I arrived, I was practically broke, and finding an affordable apartment to live in seemed nearly impossible. I hit the pavement scoping out neighborhoods, met with low-fee agents, scoured Craigslist, and enlisted the help of some old friends.

One afternoon I got a call from a college buddy now living here with an offer that seemed too good to be true: first dibs on a $1,350-per-month, large studio with newly refinished floors, a fresh coat of paint, and exposed brick on West Forty-Sixth Street in the heart of one of the city's hottest neighborhoods, Hell's Kitchen. It even had a fireplace—not in use, but perfect for candles. At this time, similar places were easily going for $2,000 or more, well out of my budget. Why was it so cheap?

It turns out the former occupant was murdered in the apartment by a man who many presume was his lover. What's more, it was bloody. He was stabbed to death. The place had been sitting empty for months while the owner cleaned and refurbished the space. The killer was caught, the rent reduced, and the apartment put back on the market.

I've never been a superstitious person. Respectful, yes. I'm a Roman-Catholic, Italian-American, fourth-generation New Yorker on both sides, my great-grandparents having come through Ellis Island in the 1890s. But superstitious? No, not really. And I figured if I wasn't willing to live in an apartment where someone died—in this case, was murdered—in New York, I might never find a place. After all, many of this city's less expensive rental apartments are in buildings over a century old.

From the moment I walked into the studio on West Forty-Sixth Street, I knew it was home. I felt a warm vibe, and it looked in spectacular condition. I signed a lease and lived there for four years before moving to live with my soon-to-be partner. In the early days of my time there, I read many articles about the crime, the murder. There were nosy neighbors who stopped me to talk about it. And people at local bars and social gatherings brought it up without prompt, not knowing I lived there.

Last fall a friend and I were talking about how that murder could have happened. What were the circumstances that brought one person to murder another? According to the news reports, the man living in the apartment had picked up a guy at the gym. That guy was down on his luck and wound up staying the night. A night turned into a week. A week into a month. Finally, the man—at the prompting of his friends—worked up the courage to kick the guy out. A fight ensued, and the former tenant was killed by his unwanted guest. The killer took the victim's credit card and headed north to Vermont. It didn't take long for the NYPD to catch him.

Anyone can look up the facts of the true story. In consideration of those facts, coupled with my own life experiences and a healthy dose of imagination, I created the story you are about to read. While the murder and my curiosity about it were my catalysts for writing this book, the world it is set in and the characters around it became just as central. Who were these men that quarreled? Lovers? Enemies? But just as important, who were the closest people in their lives before that fatal moment? Were there warning signs? Could they see this coming, or were they so wrapped up in their own lives that they missed signs? And how could this happen? How could a scenario leading to murder plausibly manifest in this apartment, in this neighborhood, in this day and age?

Within the context of fiction, *Forty-Sixth Street Smash* seeks to explore the "how" of a real-life murder—one that occurred in a place I happened to live.

CHAPTER ONE

Time. Time. Time. He wondered if it was moving around him? Was he in it now? Lying in bed, Aaron opened his eyes and checked the time. Even allowing that tiny amount of light in caused his tired pupils to sting, reminding him of how late—or rather, how far into the early morning—his night had gone. He wasn't an early riser by nature, but after several years working in an office environment, his internal clock woke him at precisely eight every morning. Last night the clocks were turned backward for daylight saving, so this morning he woke at seven. Aaron's next thought as his hangover began to wash over his consciousness was that he was getting too old for closing a neighborhood bar with patrons twenty years his junior. Eyes shut tight again and head swimming, he thought of the saying "Fall, fall back, spring, spring ahead." And for a moment, he allowed himself to fall back into last night's dream, which was all too brief.

Yesterday evening Aaron went to the Ritz on his street just one block east. It was so close that even on nights like last night, when the autumn air dropped colder than was typical and combined with a biting breeze from the nearby Hudson River, he could forgo a jacket or long sleeves, so as not to be hot and burdened once inside. Clad in just a T-shirt and dark jeans, he left his apartment at midnight to meet his friend Greg.

Dashing east the hundred or so steps from his front door, across Ninth Avenue, and to the entrance of the bar was a bit of a wake-up for Aaron. The forty seconds of solid, cold air rode right up his shirt, cutting through the warmth of the strong Red Bull and vodka he had pre-partied with while getting ready. When he didn't catch the light crossing, he decided to play Frogger through incoming traffic to get there faster. This was a decidedly bad idea on a Saturday night, when Jersey kids drove into Manhattan to do some partying of their own. But a blaring car horn and an even quicker sprint got him safely to the line forming outside.

Greg bartended at a local watering hole called the Ninth Avenue Saloon that had been open long before the neighborhood gentrified. He was tall, handsome, and somewhat lanky, though he tried to counter that by hitting the gym a few times a week and doing a half hour of pushups before going out. Working on his feet kept him slim too, even after he started taking on more of a management position. While he ran the back-of-the-house paperwork and inventory, he still bartended for the extra cash from tips during the week, when it was typically slower. He liked this schedule because it allowed him something of a normal workweek, where he could go out on the weekends—something he was rarely able to do over the past two decades. Greg liked hanging with Aaron because he felt they were both making up for lost time, Greg having worked too many weekends and Aaron having recently gotten out of a relationship.

Cutting past the front of the crowded bar on the first floor and hooking a sharp right up the stairs to the second, Aaron found Greg chatting with a muscled-up, pretty-boy bartender. The two were leaning in close to each other, engaged in a seemingly conspiratorial conversation in order to talk over the bass-heavy pop remix spilling into the room from the adjacent dance floor. Although Aaron was in his early forties and Greg was about the same, the two, Aaron thought, didn't look half bad among the mostly younger crowd of twenty- and thirtysomethings. It reminded him of what Greg often remarked during their late-night shenanigans and occasional afternoon gym sessions: being sexy in New York wasn't about being young, it was about how you carried yourself and what you did with what you had. After all, in a city where more than half of your paycheck went toward rent, there was nothing less sexy than going home with a hot young thing who lived a sixty-minute subway ride away into Queens. Maturity, and the financial stability that hopefully came with it, almost always won out.

Greg turned, spotted Aaron, and waved him over with a smile, just as the pretty-boy bartender left to serve some patrons at the other end of the bar.

"Hey, looky what the cat dragged in," said Greg, looking down slightly into Aaron's eyes. "I got you this." In one hand he held what looked like a vodka cranberry with a tiny plastic bag clinging to the side.

Fortunately, it was dark enough that when Aaron's heart rushed and face blushed with nerves, no one noticed. He quickly took the drink and shoved the tiny plastic bag into his pocket.

"Thanks, *beeeotc*h."

Aaron spent most of his twenties as a catering waiter for various event companies in Manhattan. This was back when he first moved to the city from Alexandria, Virginia, where he grew up and gained most of a degree in communications. Back then, he had too much energy, not enough contacts, and virtually no savings. While he tried to find an entry-level office job when he first arrived, he quickly realized he would never be able to make ends meet at one grade above the unpaid interns. Instead he was happy to be on his feet, working swanky corporate parties in office towers and hotel banquet halls, even if it meant attending them with a tray of hors d'oeuvres.

By the time he was in his early thirties, he found himself in a relationship living with a boyfriend of a couple of years on the west end of Chelsea. In addition to finding domestic comfort and stability—if not, at times, complacency—he also managed to land a full-time gig as a manager at an events company. Eventually, he landed a full-time role managing events for an investment bank. So while he spent more years than he probably cared for serving cocktails and bite-sized quiches to business folk, he was eventually able to transition to that coveted office job with all the perks he never had before, like health insurance and 401(k) benefits.

Now Aaron was single for the first time in what seemed like a hundred years and living on his own in a studio apartment. He was excited to finally reacquaint himself with a side of the city that— because of working events most of his adult life and being in a relationship—he had experienced only like a tourist. He had also recently realized, as those of a certain age often do, that life was short and he wasn't getting any younger—even if he was in better shape physically than he had been in years.

"Let's take these and get our asses onto the dance floor," said Greg, covertly opening the plastic bag.

"That, my friend, sounds like an excellent idea," Aaron responded.

With the extra hour of daylight saving kicking in that night and the Ritz spinning music until what should be five o'clock, an hour longer than when the bar normally stopped serving drinks, the crowd was decidedly in it to win it. The Ritz was always heaving and the dance floor full, but it usually swelled by two in the morning and tapered after three. That wasn't the case this night, as men grinded and gyrated to the DJ pumping out electrifying house-cut remixes of top forty songs interwoven with modern classics.

By five, Aaron was taking drags of a cigarette Greg bummed outside the bar, and the heat from the club was rapidly evaporating. He bid farewell to his friend—knowing he'd see him at the gym this week or out partying the next—and walked down the street back to his apartment, the whole time with a loud bass still pulsing in his head.

CHAPTER TWO

Greg and his boyfriend, Rick, met their best friend, Linda, for brunch at Eatery in the midafternoon that Sunday. Rick was out late like Greg, but at a small apartment party close to where they lived, two and a half blocks west of the Port Authority in an area he liked to refer to as SoHe, or South Hell's Kitchen.

The three settled into a large half-circle booth in the back. Rick had dark, curly hair and a penchant for wearing anything fluoro colored—shirts, sunglasses, caps, whatever took his fancy. Greg, whose head, once seated, towered a full foot above the pair, would often quote Coco Chanel to Rick on their way out of their apartment: always take off the last thing you put on.

"So what did you boys get up to last night," asked Linda, downing the last drops in her champagne flute. She was wearing a huge pair of Dolce & Gabbana sunglasses and what looked to Greg like a small-brimmed sombrero tucking back her dirty-blond hair. Greg thought to himself that Coco would probably lose the hat.

6

"Three more of these," said Rick, indicating to the waiter refills for their bottomless mimosas, which came free with their overpriced brunch. Today it was a fluoro-green sweatband on his left wrist. "I was a good boy and was only out until three. This one over here didn't climb into bed until much later."

"Aw, baby, you know I was thinking about you all night," said Greg. "I was just helping Aaron shake out some of those latent demons. That man can par-tay."

"Well, it takes two, I'm sure," said Rick.

"You're certainly not one to talk," said Linda, sipping her drink practically at the same moment the waiter was done refilling it from a pitcher. "I can remember you doing your fair share of partying and staying out all night not that long ago."

"Girl, that was the nineties," said Rick.

"Please," cut in Greg. "That was last month. Anywho, I scored us some molly and we were at the Ritz all night—not exactly shooting up in the rafters of the Limelight. Besides, it was like Aaron's third time ever, and someone's got to keep an eye on him."

"What's his deal anyway? I remember him from the apple-picking rave, but we really didn't get much of a chance to chat," asked Linda.

"He's a good guy. He broke up with his boyfriend of forever and I think he's just sowing his oats," said Greg. "Besides, I've kind of known him for years. He's been coming into the Saloon for as long as I can remember. We just didn't really hang out until recently."

"Well, you can bring him around next time we have a chillout at my place," said Linda. "It seems there's always a single guy around on the prowl."

"I don't think that's what's he's looking for," said Greg. "It's not like there are a shortage of randy men in this neighborhood. I don't know. Maybe he's looking for something more."

"Or maybe he's just lonely," said Rick. "Besides, it might be nice to have my boyfriend back."

"Whatever," said Greg. "It's not like you have anything to worry about. Aaron's a top."

"Gross," said Linda. "I do plan to eat whenever this food decides to get here."

Greg and Aaron had known each other for longer than either of them initially remembered. Back when Aaron first moved to the city, Ninth Avenue Saloon was one of the only friendly bars in Hell's Kitchen, and Greg was bartending practically every night of the week. It wasn't that Aaron was a regular, but occasionally he would find himself between catering gigs in Midtown and needed a place to sit for an hour, so he'd grab a beer. Then later, when his relationship was on the rocks and he was secretly looking at apartments in the increasingly popular Hell's Kitchen, he remembered the Saloon as a safe place and started stopping in again.

About six months ago, Greg and Aaron began socializing outside of the Saloon. Over time the two built a rapport and eventually a friendship. Being the consummate bartender, Greg listened to Aaron talk about his relationship with his ex and how it had fizzled unceremoniously. The two would grab coffee and then started meeting up at the gym they both belonged to and working out together. Rick met Aaron a few times, but the three rarely hung out together. While Greg and Aaron wanted to party and dance, Rick preferred a glass of wine—or three— and being able to actually hear a conversation. Since he was never one to be the jealous type, Rick didn't mind Greg having friends outside their regular circle, as they had been together for what felt like forever, and it wasn't uncommon for them to socialize separately from time to time. They both considered it a strength of their relationship, even if it was never formally discussed.

Rick flipped a book of matches between his index, middle, and ring fingers, then back again. It had a fork and knife logo on the back and the name of the restaurant, Eatery, on the front. It was a happening brunch spot in Hell's Kitchen. It sat on a bright corner on West Fifty-Third Street and Ninth Avenue, facing northwest. There were several tables outside on the avenue, where, in the warmer months, patrons could sit and bring their dogs, which were normally the small-apartment-friendly breeds—shih tzus, dachshunds, pugs. By November, most days were too chilly to sit outside, so the chairs sat stacked. Inside, the space was large and industrial with glass tables, heavy aluminum chairs, and a concrete floor. Despite its decidedly modern decor, Eatery was actually very warm—mostly because of the throngs who frequented the joint, often waiting up to an hour for brunch, including the ever-popular unlimited mimosas or bloody marys. Cute waiters in tight black shirts and ankle-length aprons buzzed about. Its guests included a cross of locals who spent their Saturday nights partying late on poppy dance floors, like Greg, and those who were hanging out more casually with wine and board games at a friend's apartment, like Rick.

"I mean, where does this guy get off?" said Linda, speaking of last night's trick with some Wall Street suit.

"Apparently at your apartment," said Rick halfheartedly, under his breath but clearly loud enough for Linda to hear. She acted as though she didn't.

"Can you believe he actually said to me that there is a shortage of eligible men in the city?" said Linda. "Like that was his big sales pitch."

"Well, for most women, there is a shortage," said Greg. "Isn't that what you're always saying?"

"Well, yeah," said Linda. "But it's different when I say it. He's the man. He's supposed to say some cheesy crap about how he can't seem to meet gorgeous, eligible women like me in the city."

"But you slept with him anyhow," said Rick.

"I mean, it was Saturday night and we had already been out once," said Linda. "What was I supposed to do? Tell him no?"

"Been out once?" asked Rick.

"Well, maybe not so much as out," said Linda. "More like we spent a few hours at the bar of Ted's Grill near my office building."

"Right, so is he at least hot? Are you into him?" asked Greg.

"Well, yeah," said Linda. "But that's not the point. Do you know who the eligible straight men in this town are? Lawyers, Wall Street financial types, and married guys living in suburbia who take off their wedding rings at happy hours. Thanks, but no thanks."

"Eligible, you say? Look, but you slept with him anyhow," said Rick.

"Will you shut up and order us another round before they run out?" said Linda.

"Testy," said Rick.

✎

After seeing the boys off from a boozy brunch that left Linda's head swimming behind her dark, wide sunglasses in the bright, cool afternoon, she walked home to her apartment on the Upper West Side. She grinned widely as she passed her doorman but didn't stop to say hello, catching the elevator doors opening and stepping aside to let an elderly woman with a cane walk past.

Up in her twentieth-floor, two-bedroom apartment, Linda stretched out on her sofa, which was catty-corner to a huge floor-to-ceiling window with a partial view—between a couple of buildings—of Central Park. Without getting up, she reached down next to the sofa, found a small box, removed a skinny joint, and sparked it.

Linda grew up in Yonkers, just north of the city. Her father was a director at a boutique brokerage firm, and her mother was a lawyer. Both commuted back and forth to Midtown each day. When Linda was little, she loved when her mother took her to Central Park on the occasional weekend, when she wasn't working.

11

Linda was always fascinated by all the animals moving and living in between people—largely unnoticed, independent. People had dogs, of course, and there were lots of them always out in the park. But she loved the not-so-shy squirrels, scurrying around, jumping through trees, collecting nuts, and the noisy birds that adjusted to their urban environment, nesting in this greenery in the middle of Manhattan. She remembered a story her mother told her once about a wolf who had wandered down into the park from the north. It lived there unnoticed for months, feeding on pigeons and ducks. It was believed that the lone wolf had followed the Hudson River into the city. Linda's mother told her never to wander through the park alone, because you never knew what could be lurking in the brush.

In her teen years, Linda reflected on the story. She realized there probably hadn't been wolves in North America in a very long time, centuries even, and that it was likely a coyote at best. But there was something about the story. It was said to have happened in the late seventies in New York, when Central Park wasn't the safe, manicured place it later became. Maybe that wolf wasn't there to cause mayhem. Maybe it was there for another reason. Linda felt that she was just like the lone wolf: a city dweller at heart, breaking the rules, living unnoticed where she was conventionally not supposed to survive, living in between the people. Fierce and independent at heart.

Linda took a last pull of the smoldering joint and placed it on a plate on her coffee table. She slid into the couch. At the end of high school, Linda was accepted at NYU. Her parents insisted she commute to class each day from Yonkers to save money, rather than stay in the dorms like almost all of the other students. But after her sophomore year, she moved into a small studio apartment in the East Village. She had managed to allay the reservations of her parents by pointing out that it was cheaper than living in the dorms and that this particular building was a very safe one, on a busy, well-lit corner far enough north of Houston, west of Alphabet City, and, according to some maps, practically in Union Square.

From that dingy apartment, she eventually graduated into this one. Linda had an impressive resume with a degree in business management from NYU and an MBA from Columbia, plus international experience, having worked in London for many years as a full-time business consultant. She could have secured a job as a chief financial officer or president of sales. But Linda wasn't interested in a senior management role. Instead, for the last decade, she had been a sales director, peddling advertising spots on television and radio. She was making more with a carefully guarded portfolio of clients than she would probably make at a higher level. But even if that weren't the case, she didn't want the stress of more responsibility and managing people. Sales had always come easy to her. And having never been married, never having kids, and never seeing a reason to bother with owning so much as a goldfish, Linda decided long ago to find contentment on her own—the lone wolf.

Linda sat up on her couch and propped her feet on the coffee table. She reached for a remote, which she used to turn on the recessed lighting against built-in mahogany cabinets on one wall that housed her television and electronics. With another button, she turned on music—light modern jazz, the kind without any lyrics that seems to wrap in on itself in a loop.

The afternoon was drawing to a close, and the few clouds in the sky had turned dark blue and pink. Across the park, on the East Side, it looked as though night had already fallen, and it was slowly making its way to her apartment. She thought about Greg and Rick and what a perfect couple they seemed—kind of in sync, but also completely happy to have separate nights out and social lives when they wanted. Maybe in some ways they were like two wolves that lived together. After all, Greg was able to get high and roll with Aaron, and Rick was fine with it. That's trust, she thought. Isn't it?

Linda considered Aaron, by contrast. She was curious who this guy was. She remembered him from a huge apple-picking party that Greg threw. He seemed like a fun guy, dressed for the occasion, kind of like a lewd farmer. He was smiling, laughing, and horsing around most of the time. She remembered there was also a live band with several banjo players. Aaron was swinging all these people around and do-si-do-ing. While Greg invited a ton of people that day, many of whom he met through work, he was a decent judge of character, especially when it came to letting people in the inner circle, and it seemed Aaron was gaining access.

Then Linda sighed and thought about Wall Street from last night, and what he felt like pressed against her in bed, and how warm she had felt then, despite her own best efforts. She shouldn't see him again. She definitely shouldn't reach out to him right there and then. She would seem desperate, or slutty, or both—a desperate slut.

"No one likes a desperate slut, Linda," she said aloud to no one but herself. "Except a Wall Street douche bag." Then she messaged him.

CHAPTER THREE

*K*nock. *Knock. Knock.* Aaron opened the door to his neighbor Nikki from across the hall. They had lived across from each other for over two years. Nikki was English and a redhead, though probably not naturally. She was a flight attendant for British Airways and, although based in New York, spent about half her time in the air or in London. From the first week Aaron moved into his apartment, following a brief introduction to Nikki, he started slipping twenty dollars a month under her door in exchange for her wireless Internet. Living alone, he had taken to attempting to be frugal by, for example, splitting at least one expense with someone, whereas previously he was able to split every expense when he lived with a boyfriend. Also, this way he didn't have to deal with the wires, Internet box, or paying the monthly bill.

From Nikki's perspective, she had twenty dollars a month to purchase a couple of bottles of wine, or a twelve pack of lager, which was why whenever she was having friends over for a party, she would remember to invite Aaron.

"Hey, Aaron," shouted Nikki over Britney Spears billowing from her place. "Can you pop around this evening for a boogie? I'm having some of the girls over, and my cute friend Tim, who I think took a fancy to you last time, is coming too."

Aaron laughed. "Absolutely," he said. "Probably just for a hot second, though. It's been a hell of a week, and I had an event last night that didn't wrap until midnight."

It was Friday night. Aaron spent most of last Sunday nursing a hangover, lying on his couch with his feet up on the coffee table, forcing himself to hydrate while watching really bad television. It wasn't that his late night at the Ritz was particularly alcohol infused, or that the MDMA was so intense, but he found after taking the drug the first two times that he liked countering the comedown with a Xanax the next day to mellow out. That mellow usually saw him in a fairly zombie-like state at the office on Monday. He really didn't shake it off until working out for almost two hours at the gym with Greg on Tuesday, followed by a visit to the steam room. Needless to say, by the time his work event wrapped on Thursday—a real snoozer of a panel discussion and cocktail party, hosted at the top of Hearst Tower by a bunch of investors from his firm—he was more than beat.

"Well, come by when you're ready," said Nikki. "People should be here at any time."

"Sweet," he said. "I'll just put on a clean shirt."

Back in his apartment with the door closed, Aaron slipped off his work shirt, walked over to the refrigerator, and cracked a bottle of beer. From his place, even with "Womanizer, woman-womanizer, you're a womanizer" cranking at nearly full volume next door, he could barely make out the faintest of sounds through the wall. Although Nikki's door was across from his, their two units were in the back of the building, so they shared a wall. The building was over a hundred years old, and when they chopped the floor into studio apartments at some stage long ago, fire walls were installed between the units and leading into the hallways, making them both fire safe and virtually soundproof. The only noise Aaron could occasionally make out was from his neighbor above, a bachelor who brought girls back late at night for loud, long romps. He could often hear high-pitched moaning from the girls through the ceiling, and a bed squeaking, but he rarely heard the guy make a peep. Typical.

Aaron turned on the radio and started rummaging through his closet. He was halfway through his beer when he finally decided on a T-shirt after putting on and taking off three contenders. It wasn't that he was nervous; it was just that this Tim-boy was an adorable hottie, and about ten years younger. When Aaron started getting back into the game, he also started to pay more attention to his body, specifically his midriff and that awful pouch of flab that had somehow appeared during his years of domesticity. He wasn't terribly out of shape, but after working out very regularly now, he had finally gotten himself into good enough shape that he was comfortable taking off his shirt in front of someone else.

Looking in the bathroom mirror, he readied himself to casually pop across the hall in the kind of way that hinted how he couldn't care less, but just happened to swing by. Play it cool, old man, Aaron thought to himself. He moisturized with two different kinds of pricy lotions, one for under his eyes and one for the rest of his face. He warmed some gel between his palms and pushed it through his hair, of which, fortunately, he had plenty—several inches long, wavy on the top, and buzzed very short along the sides. He never minded the gray that popped up because he figured it was better to age with grace than it was to start looking artificial. The shirt he picked was the exact shade—not by coincidence—of his gray-blue eyes. And he sprayed just the absolute tiniest mist of cologne through the air and walked through it, so as to smell good but not like a hustler from a porn flick in the seventies. He finished the last swig of his beer and he felt ready. Bring it on, Tim-boy, bring it on.

Knock. Knock. Knock. Nikki opened her door wearing a red feather boa and a red masquerade mask. Instead of Britney Spears blaring, this time it was Michael Jackson and at half the volume.

"Johnny, old chap," she said. "Come on in. We were just talking about our Halloweens and decided it was definitely costume season."

"Right," said Aaron. "But it's November now. Shouldn't they be Thanksgiving themed?"

"Oh, don't be such a literal Yankee Doodle," she responded.

He kissed her on both cheeks, walked in, and put the six-pack of beer he grabbed from his refrigerator into hers.

"Darling, you didn't have to bring refreshments," she said. "I'm making punch."

Nikki was stirring a pot on the stove with what looked like Kool-Aid, bug juice. Aaron couldn't imagine what kind of alcohol she mixed in it this time. The last time she made punch, he remembered his tongue turning red and his stomach burning after just two small cups.

As Nikki stirred the punch with a wooden spoon in one hand and emptied a label-less bottle of white hard liquor into the pot with the other, she shouted over her shoulder at the group of three sitting on her couch on the other side of the room.

"You guys remember my neighbor Aaron, don't you? I think you all met before."

Sitting on the couch were Tim-boy, drinking a beer from the bottle, and two girls on either side whom Aaron had met before, though he couldn't remember their names. The table in front of them was covered in about a dozen lit candles of different colors and sizes.

Nikki's apartment was a mirror opposite of Aaron's. Along the wall they shared was an L-shaped couch and a coffee table. The floors were wood. The wall across from the couch was brick with a fireplace, the flues of which had probably not been cleaned in decades, if not longer, so they could only be used for things like candles or storage. Nikki was using hers to house her cable box, DVD player, and other electronics, mounting her TV above it. To the right of the fireplace and TV was a queen-sized bed sandwiched on two sides into the corner. On the far wall were two large windows that looked out to the back of a building and, one floor down, a concrete backyard that was communal space, shared by all the tenants. The great thing about Nikki's and Aaron's apartments was that whereas most studios had only one room, theirs had two. There was the main room for a bed, couch, and television, and a smaller second room for the kitchen, big enough to fit a table that sat four or even six in a pinch. In the kitchen were two doors—one leading to the hallway and the other to a small but full-sized bathroom. All in all, this was a great layout for a studio apartment, as it managed to make a modest four hundred square feet feel much larger.

Tim sat flanked on either side by the girls. He wore a blue, short-sleeved, button-down shirt and an orange bow tie. His dark brown hair was slicked over to one side, and although he was in his early thirties, his face had a certain healthy youthfulness that made many hearts flutter, including Aaron's. The only trouble was that Tim could be shy at times and, on occasion, even had a hard time making eye contact. But this too, Aaron thought, was endearing. For Tim's part, he knew himself well enough to know that a couple of beers helped him relax in social situations.

The last time Aaron was over after a work event was on a Sunday. It was the middle of the afternoon, and he managed to swipe two bottles of champagne while helping break down the space. He held up the bottles when Nikki answered the door and asked if she had any orange juice. Two hours later the pair switched to vodka, and an impromptu dance party erupted with Nikki inviting a dozen people over to join. Aaron vaguely remembered trying to chat Tim-boy up in the corner to get him to laugh. Tim clearly remembered Aaron as the hot neighbor from across the hall who kept rattling off cheesy, dirty jokes.

"Tim," said Aaron, crossing over into the main room. "Ladies," he said, nodding his head as if almost in a chivalrous half bow.

"Hey," each chimed, almost in unison.

The girls to either side of Tim looked a little stoned, as if they had recently smoked a doobie. Then Nikki came over to thrust a large mason jar into Aaron's hand, filled to the brim with a bright, practically hot-pink-colored punch.

"I need to take the ladies for a cigarette," said Nikki. "Girl talk."

"Um, okay," responded Aaron.

The girls on the couch smiled at each other with droopy eyes and then looked to Nikki.

"You boys stay here for a minute and make sure the place doesn't burn down," said Nikki. "We'll be right back."

Once the door slammed shut and the pair was alone, Tim leaned back, crossed his legs Indian style on the couch, and started pulling at the corner of his shirt. Aaron, needing something to say or do, made a beeline to change the music.

"Call me a curmudgeon, but we need to turn off this Michael Jackson. It's nothing against the music, but I'm kind of over people celebrating a pedophile."

"Please, that is not true," said Tim, sitting up. "Those claims were crap. It was just money-hungry people making up lies to get a payout. MJ's music is solid."

Aaron flipped through Nikki's music library on her player, found the Scissor Sisters, and hit play. The first song on the album, "Take Your Mama," burst through the speakers. He took a big sip of his punch.

"Right, and Michael Jackson having alarms set up that went off whenever somebody walked down the hallway to his bedroom, that was normal," said Aaron.

"He was the King of Pop," said Tim. "Of course he had tight security and crazy alarms. What if someone broke in and was coming to get him in the middle of the night?"

"While he was having a sleepover with Macaulay Culkin?" asked Aaron. "Right."

Aaron crossed over from the speakers and sat on the shorter end of the couch next to Tim.

"And then that doctor who overprescribed drugs and killed him," said Tim. "It's awful. And he only went to prison for like two years."

For Aaron, it was one of those disagreements when people take a different side and stronger opinion because it's fun. It makes for good conversation to get a little rise from someone.

"Michael Jackson had so much money and power," said Aaron. "He would have found a doctor to give him what he wanted prescribed—even if this one didn't."

For as long as Tim could remember, he had loved Michael Jackson. It started when his sister, a few years older than he, began listening to his albums on a loop. Tim and his sister were close, and they would dance around and lip-synch, moonwalking in tube socks on the wood floor between their bedrooms.

Tim was getting flustered. He leaned closer to Aaron diagonally across the table, his face appearing slightly brighter from the flames of the candles.

"Doctors take oaths to protect people," countered Tim, gulping down the last of his beer. "The guy is a criminal."

"I'm not saying he's a saint or anything," said Aaron taking a swig of his punch. At the same moment, Tim shifted his right leg from under himself, which was starting to cramp from the weight of his body. This caused him to sink back suddenly into the couch. He tried to steady himself by jerking out his other foot, but wound up clumsily kicking Aaron from a seated position. This in turn forced the punch back into Aaron's mouth—a much bigger gulp than he intended—and the pink liquid dripped down the side of his face and onto his jeans.

"Jeez, you don't have to get so violent," said Aaron jokingly, wiping his mouth with the side of his hand.

"Oh my Gawd," said Tim. "I'm so sorry. I didn't mean to do that." His face was flushed. "Let me get some paper towels."

"It's fine," said Aaron. "Don't worry about it. I didn't realize you were so passionate about Michael Jackson."

Tim returned with a wet paper towel and started patting the spot where the punch landed on Aaron's jeans.

Aaron leaned in and kissed him. Tim wasn't expecting this and pulled back. Then he paused, leaned forward, and kissed Aaron back. Tim thought that Aaron tasted like sugar and fruit juice, which he liked.

This time Aaron pulled back and said, "When those girls come back, maybe you should come over to my place. I need to change these pants so I can wash them properly before they stain."

Tim smiled, laughing a little under his breath. "You cheeseball," said Tim. After a moment, he said, "Sorry, what I meant to say was, that sounds like fun."

What Aaron didn't know was that before he arrived, Tim was in on the plan that Nikki devised to get the girls out of the apartment so he and Aaron could be alone. They figured this way, the two could see if there was any real chemistry. But what none of them could have guessed was just how much chemistry the two would have—or how quickly they would start hooking up.

CHAPTER FOUR

"You got it. Yes. Almost there. Three, two, one. Nice!" said Greg as Aaron lowered the barbell back onto the bench press's frame. Greg and Aaron often hit the gym hard on Saturday mornings, but today Aaron seemed to be really pushing himself.

"You are definitely lifting more than me now," said Greg. "I'm going to drop this down by thirty for my first rep." He squeezed and then pulled off the clamp on one side of the barbell as Aaron rose to his feet, moving to the spotter position behind the top of the bench.

Urban Workout had only two locations in the city, one in Midtown, where Greg and Aaron went, and the other in Chelsea, thirty blocks south. The Chelsea location housed a pool and yoga studios, and its clientele seemed to be predominantly models and housewives. The Midtown location was comprised mostly of Broadway actors by day and the office crowd in the evenings. Both locations maintained fairly upscale amenities, including a sauna, steam room, and towels.

"Do you feel like checking out Pasha tonight? Or maybe seeing what's happening downtown?" asked Greg. "Rick mentioned that Linda is having some people around her place tonight too, so that could be fun."

"Not too sure about going out on the prowl tonight," said Aaron. "Remember my neighbor Nikki? Well, I went over to her place last night and wound up hooking up with one of her friends."

"Oh, well, do tell," said Greg. "What's his deal? Is he hot?"

"A real cutie," said Aaron. "His name is Tim, and we were hanging out at Nikki's across the hall and then he came back to my place. We wound up going at it most of the night."

As Aaron spoke, Greg lifted and lowered the barbell high above his chest. His brow was starting to sweat, and his torso was getting tighter and tenser.

Aaron continued, "He just moved into an apartment with a roommate somewhere uptown. I think it's just below Harlem, by the sounds of it. I told him I'd rent a car with him to make a run to Ikea this afternoon."

Greg lowered the barbell very slowly down for the final rep of his set. He was breathing heavily and his speech was labored between breaths.

"You're renting a car and you're spending the afternoon driving this guy to Ikea and then up to his place in Harlem?" asked

Greg. "This Tim either has the biggest cock on the West Side or you're nesting after one night."

"It's neither of those things, he's supersweet, and we had a really fun time last night. Besides, it's just what New Yorkers do for each other: help each other without asking for anything in return."

"No, they don't. Who are you anyway?"

The two made their way to a stretching area with mats on the floor and mirrors on two walls. Aaron swung his arms outward, gaining momentum and loosening his back muscles. To his right, Greg was rolling his shoulders in small, circular motions forward. Even though Greg was almost six inches taller than Aaron, and his shoulders were broad, Aaron's stature still looked somehow larger. His chest appeared huge in a white tank top, and even his legs looked so muscular that they could belong to a hockey player. Greg really admired Aaron's dedication and his quick turnaround. For a guy in his early forties who only recently became serious about hitting the gym, his body was already shaping up to look beefy and chiseled.

"When you finish with your Swedish meatballs later, you should come by Linda's," said Greg. "I'll be there then with Rick, and I know Linda and everyone else would love to see you."

"Think it's all right if I invite Tim?" asked Aaron. "I don't know that he'll want to hang out afterward, but I don't think we'll be sick of each other or anything. He's a little shy, but he has a wicked sense of humor."

Greg and Aaron finished stretching. They were at it almost ninety minutes that morning. They mostly worked out as a team when they were together, helping each other with spotting and stretching. They encouraged each other to do larger weights and longer sets.

"I'm beat," said Greg. "Let's head down to the steam room."

"Don't hate me," said Aaron. "I really need to shower and then jet. I'm meeting Tim at the rental car place in an hour."

"And so it begins," said Greg.

"Okay, okay," said Aaron. "Even if this boy doesn't want to go to Linda's later, I'm in. It's Saturday night after all."

"And it's one thing to help a guy make an IKEA furniture run," said Greg. "It's another to spend all night building it for him."

Down in the locker room, Greg stripped down and wrapped his waist in a towel. There were several men around in various states of working out, either changing into their gear or packing up to head home. Saturday morning didn't have the usual businessmen working out, most of who lived outside the city and commuted to Midtown to work and play. It did, though, have plenty of locals, including hospitality staff, like him, who were probably working later. There were even a couple of guys he recognized as dancers from clubs, pumping up before their shifts that evening.

Greg sat in the steam room with his legs stretched out in front of him. Through the fog he could see that there was one other guy in the room with him, with a towel over his head, and he was leaning forward with his elbows on his knees. Greg leaned back and allowed his head to rest on the tiled wall behind him. From where he sat, he could barely see the door through the steam that stood less than eight feet in front of him. It was very warm and he felt very relaxed. He let out a deep exhale.

Greg had been working out for years. Like most men over thirty who still had enough youth left to take their shirt off on a dance floor occasionally, Greg wanted to keep everything in the right place. He had this idea that working out was the kind of thing you did, whether you wanted to or not, for as long as you could still do it. Eventually, he wouldn't do it anymore, and then all of the work leading up to then would come into play, sort of like retirement. He thought of it in the same way he thought of working at the bar. The name of the game was to work as much as possible for as long as he could, so that one day when he couldn't anymore, he wouldn't be poor and homeless. He had seen it before—men in New York who spent too much time partying, using up all their money and energy, leaving themselves financially strapped, physically exhausted. Preservation wasn't enough. It was about improvement and growth.

All of that didn't mean that he didn't like to have fun at times. And as far as he was concerned, most rules were meant to be broken. While he worked hard and saved and tried to always keep Rick a priority in his life, he also knew that he wasn't a robot. Life was best when enjoying it, feeling it, and making the most of it. When Greg went out and danced, he felt alive. He loved the crowds of people, laughing, grinding, living, connecting.

Without a doubt, Greg was the social butterfly in the relationship. Whereas Rick was happy to hang out with a few people on a Saturday night, have dinner, banter, play a board game, Greg needed way more than that to stay entertained. The more the merrier, he thought, and there was never a reason to exclude people. This was the case when they planned a day-trip to go apple and pumpkin picking in Upstate New York. Rick had been excited about it and set up an invite online and included a few of their closest friends. But then Greg, working at the bar and running into so many others who came in to visit, kept extending the invite. He would also be surfing the Internet some nights—weeks before the day—after he came home late from bartending and Rick was already in bed. He would be a few beers deep and one thing would lead to another and before anyone knew it, what started as a day with a few close friends turned into a kind of unofficial Manhattanite takeover of a rural farm sixty miles north of the city. The owners of the orchard probably didn't know what hit them, but they didn't seem to mind, too much. Manhattan came in like an infestation, cleaning the place out of thousands of apples, hundreds of pumpkins, cases of cider, and as many cinnamon doughnuts as the country store clerks in the barn could package.

While most of their group was well behaved, there were a few bad seeds. Some were reprimanded by staff for general mayhem, such as climbing the trees and hooking up in the corn maze. A total dance party took over the square-dancing pit. Others went so far as to smoke pot on the premises or take other illicit substances. And there was plenty of alcohol smuggled in to make the rural day of family fun just that much more rousing.

At first Rick could not help feeling like his Martha Stewart, romantic day out with a few close friends was dashed. But by the end of the outing, he had to admit that it was a blast. And Greg understood. Over the years they were together, Rick had gotten used to this sort of thing. While they might not have known everyone who went intimately, Greg was still sort of the life of the party, almost the ringleader of the whole herd. Rick liked seeing Greg pumped up by this and loved being at his side. And Greg knew Rick liked being there. That was their arrangement, their balance.

The door to the steam room opened, interrupting Greg from his thoughts. The man with the towel over his head now had it around the back of his neck. For the first time, Greg noticed that he was attractive with a shaved head, huge arms, and a wide chest.

"Hey, Hank, how was your workout?" said the man who just entered. He was rather built but slim. Greg thought he looked like an actor, or maybe a model.

"Yeah, great," answered Hank. After a minute, he asked, "Sorry, what was your name again? I've seen you in the weight training room and I know we've met before, but I'm bad with names."

"Perry," he said taking a seat next to him. "You got workout supplements for my friend last week, Vinnie—with the out-of-control mustache?"

"Oh, that's right," said Hank. "I know Vinnie. We've lifted together a few times."

Perry interlaced his hands behind his head, keeping an eye on Hank. Hank seemed to take notice of Perry's chest, lean and long, but looked away. Then Perry stretched his arms in front of himself, still holding his hands together, pulling on one wrist and then the other. He pushed his right arm out, bulging his triceps as much as possible while massaging it. His arms were as slender and toned as the rest of his body.

"I got this new gig down at Pasha dancing on weekends," said Perry, clearly thinking that he had Hank's attention. "You know, you should come down and visit me sometime."

"Sure," said Hank. "I like Pasha. It's a pretty decent space. The drinks are overpriced and there's always a cover, but it's usually a good time."

"I can get your name on the list," said Perry.

"Really?" asked Hank.

"Sure," said Perry. "We are allowed to put a couple of names down each night, if we get them in by nine. The promoter is a pretty cool guy. He wants the place packed."

There was silence between the two men as fresh steam loudly kicked in through a grate on the wall over the door. Its hiss started to wane just as the air became hotter and dense again. Greg closed his eyes; his body felt wet, saturated. But he was content eavesdropping on the conversation and wanted to see where it was going, wondering if this Perry was making an overly eager pass at Hank, who seemed like he might not actually be into guys.

"Sure," said Hank once the room quieted down. "Maybe tonight, if you're working."

"Yeah, yeah, done," said Perry. "You know it's been tough keeping up the bulk for this gig. I've been working out like seven days a week. You know how it is."

"Sure," said Hank. His body was so big and perfectly sculpted, he looked like he maybe had the opposite problem.

"Any chance I can get some of those supplements you got for Vinnie?" asked Perry. "He says they work really great. He's been taking them for less than two weeks and he's already looking bigger. He said he's feeling like he can lift way more too."

"Yeah, sure, I can," said Hank. "Have you taken them before?"

Greg opened his eyes, but not before rolling them as far back into his head as they would go. Oh brother, he thought. 'Roids. Unbeknownst to Greg, Hank was looking straight at him. Greg looked down, grabbed the towel around his waist tighter around the front, stood up, and left for the showers, leaving Hank and Perry to close their...whatever that was. Greg was the last person to judge anyone for doing drugs, but he had seen enough acne-covered muscle marys on the dance floor to know 'roids were bad news.

CHAPTER FIVE

Cocktails and tapas at Linda's apartment snowballed into a much larger affair within hours. Originally, the plan was for Linda, Rick, and a couple of mutual acquaintances to get together. Linda was going to make her specialty tasty tapas from some simple, trusted recipes she had perfected in her college days, which were also by coincidence when she first discovered her affinity for marijuana. She eventually figured out that marijuana served with tapas was an outstanding combination, and Rick was going to top it all off by bringing over a carefully selected, yet abundant collection of wines.

When one acquaintance brought another, and that guy brought another guy, Linda decided to drink a Manhattan instead, given the new mood of the party. Greg called to say he would be coming, which meant a few more people were texted to join. Before she knew it, not only was it a party, but something of a second or third date after her Wall Street guy, Allen, took the bait of her text and was wandering around somewhere. She supposed he could be in her bedroom in her underwear drawer, as apparently that, of all things, was his thing.

"Everybody needs a thing," said Linda to Rick, who was fixing mixed drinks for a couple of people she didn't think she recognized. Fortunately, Linda had a fully stocked bar for just such an occasion. Greg walked in with two bags of ice, and Allen—in what felt like his typical big-brass-balls manner—brought a case of Bollinger Rose Champagne. Not that she was complaining.

"What did you say?" asked Rick, pouring the drinks from a shaker into tall glasses. He was wearing dark jeans and a sports jacket with a hot pink camouflaged T-shirt underneath.

"Everyone needs a thing. You know, a hobby," said Linda. "Like you've got Greg, I've got my tapas, and Allen has my panties."

"Gross," said Rick. "You're already drunk."

"I am not drunk," said Linda, picking up an open bottle of the champagne and pouring it into an empty glass for herself. She figured one Manhattan was enough.

"And Greg is not my hobby, he's my life partner," said Rick.

"Now who's being gross," said Linda.

Rick loved hanging out with Linda, not because she had this fantastic apartment, usually knew how to hold her liquor, or hooked up with suspiciously good-looking men, but because she could be just as snarky as he. Rick spent all week directing the talent managers for one of the bigger record labels. When someone wanted a star to appear on a late-night show or to endorse a product or to make a speech at their son's high school graduation, someone would call someone who would call Rick. It was like being the guy who picks up the poop of the guy who picks up the poop of a dog. The dog being the musician, thought Rick, and the poop being the graduation, or whatever. The point was that all week, he was polite and professional and rarely had conversations of any real substance. So on the weekends, he liked chilling, being impolite, and talking, as Linda called it, a whole lot of smack.

"Come on, Lindy darling," said Rick. "Let's go find Wall Street and get him to show us his nipples or something."

"Down, girl," said Linda. "He's mine."

The two topped up their drinks and walked from the open-room kitchen, past a few revelers, down a short hallway, and into Linda's bedroom. Linda's bedroom had a similar partial view of Central Park as the living room did—only it was on the northeast corner of the building, so it also looked straight up Columbus Avenue. There was a king-sized bed with many coats already piled up, a second bathroom, a full-length vanity mirror, and a dresser. Instead of finding Allen, they found Aaron making out in front of the large window with some young guy. But instead of interrupting, they stopped dead in their tracks and made a U-turn back into the hallway.

Aaron's and Tim's mouths had been fully locked for at least ten minutes, which was about how long they had been at the party. When they arrived, Greg let them into the apartment and told them to drop their coats on the bed in the next room. Afterward, they paused at the window to look at the view—a couple of tall apartment buildings, the paths and roads of Central Park lit up by lampposts, and the East Side in the distance. The sky over Manhattan was rarely completely dark because of all the lights in the city. Tonight, because of a low cloud cover, it looked completely illuminated in a pinkish hue that reflected from the buildings below.

"You're a really good kisser," said Aaron, breaking off from their embrace.

"I guess it takes two," said Tim.

"You must be getting over me," said Aaron. "I feel like we have been together for two days straight now."

"Well, it's technically only been thirty hours with a break for the gym," said Tim. "But who's counting."

Once Nikki returned to her apartment from smoking cigarettes with the girls the night before, Aaron and Tim said they were going across the hall for a few minutes so Aaron could change and they could grab some better music. Nikki saw right through that and told them on their way out, and not so coyly, that there was no hurry.

Back in Aaron's apartment, he and Tim found and put on some music. They also poured drinks, messed around, returned to Nikki's, and repeated that circuit three more times until it was after four in the morning and they decided to just stay at Aaron's and crash.

In the morning, Tim said he needed to go back to his place on 119th Street to try to get his room in some kind of order before taking the ferry over to Red Hook to buy a bed frame and dresser. He had moved into a three-bedroom apartment a few days before—with two roommates already living there—and had been sleeping on a mattress on the floor and living out of garbage bags. The room he had prior to this place, he said, came fully furnished, and he had moved there with essentially nothing but suitcases when he first came to the city about a year ago.

Aaron's heart sank when he thought of this superhot and supernice guy living like a squatter. Besides, Aaron had been there and he remembered what it was like, just getting by without much money or stuff and needing a helping hand. The idea of Tim in his now wrinkled, short-sleeved, button-down shirt and crooked, clip-on bow tie wrangling huge, heavy boxes onto a ferry and then onto a subway was just too cute to bear. He felt he had to help, so he offered Tim a ride in a rental car that he could get a corporate discount on through his job.

Between the ride there, the walk around the showroom, and the ride back across the Brooklyn Bridge, they had plenty of time to talk and get to know each other. While this might have seemed like a long time for two people who barely knew each other to spend together, Aaron and Tim felt comfortable. Aaron filled Tim in on his time in New York, working from catering events to corporate events, and about his time in Chelsea, carefully omitting his ex-partner's name from the narrative. He referred to him only as his ex, and only when necessary.

Tim shared his story with Aaron, though somewhat reluctantly and not in its entirety. Tim told Aaron about growing up in Long Island with his parents and sister. He also told Aaron about living at home during most of his twenties and studying graphic design at Briarcliffe College in Bethpage. His father left when he was a teenager, and then his sister, who was four years younger than he, got pregnant when she was a senior in high school and needed help raising the baby.

What Tim didn't tell Aaron was that as the years went on and his nephew grew, his sister wound up needing much more than just general support. Their mother started drinking heavily again, which Tim thought was probably one of the reasons why their father left in the first place. And his sister started taking advantage of Tim more often, at first relying on him for extra cash, and then later for cleaning, shopping, and even cooking. If Tim didn't cook dinner for her and his nephew, then his sister would pick up unhealthy fast food—burgers, fried chicken, pizza—every night of the week. Once, as an act of defiance and as an experiment to see how long this could go on, Tim didn't cook for two whole weeks. When he confronted her about it, she told him to mind his own business and that it was her son.

The neglect of his nephew didn't stop there. Outside of the little time Tim could dedicate to his nephew, he had virtually no upbringing or childrearing until he started going to kindergarten. He was often dropped in front of a television for entire days. Tim would go to class in the mornings and occasionally stop home in the afternoons before work. It seemed to him that his nephew never left the living room. And his sister and mother during these times would be elsewhere in the house, often not even within earshot. He sometimes wondered if that was intentional.

It took more years than it should have otherwise taken, but Tim managed to finish school. He found consistent freelance work and volunteer jobs, building up his design portfolio. He never made enough money to quit serving tables at various local feel-good chain restaurants, but he kept optimistically applying and submitting his materials to agencies. He spent all of his money on his sister and nephew, and eventually, it would seem, even that wasn't enough for them.

Tim's mother, unbeknownst to him, had secretly taken out multiple credit cards under Tim's name and maxed them out, never making a single payment on the bills. In college, he took student loans through the government because of his and his parents' low incomes. He wanted nothing more than to be financially stable and independent, so he never took out a credit card of his own and only paid for things in cash or by using his debit card.

Years later, he finally found out what his mother was doing when he applied for what he thought was his first credit card. He was rejected several times by different companies over several months. He finally ran a free credit report online. That was when he learned that in addition to the eighty thousand dollars he owed the government for his four-year education, he also owed another twenty-four thousand on seven different credit cards.

Tim thought he could probably buy two of the houses he grew up in for the amount of debt he had hanging over his head. He was still living at home. He confronted his mother, but it was no use. She denied everything. She was so deep in a drunken stupor almost all of the time then. To him, she seemed emotionally comatose and completely useless. It was another two years before he would finally make the move to Manhattan. He landed a part-time design gig at a fledgling agency and was determined to give it his best. So he hugged his nephew, then nine, apologized for leaving, packed two suitcases, and headed west on the Long Island Railroad. Within three months, he was offered a full-time position at the company and started to learn how to breathe again, or perhaps even learn how to breathe properly for the first time ever.

Linda's party humming in the next room took a turn. Someone changed the music to early Madonna, and a couple of people were singing along. Linda's bedroom was also starting to heat up, and Tim thought that unless they were about to really get it on in this stranger's apartment, he and Aaron better take a break and join the group.

"I'm thirsty," said Tim, pulling back. "What do you say to the best cosmopolitan on the West Side?"

"That sounds like an offer I can't turn away," said Aaron. "Listen, before we go and join everyone, I had a really great time today."

"Me too," said Tim. "And thank you again for helping me buy all that stuff and lug it back to my apartment."

"It was fun, and I mean it," said Aaron. "If you need help building everything, I don't mind. I'm pretty handy with one of those little wrenches."

"You have already been so good," said Tim. "If it wasn't for you and Nikki, I don't know how I would have coped with this move. She let me sleep on her couch for a week until the last person moved out of my new room."

"Have you known Nikki a long time?" asked Aaron.

"Pretty much since I moved to the city," said Tim. "She was dating a coworker of mine from the agency briefly. We met at a happy hour and I kind of stole her from him."

"No hard feelings, though?" said Aaron, smiling.

"He's a bit of a player anyhow," said Tim. "A decent guy, but it wasn't serious or anything. Besides, Nikki and I kind of bonded checking out this hot bartender and trying to decide his type."

"Well, that sounds about right," said Aaron. "Best to make friends with the person making your drinks. Speaking of which…"

"Right, let's do this."

When Aaron and Tim entered the living room, the Madonna sing-along appeared to have shifted to Journey karaoke. Several people, including Greg, who had one arm wrapped around Rick's shoulder, were standing in front of the entertainment center, where the words to "Open Arms" were being displayed on the television. It appeared to Aaron to be one of those corny homemade Asian karaoke YouTube videos. In the background were photos from what looked like some random couple's honeymoon on a beach. In front of the oversized screen, three girls sat on the sofa chatting away, laughing, and talking over each other rather than to each other. Four primped guys stood around the island in the kitchen near the bar, cracking loud jokes and discussing the latest season of *RuPaul's Drag Race*.

Although it was close to midnight and November, it was a mild enough night, and hot enough in Linda's apartment with so many people, that she and Allen could step outside onto the balcony for a few minutes. Linda's balcony was just big enough to hold two chairs, a small, round, outdoor, glass-top table, and a large potted evergreen tree that the previous owner of the apartment left because it had grown too big to move. Linda sat, pulling her skirt over her knees and wrapping her shoulders in a tight, black knit top. Allen stood with his lower back against the balcony's railing in front of her, surveying the scene inside through the sliding glass doors.

"Thanks for bringing the case of bubbles," said Linda, bottle in one hand and half-full glass in the other.

"Champagne," said Allen.

"That's what I said," said Linda. "Bubbles."

"Bubbles are what you put in a bath," said Allen. "Champagne comes from France, is two hundred dollars a bottle, and tastes buttery like a fifteen-year-old's nipples."

"You did not just say that," she said.

"What?" he asked with a boyish grin on his face. "That real Champagne comes from France?"

"You're disgusting," she said.

"You're sexy when you drink," he said.

"Jeez," she replied.

Linda took Allen in from head to toe. He was about six feet tall, had short-cropped brown hair, brown eyes, was closely shaven, and wore a gray jacket, dark jeans, and expensive dress shoes. He could probably stand to lose twenty pounds, she thought, but he carried his weight well. Beyond his exterior, she felt there was something more there, something more to him. Maybe it was pheromones or chemistry. Maybe it was the way he listened when she spoke, the way he looked at her. It was like he was taking her in fully, without touching her or saying a word.

"Tell me something about yourself that won't make me hate you," said Linda. "What do you do when you are not doing whatever it is that you do for work?"

Dating questions still, he thought. "You mean like ride my bike in the summer, ski in the winter, or go to the Metropolitan Club for happy hours?"

"I've been to the Metropolitan Club," she said. "It's downtown, Broad Street. One block from the Stock Exchange."

Allen raised his eyes to hers dubiously. "You've been to the Metropolitan Club?"

"Well, you don't have to look so surprised," said Linda. "My father worked in finance. He was a Wall Street suit too. He started bringing me to those types of places when I was a teenager. We went there once. I remember there being all these candles, and the walls were all huge and lit red."

"Yeah, apparently it hasn't changed much over the years," said Allen, leaning over, taking the bottle from her hand, and filling his glass. "So I guess that's why you are into me? You're still daddy's little girl?"

"First off," said Linda, downing her glass and snatching the bottle back from him to refill it, "I don't have daddy issues. My father was a perfectly kind gentleman growing up. Still is. And second, what makes you think I'm into you? I thought we were just having fun."

"Really, Linda," he said. "The relationship talk, already?"

"You brought it up," she said, shifting in her chair and tugging at the back of her sweater, which was all bunched on one side.

"You have great tits," he said as she adjusted her top.

"Right," she said. She had to give it to him. He was persistent. And it was nice to have at least one of the guys at her apartment that night noticing her.

Allen was not used to meeting women who were as smart as he—or who were as well-off as Linda, he thought, judging by her apartment. Most of the women that he was used to meeting were bridge-and-tunnel commuters, office workers at happy hours on the East Side, secretaries who were more looking to score a husband than have a good time. While Wall Street and trading was an industry dominated by men, there never seemed to be a shortage of women available, all looking for something. And money bought everything.

It was Saturday night, and Allen should have been out with the new trainees. Instead, he was sitting on this balcony with Linda, getting drunk, and he could not have been more relieved.

Allen started manning a derivatives trading desk just out of college. Eventually, with a lot of politicking and back-scratching, he graduated to currency trading. Derivatives required fewer and fewer people those days, though it was still an entry-level position for many wanting access to the riches of Wall Street. Every six months or so, a new, young group of eager, recent graduates would be hired to man phones in a building close to the trading floor for up to twelve hours a day. Nearly everyone started this way, and absolutely everyone needed to pay dues. When new trainees came on board, the more senior members of the team would break them in and teach them the ropes. Saturday nights were part of the initiation.

This involved getting the new trainees as drunk as possible for about five weeks straight, until they could not tell the wolf from the sheep. It was a frat mentality, and if everybody didn't see it, Allen certainly did. In his first year trading, he gained a bunch of weight. His more senior colleagues joked that it was his freshmen fifteen. They would take clients for lunch at the best and most expensive restaurants in the world. Bottles of wine priced at a half grand each, everything getting billed back to the firm. It was literally the 1 percent of the 1 percent, and the trainees who seemed promising would occasionally be allowed to go on an actual lunch call.

A fresh batch started two weeks ago. For the first time in a couple of years, Allen was not that guy in charge of breaking in the trainees. He tagged along two weekends ago and had many late nights out, vomiting in excess, blowing thousands of dollars on private dancers, putting more crap up his nose than he cared to remember. But since he managed to extradite himself to currency trading, where he could work fewer than ten hours a day, he was able to pull back from the bulk of what sometimes felt like fraternity inductee childrearing. He felt he earned it. His liver earned it. His gut earned it.

On occasion, Allen went to back-to-back lunches with different clients. The rule was one that he learned back when he was a trainee. Always order the most expensive thing on the menu to make the client feel comfortable, so that he would, in turn, order whatever he wanted. All of this in hopes that the client would decide to invest copious amounts of money with the brokers.

The Thursday he met Linda was one of those days. He had finished a second late lunch with a couple of clients and a partner on the account and was in a part of town he didn't frequent, Midtown. After he said his good-byes, he saddled up to the bar of the restaurant in the lobby of the Time & Life Building. It was five o'clock, and Linda was sitting at a high-top near a window with two female colleagues. He could not take his eyes off of her, with her dirty-blond hair just touching her shoulders and that tight, fit body. He ordered a round of drinks to be sent over to their table and eventually went over himself, chatted briefly, and gave her his number. He wanted her, and he knew it would require just the right about of deal closing, bravado, forwardness, and feigning a lack of confidence.

Then Linda phoned him up—not the typical woman by a long shot. She was forward and actually confident. One call from her and he knew he was able to close the deal. It was signed, sealed, and delivered to the tune of spending last Saturday night banging all night at her apartment. Then she texted him the next night for round two. When he actually wanted to go, he knew he was onto something. He called her on Tuesday and then again on Thursday. He did so just to chat briefly. Women liked that sort of thing, and he knew from work that when he had a buyer on the line, the secret to closing again and again was talking in a charming way and not stopping. Sure enough, late that afternoon when he was ready to meet the guys for another week of the latest recruitment training, Linda texted to invite him to this impromptu party at her place. So he picked up the two boxes of Bollinger Rose Champagne he had ready for the party bus reserved for his colleagues and loaded them into the back of a cab going in the opposite direction.

Allen leaned over the table and kissed Linda. He slipped his tongue into her mouth at the same moment he slid his hand up her thigh.

Linda's eyes were half closed when she said, "You've got great hands, but they're cold. Let's go inside."

Back in her apartment, things seemed to be winding down. Aaron and his boy Tim sat along the island in the kitchen on stools. The counter was littered with empty glasses. A mostly melted bag of ice was deflating in the sink. Next to the garbage can were two Bollinger boxes with six empty bottles in one and dozens of empty beer bottles haphazardly piled in the other.

"Will you call me tomorrow?" asked Aaron.

"Of course," answered Tim. "We should definitely get together this week—maybe for happy hour or something."

"Sounds perfect," said Aaron. "Let's invite Nikki too, if she's in town. I'll text her to see if she's flying that day."

"Into it," said Tim.

"Into you," said Aaron.

Greg was holding court in the living room, sitting on the coffee table while Rick and a few others sat on the couch. The music from the television was lower and playing R&B. The entertainment center's recessed lights were dimmer than before. The apartment felt warm, soft, and open.

"That is why the Republicans don't stand a chance in the next election," Greg was explaining. "They have completely decimated their base. There are fewer and fewer white men voting in this country every election."

Rick was the only one completely engaged. The others looked in a slump, as if all the liquor they consumed that night had suddenly, and simultaneously, turned heavy in their bodies.

"With the tea party pulling the strings of the House, a few members are able to wield disproportionate power," said Rick. "Look what happened with the last bill the Republicans tried to pass. It was filibustered."

Greg and Rick could go on like this for hours. When it was just the two of them at home, their conversations would often turn into what would probably sound to an outsider like an episode of a Sunday morning political show.

"Those people won't get reelected," said Greg.

"I definitely disagree," said Rick. "The people voting the tea partiers in could not be happier with what their representatives are doing."

Greg cut him off and said, "Of course you disagree," shaking his head and smiling. He leaned forward and kissed Rick, who kissed him back but did not miss a beat.

"All I'm saying is that these people were voted in as tea partiers and now they're doing tea party things, which is why they were elected," said Rick. "All they're really doing is what they were hired to do."

Linda walked through the living room, leading Allen by the hand from the balcony. They passed Aaron and Tim chatting in the kitchen and Rick and Greg talking with a group in the living room. They headed down the hallway to the bedroom. As he was led, Allen kept his eyes on Linda's backside. Then everyone in the room went quiet as they heard the bedroom door shut with a thud.

Tim was the first to speak saying, "Um, my coat is still in there." Everyone erupted in laughter, with Rick laughing until he was red in the face, finding this so funny he momentarily lost his breath and doubled over onto Greg's lap.

CHAPTER SIX

About a dozen tourists loitered in one section of the Highline off the main reclaimed, reimagined industrial causeway. It was somewhat detached with platform seating and a large window suspended above the street offering a view east, straight across Manhattan.

Aaron sat with his mother, Barbara, the two sipping hot drinks from paper cups—his black coffee, hers apple cider. Although there was a bite in the air, the sun was high and bright. She looked to the cars below and then through the tunnel of buildings that rose up on either side clear across the city. In the far distance, she thought she could just about see water. She wondered if that was the East River.

"This city sure is beautiful," said Barbara. "I always dreamed about moving to New York when I was little."

"You did?" asked Aaron. "I didn't know that. I thought you and Pop were always happy in Virginia. I figured that's why you stayed."

"We were, are. We are happy," she said. "When I was a little girl—maybe eight, nine years old—every Friday night I'd watch the double feature on television. It was after your grandmother passed, God rest her soul. I'd get into my pajamas and curl up on the couch in our living room. Your grandfather would watch some of it with me, but eventually I'd be alone. I must have watched *King Kong* a hundred times. After it aired, they'd play it again from the beginning. I always tried to stay awake to watch it all the way through the second time."

"And that's why you wanted to move to New York? For *King Kong*?" poked Aaron.

Barbara gently smacked her son's shoulder with the back of her hand. "No, Son," she said. "It was because New York seemed so magical, so glitzy. So full of dreams and potential. Like anything could happen here."

Aaron and Barbara sat in silence for a moment, enjoying their beverages, the heat from the sides of the cups warming their fingers.

"How is Pop anyhow?" asked Aaron. "Enjoying semiretirement?"

"I think so, as much of it as he can."

"What do you mean?"

"His firm keeps asking him to work on new contracts—at least that's what he's telling me," she said. "Honestly, I wonder if they keep asking or if he keeps volunteering. I think the idea of retirement, and being home all day, scares him. He likes to stay busy."

"Oh, I know," said Aaron.

Even in childhood, Aaron recognized that his pop, Henry, was something of a machine. He left for work most mornings while it was still dark outside. Aaron was often awake, eating cereal, watching cartoons before school. Henry dressed in a full suit. His company ran the office setup and day-to-day maintenance of other companies, agencies—the initial leasing of space, moving in desks, wiring phones, buying and setting up computers. For bigger accounts, they would also manage ongoing jobs such as daily cleaning services and building security. In Alexandria, the federal government was a client for a lot of industry businesses, the Capitol being less than twenty minutes north. But for Henry's company, government was almost all of his business. When government agencies expanded and shrank or moved offices in and around Virginia and the District, Henry's company went to work. Growing up, Aaron and his younger sister used to joke that their father was actually a secret agent, working for the CIA or even directly for the White House. Henry disappeared in a jacket and tie like clockwork every morning and returned late in the evening, often going directly to his home office to empty his briefcase.

Meanwhile, Aaron's mother was always there. Barbara was the PTA mom, the one who volunteered for school trips, hosted Aaron's and his sister's friends after school, and carted them around to activities, including his sister's basketball games and his guitar lessons.

"At least I have Daisy and Meep around to keep me company while your father pretends to take it easy," said Barbara.

Daisy and Meep were her two cats. Growing up, the family had a cat named Lightning—on account that from the day they got him, he ran through the house almost exclusively at top speeds. His parents adopted Lightning when they first moved to Alexandria. He lived until he was twenty-two—probably so long, thought Aaron, because he managed to get so much exercise running around, despite being an indoor cat.

After Aaron moved to New York, his mother found Daisy on the side of the road near their house and took her in. She was driving home one afternoon from the supermarket and spotted a cardboard box. She thought she saw it move, and, after slowing the car and looking closer, she found three kittens. Two of them were in bad shape—such bad shape that they didn't make it. Daisy made it through though, Barbara nursing her back to health. Daisy was very loyal to Barbara and followed her around the house. She was also very skittish around strangers, usually hiding when people came over.

After Aaron's sister went away to college, Barbara found Meep. She was a Russian Blue who wandered into the backyard one day and never left. She must have been lost or abandoned. In either case, no one ever came looking for her, and eventually Barbara took her to the vet to get looked at before letting her inside. Fortunately, Daisy and Meep both had good personalities and got along, often cuddling up with each other to sleep. Aaron and his sister used to joke that cats replaced them. Barbara denied it and laughed it off but secretly thought it might be true. She did like to refer to Daisy and Meep as her kids, after all, as in, "Did I remember to feed the kids this morning?" Or, "This storm is so loud, I hope the kids are okay."

"Do you think the no-kill shelter in New York is a good place to find a cat we'll like?" he asked. He thought briefly about Tim-boy. Tim would love a cat.

"I have no idea," responded Barbara. "Have you been in there before?"

"Just once the day before you arrived," he said. "I feel a little bad getting a mouser."

"Don't worry about that, Son," she said. "You're obviously going to love and take care of it. Did you actually see a mouse?"

Aaron thought about lying to his mother but didn't have the heart.

"Well..."

"I knew it," she interrupted. They had been discussing adopting a cat for about a week while she was visiting. Aaron said he wanted her to help him pick one, since she was the family's resident cat rescuer. "Don't tell Pop that's the reason you're getting one. He'd probably insist you have an exterminator come in. All those chemicals are the last thing anyone needs. What did you see exactly?"

"It's more what I heard," said Aaron. "I was lying in bed and something small and furry definitely scurried across the floor."

"Oh, Aaron," she said. "That's terrible. Maybe you should find another building."

"Another building?" asked Aaron. "This could happen in any building. Besides, I'm in a relatively cheap apartment in one of the city's most popular neighborhoods. Where else am I going to go?"

"I'm not sure I'm comfortable sleeping there," said Barbara. She drank the last of her cider. "We should get you that cat."

"Really, Mother?" questioned Aaron. "This is a cat adoption emergency? I can see right through you. You just want a proxy grandson."

"Or granddaughter," she said.

Aaron and his mother rose, climbed the wooden steps to the main thoroughfare of the Highline, tossed their empty cups into the trash, and headed north. They walked up the Westside Highway, passed the *Intrepid*—a World War II aircraft carrier converted into a military and maritime history museum—and turned back into Hell's Kitchen. Barbara was visiting Aaron for four nights while her husband was out of town for a conference. Usually Aaron visited her, mostly for holidays and sometimes in between, but she wanted to come to the city, see where he lived, and take in a Broadway show. But now there was a mouse, and a mission.

Barbara grew up in the country, so she was no stranger to rodents, but she still feared them in her living space. The more she thought about it on their walk back to his neighborhood, the more she became convinced that a cat was just the thing he needed. It would certainly keep him safe from all sorts of city critters but also might help keep him grounded. Even though he had been living in New York for over a decade, she still worried that because of the city and everything it offered, he was going out all the time, partying and getting up to God only knew what. Aaron was so passionate about everything and always tackled life so head on. To her, he always seemed to be living life a little more at any given time than most people she knew. She worried he would burn out or, worse, something would shadow his good nature.

It was already three in the afternoon, and they had tickets to a show that night. She told Aaron that she thought the best thing for them to do was to go directly to the shelter, then home. This way they could get the new little arrival settled before giving him or her a few hours alone to get comfortable with the space.

City Bitches was a small, no-kill shelter that Aaron passed often in his neighborhood. It was two blocks north of his apartment and attached to a nonchain pet store. It was also a little famous. Besides its tongue-in-cheek name, its front window was usually filled with adorable puppies and neighborhood volunteers playing with them. Cute young guys with a passion for animals, but without the money, space, or responsibility to own one full time, worked at the shelter. Between cleaning, feeding, and grooming, they would take turns in the front window cuddling and cooing new litters, much to the delight of onlookers. Post-happy hour in the early evenings, a half dozen tipsy folks could usually be seen ogling some tank-topped twentysomething while he wrestled a pup with a rope or tossed around a ball. While this display gave the place some notoriety, its reputation was actually built on saving thousands of animals and finding them good homes.

Aaron, like his mother Barbara, held some pretty strong feelings about adopting from shelters rather than buying from pet stores. With so many animals in need of homes, neither saw the point in supporting pet factories.

"Most of these little guys came in sick or injured," explained a lanky shop worker. "All of the animals get looked at by vets. They are treated with medication if needed, so every one here is healthy or far enough rehabilitated that he or she could be adopted today."

Aaron and Barbara circled the room slowly with Aaron leading the way. Many of the caged kittens and cats were lying down, curled up, lethargic looking, or flat out sleeping. A small card attached to the front of each cage displayed the animal's name along with a few notes, including its specific story or disposition.

There was Taco, who was fully matured, tan colored, and, unlike the others, fully awake, sticking one paw way outside his cage as if swatting something invisible. He looked a little crazy to Aaron. The card on his cage revealed that he was given his name because he was found wedged in between two buildings. Apparently, he preferred a very active home with lots of people around to play with him.

Two cages down from Taco was Ms. Suey. She was white with long hair and very long whiskers. Curled up in a ball with her chin resting on her tail, facing outward, she looked up at Aaron with big green eyes. Ms. Suey was brought in by some overzealous tourists who said they found her living in the entranceway of an abandoned building next to a restaurant in Chinatown. They were worried about her welfare.

There was also Oreo, who was mostly black with some white on his belly, Meatball, who was brown and rather round, and Buttercup, who was a sort of midget tabby.

"Do all these cats have food names?" asked Barbara.

"We give the dogs names of movie stars. We find it makes them a little more relatable and gives them a zing of star power. The cats getting food names was just something one of the founders started. She says it's because they are all so cute, she wants to eat them up."

"That's a little creepy," said Aaron under his breath to his mother. Just as the words left his mouth, he came across Mr. Boo Berry.

Mr. Boo Berry was a Russian Blue kitten with a dark gray coat that had almost a bluish tinge. His legs were short and his frame small. As soon as Aaron stepped near, he immediately jumped to his feet and stumbled to the front of his cage. When he opened his mouth to meow, almost no sound came out. Besides obviously being given his name because of his breed, Aaron thought maybe it was also because he looked as if he was trying to be scary, but failing in spite of himself because he was so cute.

"This one just says he was rescued from under a Dumpster," said Aaron.

"Ah yes," said the store clerk. "Mr. Boo Berry comes to us all the way from Brooklyn. His breed stays rather small. A family brought him in along with his siblings. They found a litter in their back-yard. There were four all together. Mr. Boo Berry seems to be the last one here."

"Oh, Aaron," gushed Barbara. "He's so adorable. He reminds me of Meep. He could be her cousin."

"I could see that," replied Aaron. "Do you think he looks tough enough to protect my place?"

"Of course he is," said Barbara. "He'll put a few pounds on in no time at all. And it's good to give him a home while he's so young. See how he's looking at you? He loves you already."

"Ma," proclaimed Aaron. "How can he love me already? He doesn't even know me." But Aaron had to admit—bending down and looking nearly eye level with Mr. Boo Berry—his heart was melting. He had always wanted a cat, but his ex was terribly allergic.

"You're not getting a cat because you saw a mouse or something," said the young, lanky clerk. "We definitely frown upon that. We're looking for good owners who are going to give these animals good homes."

Aaron and his mother adamantly denied that this was the reason, which was mostly true. They both knew the mouse Aaron thought he heard was mostly just an excuse. Barbara felt better about her son not being alone in his studio apartment. He needed a little companion to care for and keep him company—something to rely on him so he wouldn't be out all the time. Aaron considered this new little buddy of his another symbol of his changed life, the one that started when he split with his ex and leased a place in Hell's Kitchen on his own.

"Do you want to come home with me, Mr. Boo Berry?" asked Aaron. It would seem, by the kitten's practically muted, mini roar in response, he did.

CHAPTER SEVEN

E very year Greg and Rick went ice skating in Central Park. It was still technically the preholiday season, but tourists were already flocking to the city in record numbers. When people thought of Christmas, they thought of New York—the windows decorated at Macy's, shopping for presents along Fifth Avenue, the giant tree at Rockefeller Center, and snuggling under a blanket for a ride in a horse-drawn carriage. Also, for many, ice skating.

There were three places to go ice skating in Manhattan. The rink at Rockefeller Center under the giant Christmas tree was the most iconic. The downside was that it was the most popular and also the smallest, so wait times were the longest. Bryant Park also had a rink set up next to the New York City Public Library on Fifth Avenue, where, under the watch of two lions guarding the building with big red bows wrapped firmly around their necks, people lined up around the block to skate. There was also a gift market where people shopped for artisan goods and novelty crafts, strolling between wooden stalls, strung lights, and sporadic, well-positioned heat lamps. But the biggest and least crowded ice-skating rink was in Central Park.

Completely outdoors, Wollman Rink was resurrected for four months each year with short walls surrounding six inches of crisp, clean ice. Below the ice was concrete that in the warmer months hosted the park's small amusement park, intended mostly for kids. Entrance into the rink was inexpensive by New York standards, easy to get to for anyone in the city, and large enough to house what grew over the years to become a massive takeover by Greg, Rick, and every person that they knew in Hell's Kitchen, the West Side, and most of New York.

Layde Licious was one of Hell's Kitchen's premiere drag queens. She performed in a classy, showgirl style that ushered back to a different era when poise, diction, and presence were more important than heckling the audience and lip-synching pop songs. Layde also truly stood out when she performed because she actually sang at least half her numbers. She would scoot up on the bar, crossing one long, muscular leg over the other, thrusting her sequenced stilettos in front of her. The lights dimmed, the crowd silenced, and the barback shined an over-sized flashlight on her face from below. She sang from deep in her chest, and her voice washed over the audience, daring any-one to interrupt, talk, or even try to entertain a thought that didn't involve her. She knew how to own a room.

Rarely lacking performance invites, Layde worked nearly every week of the year at some gig or another. But most of the younger patrons never realized she had been around since they were in diapers. They saw her performing at their favorite bars and assumed she was just another fresh talent. Layde had the ability to charm crowds with her perfect body, large eyes, and impressive voice as much then as she did when she first came onto the scene.

Layde strapped on her skates, tightened her laces, and with one long, confident glide strode onto the ice in full winter drag. This was her third skate session at the rink this year, and, as with all appearances, she was dressed to the nines, wearing a knee-length, red, sparkling dress, a short, white fur coat, green mittens, green, sparkling lipstick, and a green beret to hold in place her neatly braided hair. Her presence was augmented by the full foot her skates seemed to add to her height.

With a bellowing voice that echoed across the ice, through the skaters, and into the recently winter-bare trees beyond, she declared, "Make some room and show me those backsides, because I'm Layde Licious, bitches!"

Those who knew and loved her clapped. But others who didn't—tourists, couples, families visiting from near and far— had slightly less encouraging reactions. A young, Midwestern, newlywed couple looked from Layde to each other as if to say, what on God's good earth is that? A group of Japanese girls, students on a weeklong class trip, squealed in delight. A father, out of sheer reflex, not malice or misunderstanding at what he was seeing, lifted his seven-year-old daughter, dressed in white like a winter ballerina, straight in the air as if the ice were on fire. Layde's massively long legs meant she was skating fifteen feet with every stride, so just as suddenly as she appeared, she disappeared, a throng of skaters parting and receding around her in a flash.

"Dance party!" shouted someone over the holiday music.

"Girl, it's on," came a reply from somewhere across the ice.

Nearly half the people were locals, friends of friends of the annual event, with others from the Greg-Rick group still arriving, soon to take the ice. It was two in the afternoon on a Saturday, yet late enough that some people had already worked off yesterday's hangover and were ready to start anew. At least a few, who were the most boisterous, pre-gamed for the event with a boozy brunch, re-shampooing from the night before.

From tiny speakers overhead, soft classical music tinged above the ice. Midsonata it came to an abrupt stop and was replaced, after a short pause, with house music at twice the volume and three times the speed. This new music was warmer, sexier, and clearly better suited to a late-night dance floor than a daytime winter fairyland. Someone must have convinced—or bribed—the staff to allow them to take over the sound system.

It was easier to spot the outsiders now, as they were starting to become outnumbered. Young kids in puffy suburban ski coats looked to their parents for clues on how to react to the circus that was descending around them out of seemingly nowhere. Some of the tourists shrugged it off in good humor, thinking they were having a real New York experience. And an elderly couple who had been slowly making their way around the edge of the rink stayed in place and started wiggling to the beat.

Layde was now in the center of the ice, spinning slowly, facing outward.

"All right, boys and girls," she said. "It's time to form a circle. Everyone take the hand of the person on either side."

Aaron, Tim, Nikki, and Wall Street Allen had no idea what was about to unfold. Greg, Rick, and Linda had seen this once before. The problem with inviting a hundred or so people to go ice skating, especially people that were treating this like a dance party, was that not only were many already in various states of intoxication, but few actually knew how to skate. And joining a circle with dozens of them to spin in one direction while the rest attempted to skate around them in the other was more than dizzying; it could easily turn into a blizzard of chaos.

Aaron was a fairly decent skater, having practically grown up at a roller-skating rink in Virginia. It was a short bike ride from his house, and he and his friends spent nearly all of junior high skating and hanging out at the concession stand. The ice required slightly more coordination, but after he took a few minutes to get acclimated, he proved to be quite graceful.

Tim was naturally spry and had good balance but had only gone ice skating once before, when he was young. It was one winter when his mother seemed to have her drinking under control, so his father attempted to take the family skating for his sister's ninth birthday, departing from their usual family tradition of celebrating birthdays, which was to take the family to McDonald's for Happy Meals before devouring an entire ice-cream cake from the box with only spoons.

Nikki was fairly competent on the ice. She grew up outside of Cornwall in England. Her older sister went through a brief stage of wanting to be a professional ice skater and managed to cajole their parents into paying for lessons. That interest lasted only about a year before she moved to her next obsession, but Nikki accompanied her sister often to the rink and skated in the public area while her sister met with an instructor.

Greg grew up in a hockey home in an affluent suburb outside of Chicago. His father played Division I hockey in college and even lasted for a couple of seasons in the minor leagues. As a result, Greg and his brother were practically raised on the ice—being groomed to pick up their father's mantle—until each brother's skill plateaued, both in high school.

Rick took up roller blading as a teenager where he grew up outside of Columbus, Ohio. And although the winters there were less than hospitable, and part of the year was spent mainly indoors, he and his friends owned the summer on blades. It didn't hurt that he had a massive crush for two years on one of the older guys in his neighborhood who also happened to be into roller blading. The two were nearly inseparable, though Rick was slower and often trailed behind.

Linda and Allen opted not to skate but sat instead on bleachers, watching everyone start to form circles. They brought giant coffees, which Allen spiked with whiskey from a silver flask. Despite Linda's agile frame and general gumption, she felt as though she never possessed a decent sense of balance. She was more content anyhow this year to be wrapped in one side of Allen's giant coat with his arm around her than to be down below.

"Let's go, everyone," shouted Layde over the music. "Enough clowning around."

Slowly but surely, people started joining hands and moving in one direction.

"Whatever you do," said Aaron to Tim, "don't let go of my hand."

"Don't worry," said Tim. "I think I need you more than you need me."

Greg was circling around the outside, herding the crowd tighter, away from the edges of the ice.

"Baxter, Carlos," said Greg, waving over two burly men not paying attention. "You guys over there. We need you." The pair looked up and skated over, not wanting to displease their favorite Hell's Kitchen bartender.

"We're in too, Greg," shouted a handsome blond man. A woman trailed him, looking decidedly less steady on her feet.

"Don't go so fast," someone from closer to the middle was already shouting. "I haven't done this before."

The circle started going around with about twenty or so people. Another chain of five joined them, and then another. The group skated clumsily, but with speed and determination, their shoulders facing inward, all holding hands—one hand with the skater in front of them and the other with the skater behind.

Layde stood in the center with her mittens above her head as if she were a deranged orchestral leader trying to will her musicians to play an impossible, never-before-rehearsed piece.

"Remember, my little elves," said Layde. "Hold on tight!"

"I feel like I'm flying, Jack," slurred a young guy not dressed properly for the occasion, wearing only a tank top with a Santa hat, scarf, and gloves.

Another poorly prepared person, three people down, responded, "Shut up, Rose! You're high, and I told you, I'm into your fiancé."

One person between them said, "Christ, I'm not going down with this ship."

A girl on the other side of the circle cheered in delight, while three others chanted, "Faster. Faster. Faster."

From Linda's and Allen's vantage point, they could see that the group was starting to fracture. One section of it was distinctly lopsided, creating an oval shape to the circle, where some man-child with the hips of a six-year-old was being lifted into the air with each push of a skate, weighing down the skaters holding his hands on either side.

"I lost count," said Allen. "I think I have seen your friends go around at least twelve times."

"I think I'm going to be sick just watching this," said Linda.

Skaters from the outing who weren't in the main circle started skating around in the opposite direction, some holding hands.

"I don't see this ending well," said Allen.

Back on the ice, Greg and Rick were laughing so hard both of them were winded.

"I think I have to break off," said Rick, shouting over the music, which was a decidedly appropriate song, a remix of Kylie Minogue's "Spinning Around."

"Don't you dare," yelled Greg from behind him. "It can't be you again this year. You have to hold on."

I'm breakin' it down, I'm not the same.

The music was blaring overhead.

"This is bloody brilliant," said Nikki, the next link around behind Rick and Greg.

"I can't hang on much longer either," said Tim from behind Nikki, grasping her hand and Aaron's behind him. "This is getting out of control. I can't skate this fast."

I know you're feelin' me 'cuz you like it like this.

"I'm being pulled from behind too much," said Aaron in the caboose of their group.

The order in which things happened next was hotly debated for years to come.

The man wearing only the tank top vomited, which, because of the momentum of the group's spinning, ricocheted onto the next several people behind him to varying degrees—the ice moving swiftly behind him now having turned a foul shade of brackish pink.

The man-child who was being lifted off the ice in delight suddenly took so much air his legs flung completely behind him, causing his partners on either side to lose their grips. He landed, spinning face down on the ice like a windmill lawn ornament that lost its stick in a big gust, yet managed to keep turning. As he whirled and simultaneously slid, he started taking down the skaters who were circling in the opposite direction from under their feet.

Rick and Greg lost grip of each other's hands, causing Rick, in the front, to swing outward like the end of a roller coaster that was suddenly fishtailing off its track. He managed to wriggle from the hand holding him, which only succeeded in launching him faster into the unknown.

Greg, now rogue and leading a succession of a dozen skaters—including, directly behind him, Nikki, Tim, and Aaron—cut swiftly through the masses like an overeager conga line leader, disrupting any semblance of order that the entirety of Wollman Rink might have still held.

Linda and Allen rose to their feet from the stands. From their vantage point, it looked as if a natural disaster had suddenly struck the ice, an unseen tornado blowing through the rink.

"Dear God," said Linda. "I hope no one was hurt."

"What the heck just happened?" asked Allen.

The pair rushed down to the edge of the ice, bending in close to survey the damage. The music, which was previously at a loud roar, stopped as the staff selling tickets and skates from off the ice scrambled to see what was happening, having heard the shouts and commotion from afar.

Out of the couple of hundred people on the ice, about a third were either no longer on their feet or in some stage of trying to get back onto them. The small girl whose father scooped her up earlier was crying, not because she was injured, but because her white skirt was now splattered in pink vomit. The man-child was still down, arms flailing, pushed up against three people who were sandwiched against the wall.

Rick leveraged himself against the two sturdiest skaters he initially came in contact with, the burly Baxter and Carlos. The trio was tangled, moving as a single, clumsy, unstable unit.

Greg's conga line fell from the back, each pulling the person in front of the other down in a hopeless attempt at holding ground. Then Greg fell, spread eagle, eventually coming to a standstill as if he were trying to make a snow angel. He stared up to the blue sky, laughing.

The only person who seemed unaffected by the tornado of skaters was Layde, who was standing in the same place she was spinning when the storm erupted. She turned slowly, surveying the damage, letting out a humph as if she had just figured out the solution to a complicated physics equation—presumably that being what happens when a hundred people, half of whom are wasted or can't skate, attempt a highly synchronized sport.

"I'm never doing that again," said Aaron, steadying himself on one knee.

"Bloody hell, that was a fun time, let's do it again," said Nikki. She and Tim were the only two from their section still holding hands, though they were down on the ground. "We don't skate like that in England."

Tim grumbled. He said, "We don't skate like that in America." His head was raised and he was leaning on one shaky elbow.

As if on cue, the two Japanese girls grappling each other smiled widely, one of them saying in broken English, "Only in New York."

Someone must have called park services, or possibly the police. A voice came over the loudspeaker. It was not a friendly one. It said, "Folks, the rink is temporarily out of service for cleaning. Please remove yourself from the ice immediately."

After the ice-skating event, the group broke off into factions and scattered. The largest contingent, including Layde, walked south to find an open bar in Hell's Kitchen—some limping with bruises starting to turn black and blue. Yet everyone was—for the most part—in high spirits, having considered the day a huge success.

"Allen and I are going back to my apartment to freshen up," said Linda. "We can meet you guys in a few hours if you're hanging out."

"Sure, freshen up," said Rick. "We got it."

"It's not like that," said Linda. "All right, well, it's a little like that."

Linda and Allen broke away, walking west back to Linda's apartment.

"Let's go back to my place," said Nikki. "I'll whip us up some hot chocolate and we can chill out for a few ticks."

Aaron and Tim looked at each other as if in agreement.

"That sounds fun," said Aaron. "I think I have some Baileys too."

"Right," said Greg. "And let me guess, that will give you and Tim a chance to freshen up?"

"Shut up," said Aaron.

"You are such a dork," chimed in Rick to Greg.

Aaron, Tim, Nikki, Greg, and Rick worked their way south, following in the wake of the day's other skaters, through the winding paths of Central Park, crossing Columbus Circle and down Ninth Avenue. As they walked, they relived the afternoon and debated what precisely went wrong with the skating circle and who was at fault. Aaron and Tim said it was the ill-timed vomiter. Nikki blamed the flying man-child. But Greg and Rick both secretly believed it was their fault for losing grip of the other's hand. As if to make up for it, they held hands all the way back to Aaron and Nikki's front stoop.

CHAPTER EIGHT

T he Ninth Avenue Saloon was one of the older neighborhood bars in Hell's Kitchen. Back when the area was crime ridden and the streets were not as safe to walk, it offered locals and visitors a refuge from the chaos outside. Inside, it was long, narrow, and high ceilinged with a well-polished bar along one wall and a pool table in the back. The Saloon was also home to some of the longest-serving bartenders in Hell's Kitchen.

Greg had started as a rookie almost fifteen years prior. It was one of his first bartending gigs in the city. Back in those days, the owner, who was also an active bartender and manager, used to give him the worst shifts, saving the weekend nights for himself.

Being the only staff member save the occasional barback that would be scheduled alongside him, Greg worked shifts early in the week until four in the morning. Occasionally a group of young actors would venture a couple of avenues west from the Theater District after performing a show. But for the most part, the regulars of the Saloon were late-night, local boozers who nursed beers hour after hour. They presumably used the place for company outside of their small, lonely apartments, or even for its generous heat in the dead of winter. Despite the Saloon's twenty-foot ceilings, heat in the old building came from giant radiators, which, once winter hit, seemed to be stuck permanently on swelter.

Regardless of what brought his patrons in on those quieter shifts, Greg served them with gusto, chewing their ears off when they let him, keeping a fairly tight-running bar, treating the place as if it were his own—cleaning, stocking, polishing, creating a welcoming atmosphere in an otherwise relatively modest, if not desolate space.

As the years passed, another person bought into the business, and Greg started getting the more coveted shifts—later in the week and sometimes weekends. Not only did this mean he was making more money because there were more patrons, it also meant he had more colleagues. On the weekends, a second bartender was scheduled along with the barback. This made his shifts seem faster and more fun. The music selection evolved too as Greg enlisted disc-jockey friends to build playlists for when the jukebox was not being fed. Later he'd make the playlists himself.

It was also during these later years that the Saloon's clientele started changing. Whereas previously it felt like the place was a hangout for the local refuse of the neighborhood, it started attracting a hipper crowd.

Toward the front of the bar, closest to Ninth Avenue, a small faction of regular local women took up residence. They hung on each other, danced, held hands, and even helped keep the peace should any riffraff or unruly types try to cause a ruckus. Bifolding doors were installed in place of the front windows, and in the shoulder seasons, when the city wasn't blistering or snowed over, Greg opened them to the street.

The middle section of the bar was unofficially reserved for younger tourists, which inevitably meant it also became the hunting ground for older, neighborhood men trying to get lucky. It was a dance that occurred in most bars in and around Midtown, given the high influx of regular visitors to the city.

The other end of the bar, opposite the women, farther away from the street, was staked out by local twentysomethings. A brief period passed in which some were on the prowl for paying johns or out and about between tricks. But that too, as the years went on, seemed to diminish. Eventually it became the corner for any cute guy, be it bridge and tunnel in for the night from the outer boroughs or neighborhood regulars who were often there at the invite and hospitality of the staff.

Some patrons played pool or sat close by, occupying the few small bar tables off to the side while playing. But all the way against the back wall, there was an open anteroom of sorts with a bench built into the wall. It was opposite the bathrooms but still within full view of the entire bar and became a kind of safe zone commandeered for an unofficial club of men who preferred to dress— as often as their lives allowed—as women. Beyond them and the bathrooms was a door that led to the back entrance of the Saloon, where a narrow, short alley gave way to the street. The men who preferred women's clothes gravitated here, so that if trouble arose in the front of the bar—be it from regular clientele or local authorities—they had an escape route close by. They mostly drank beer from bottles, never draught, which Greg always thought funny. He also remembered to give them a straw in each bottle, as they preferred, so that they wouldn't smudge their lipstick.

After fifteen years of bartending at the Saloon and helping transform the place from a dive bar to a thriving, pulsating neighborhood scene, Greg graduated to management, helping place orders with the distributors and scheduling staff. Tonight was Friday, his favorite night to fill in working when needed, since for about an hour, starting at ten o'clock, the entire back half of the Ninth Avenue Saloon transformed into what Greg liked to refer to as the best little drag bar in New York.

The pool table was covered with thick plywood, and the few small tables around it pushed to the side. The back bench along the wall in the open area of the anteroom was converted—with the aid of a large, wooden, custom-cut board and two huge, interconnecting blocks—to a stage. After the ice-skating outing the weekend before, Greg called Layde to ask her to perform at the Saloon. She had performed there many times over the years, but not in recent days. She took one look at her calendar, saw that Friday was open, and accepted the invite. She had a soft spot in her heart for the Saloon and more so for Greg, who always remembered to invite her to his outings.

"I don't know if I can sit that close to the stage," said Tim. "I'm always afraid drag queens are going to pick on me."

The crowd that night was a mix of late happy hour revelers, most of whom were four to six drinks deep into the two-for-one specials, and what Greg like to refer to as the midtermers. The midtermers were the people who came after happy hour but before midnight. It was a slight lull in an otherwise typically jam-packed night, though anyone would be hard pressed to call the place even remotely empty.

"Don't worry, I know Layde," said Aaron. "I've been coming here off and on for years. She tends to attack the tourists in the middle of the bar, if anyone at all."

"Oh, that's reassuring," said Tim.

The truth was Aaron knew Layde fairly well. Several months back, he helped close the bar with Greg. Layde—known as Andy when she was out of drag—was there with them. It was a quiet night, and Aaron had recently finished a particularly laborious work event, so he was taking the next day off to make up for his overtime. Greg, Aaron, and Andy wound up sipping tumblers of Johnnie Walker Black and smoking a doobie at a table in the back. This was after hours, the bar closed, doors locked, curtains drawn. Andy was quite fetching as a man, no makeup, fit, all smiles. Although he was more than a decade Aaron's senior, whether it was the whiskey or smoke, they wound up kissing for a brief spell while Greg was distracted sorting a drawer of paperwork. Nothing more happened or ever came of it, but when they saw each other since, they smiled and nodded, acknowledging that they had shared that sexy kiss between them.

"How about we sit over there next to the service bar," said Aaron, indicating the end of the bar on the stage side, but with the pool table between. "That looks like it should give us plenty of protection, and we'll have access to Greg for drinks."

"Hey, boys, how are you sexy beasts doing?" asked Greg. "Glad you could make it."

"Wouldn't miss it for the world," said Aaron. "Tim here is a little nervous that Layde is going to give him a lap dance or make fun of him or something."

"Am not," said Tim. "It's just that whenever I see a drag show, the drag queens always seem to call me out."

"That's because you're so damn cute," said Aaron, reaching over and straightening Tim's bow tie. While Tim was in his early thirties, he was baby faced. Aaron thought he looked angelic.

Tim hadn't worn a bow tie since that first night that he and Aaron slept together, which was exactly one month ago. Tim was reminded of this when, earlier that night, Aaron had presented him with the one he was now wearing, wrapped in a box with a card that read, "Happy One-Month Anniversary, Tim-Boy!"

"I think I'm ready for a drink, Greg," said Tim, keeping eye contact with him. "And a shot."

"Coming right up, kiddo," said Greg. "What'll that be? How about a couple of kamikazes?"

"Perfect, thanks," said Aaron. "And two Coronas."

"You got it," said Greg. "Rick is probably stopping by too. He was just finishing up with coworkers around the corner last I heard."

Two guys were sitting along the bar next to Aaron, who had his back to them, as he was facing Tim.

"Is there actually a drag show at this place?" asked one of the guys, who had a buzzed head and looked like he could have been a bodybuilder.

"Yes sir," answered Greg. "Layde Licious in the flesh and blood."

"Yeah, what's left of her," said the bodybuilder's friend, a tall lean guy with a chiseled jaw. "I thought that old queen was washed up."

"Well, she's not," said Greg. "She's actually not that old, and she's coming on at ten. She's doing a few numbers."

"Was this place always like this?" asked the bodybuilder.

"Like what?" asked Greg.

"I don't know, man, maybe it's this whole neighborhood," said the bodybuilder. "I mean, I haven't been in New York that long, but this neighborhood, this scene. It's a bit much, if you know what I mean."

Greg didn't. He thought he recognized the guy, maybe his voice. But he was too busy trying to serve the other patrons at the bar to think about who he was or what he was trying to say.

"I have to be at the club by ten," said chiseled jaw. "This show probably won't actually start until much later anyway. Drag queens never start on time."

Aaron overheard everything and leaned back, turning to the duo. "Hey, they really only book an act here every now and again for a couple of hours," he said. "It gets way too crowded by midnight to have a full show. They need every last inch of this place for people, so they pull apart that stage afterward. It'll start on time."

"I just want to find a dark place to dance," said the bodybuilder. "You know?"

"Like hitting the clubs or something, man?" asked Aaron, putting an emphasis on "man."

"Yeah, you know. That's the thing this neighborhood has," said bodybuilder. "Really decent DJs and dance floors."

"Ah, I see," said Aaron, thinking that this guy just liked to get messed up and enjoyed the scene that Hell's Kitchen offered. He seemed like kind of a local tourist, someone who just came into a neighborhood to participate in it but then went back to his own. It's kind of nice in a way, thought Aaron. His neighborhood was inclusive enough to attract and welcome people from outside of it, even if they didn't necessarily fit there, exactly. "I hear you. I like the dance floor around the corner at the Ritz. It's small, but the crowd is good."

"Right on, man," said the bodybuilder. "I've only been going to Pasha. This guy works there. He gets me in for free." He said this with a hint of pride—either of the chiseled jaw guy or the free admission to a twenty-dollar club, Aaron could not tell.

"The dance floor at Pasha is twenty times the Ritz's," said chiseled jaw, hearing that he was mentioned.

"Well, yeah, of course," said Aaron. "But that's not the point. I mean, whatever. They are two different places."

"I'm getting out of here," said chiseled jaw. "You can stay if you want, but I have to get to work. Are you staying?"

"You just ordered us drinks," said the bodybuilder. "I was going to stay and finish them."

"Suit yourself," he said, stood up and left.

As Aaron turned his attention back to Tim, he saw that Tim was fixated on his empty shot glass.

Tim had moved into his new apartment just over one month ago. It was practically the same day that he and Aaron spent their first night together. Since then, he had slept at Aaron's place several times a week and, as a result, still hadn't fully unpacked. Although Aaron came over and helped him build his bed, he never got around to building the dresser, which sat in a corner of his room, still in its IKEA box, unopened. As soon as Tim's new bed was in place, they immediately christened it, left to grab a bite at the diner around the corner, and headed back to Aaron's.

Tim's apartment was bigger, but he had two roommates—two girls who had lived there for years. They were very comfortable camping in the living room in their sweatpants night after night. At least at Aaron's place, even though it was a studio and smaller, they had privacy. Plus, Tim had to admit that he had fallen for Mr. Boo Berry, Aaron's new little kitten, even if he hadn't quite fallen for his owner completely. Kids always complicate things, thought Tim, trying to suppress a laugh.

"What are you smiling about?" asked Aaron.

"Nothing," responded Tim. "Just wondering if Layde would remember me from ice skating last week."

"You are too cute," responded Aaron, who took a deep breath and surveyed the room. He was feeling happy and relaxed. The uphill climb of the last few years was melting away. For the first time perhaps ever, he thought, he felt stable with a solid job and a few dollars tucked away. For too long he worked from gig to gig without health insurance or sick pay. Now he had a career, was living on his own, and was loving life in New York again. He worked hard to get to this place and thought about how comfortable he was in his own skin. He thought that it was funny how he grew more confident as he got older. He always considered that one trait something he had to strive for, not realizing it would grow organically over time.

It was a quarter to ten, and Layde walked into the Saloon in drag, but wearing a dark shawl to hide her head, wig, and make-up. Within fifteen paces—having to lift her drag bag over people's heads—she passed the bar, made eye contact with Greg, weaved around the pool table, and disappeared into the bathroom. She was as stealthy as a six-and-a-half-foot drag queen could be. She wanted to finish getting ready and into character without revealing too much to her audience in advance of the show.

"Aaron, Timmy, how the heck are ya?" asked Rick, seeming to appear from nowhere, having drifted to them in Layde's wake. "I just had the most boring drinky drinks with my coworkers and ditched them to come here. I hear Layde is performing."

"She sure is," said Aaron. "You're just in time."

"Excellent, there's my beautiful guy," said Rick, leaning over the bar to kiss Greg, who was in the middle of taking drink orders from three tall lady-boys.

"Whoa, easy there, tiger," said Greg, stopping, smiling, and leaning in to give Rick a peck on the lips. "Let me finish with these guys. You want a water to start, babe?"

"A water?" said Rick. "It's Friday night. We need shots."

"I second that," said Tim. "Let's do shots, and get some more beer, please." But before he could finish, Greg was back talking with the lady-boys, pouring drinks.

"You're feisty tonight," said Aaron.

"No, I'm not," said Rick.

"I was talking to Tim," said Aaron.

"Okay, boys, sorry about that," said Greg. "What can I get you?"

"I think we need a lot of liquids," said Aaron.

"Three shots," said Rick.

"Three beers?" asked Tim.

"And water," said Greg, looking at Rick. "And I have a surprise for Rick."

The bodybuilder, still sitting next to them, finished his drinks and looked around uncomfortably. Rick was practically shouting over him.

The Saloon was getting more and more crowded. People arrived in anticipation of Layde's show. Others were there because happy hour had ended someplace else, and they figured for full-priced drinks, they might as well get a show. Nearly all were in some state of intoxication.

"So why did you go to happy hour with your coworkers if you think they are so boring?" asked Aaron.

"What?" responded Rick. The volume in the Saloon was growing louder by the minute. More people clambered in, and the second bartender, Sean, had jacked up the music at exactly five minutes to ten at Layde's request, who wanted to get everyone in the spirit for her performance.

"I asked, why did you drink with coworkers you hate?"

"I don't hate them," said Rick. "They are just boring. And they are half our age, and prettier than us."

"Speak for yourself," said Tim, just loud enough so that Aaron could hear, but not Rick.

"Dude, you are yelling directly in my ear," said the bodybuilder, just as Greg came back with the drinks.

"Shots, everyone," said Greg, setting down a metal martini shaker, then three shot glasses, three pints of beer, and a bottle of water.

"Thirsty! Thanks, mister," said Rick.

"Hang in there, guy," said Greg, noticing the bodybuilder's annoyance. "Here, have a shot. There's plenty to go around."

Greg produced another shot glass from under the bar and began filling them all to the brim.

"Thanks," said the bodybuilder, who immediately downed it and stood up, reaching for his jacket.

Greg, Aaron, and Tim looked at each other as if to say, thanks for waiting so we could do that together. Rick didn't seem to notice what happened.

Aaron shrugged, lifted a glass, and said in his best Jewish-New York accent, "*L'chaim, mashuganas.* To life."

"You are not staying for Layde's show?" asked Greg. "It will be starting any minute."

"Right," said the bodybuilder. "See you guys around." He looked directly at Aaron, who was looking at Tim, who appeared to be scanning the room for someone. Then he turned and passed through the crowd to the front entrance.

At that moment, every light went out, along with the music, leaving only a dozen or so candles between the bottles of liquor behind the bar to light the entire room. Some in the crowd jeered, while others made shushing sounds.

"Ladies and gentlemen," shouted Sean from behind the bar. "It is with great pride that the Saloon presents to you tonight the hottest trick in town, Layde Licious." He flicked on an oversized, handheld flashlight above his head, directing it toward the back of the room, just as the first few notes of Shirley Bassey's "History Repeating" came up in full volume.

Layde was standing tall on the makeshift stage in a tight, short, gold-sequined cocktail dress, her wig piled high with light brown hair and streaks of blond pinned in an intentionally untidy beehive. Her earrings were enormous gold loops, and she was wearing vintage-style, black, crushed velvet, arm-length gloves.

The word is about, there's something evolving.

Layde's face was fierce and her mouth tight as she lip-synced, her arms stretched out wide with her palms facing upward and her hips swaying side to side in samba-like pivots. Her body invited the audience in, and they were clamoring for access.

Whatever may come, the world keeps revolving.

Closest to the stage was a group of middle-aged men with huge grins. They positioned themselves there an hour before the show, having seen Layde before and turning out just for tonight's performance, one of them having gotten wind from Greg while at the Saloon earlier in the week. They cheered from the moment she appeared.

Sandwiched next to them and along the bar wall was a group of younger guys, several of them with their mouths opened in awe. The shortest one was standing on his tippy-toes trying to get a better view. His heart was pounding so hard, it felt like it was going to explode from his chest.

The pool table was covered with a large wooden board to protect the green felt below. Some patrons, the ones wedged immediately around it, were leaning over it, fixated, mesmerized.

Beyond them at the edge of the bar sat Tim, Aaron, and Rick. Greg stopped serving and was giving his best cat whistle with his thumb and middle finger between his front teeth. Layde looked across the crowd, down at him, and winked.

The whole bar up to the front door was jam packed, and if music had not been playing at that moment, you could have heard a pin drop.

But to me it seems quite clear. That it's all just a little bit of history repeating.

Trombones and trumpets blasted overhead as Layde swung her hips further, swaying to the beat. She leaned her long body over and took one fellow's face between her gloved hands, blowing him a kiss.

Just as she was coming on to the chorus for a second time, she began one long, swift stride from the front edge of the stage through the crowd to the covered pool table. Planting a giant heel firmly in place, she catapulted herself over the heads of those below onto the table, flashing those directly under with more than they had bargained to see had they looked directly up. Not missing a word of the track, her lips accentuated every syllable with complete and absolute precision.

As she moved to the middle of the pool table, which was nearly the size of the entire stage she just left behind, the crowd shifted to adjust to her new position. Tim let out a small gasp, as he thought she was going to topple over into the audience and take half of them down with her. But she didn't. She made a slow whirl, her tight dress plumping out from her muscular thighs, seductively wiggling her backside until she was back in position facing front once more. The bar erupted in a roar of cheers.

After Bassey belted the last verse and Layde's lip-syncing came to a close, the recorded brass orchestra blasted for a final sixteen-bar instrumental. Slamming one heel down sideways and rotating around to the rhythm, she spun again, this time not stopping to face the front. With each beat she thumped her foot down and pivoted around, again and again, faster than the refrain, until she was fully spinning, her long arms up, her gloved fingers reaching into the air, dancing, creating space where there was none before. From behind the bar, Sean made the light's focus Layde's hands, her face falling into shadow as she spun and danced, spun and danced. From her vantage point high above, the crowd appeared to be spinning and dancing around her, their faces cast in shadow too. She steadied herself by picking out an imagery point on the wall in the darkness and then closing her eyes.

When the music stopped, the crowd erupted in applause. The lights came back up, dimmer this time. Sean flicked the oversized flashlight off. He and Greg resumed serving, pouring drinks rapidly, taking the next orders while fixing previous ones. One patron offered a hand to Layde, who took it as she stepped down from the pool table, people parting around her, pushing up against each other to make room.

"Thank you, darling," she said, gliding off to the restroom to fix her hair and makeup.

"Wow, that was some performance," shouted Tim.

"It sure was," said Aaron. "Glad you liked it. And you didn't get attacked."

"Hardy har har. I swear I thought she was this close to toppling over," said Tim, holding his thumb and index finger tightly together.

"And she's back on with a second number in fifteen," said Greg as he cleared empty glasses from in front of them.

"Just enough time for more shots," said Rick. He was speaking much louder than he needed to.

"What's up with you tonight, Rick," asked Aaron. "You seem like you're out to get drunk or something."

"Whatever, buzzkill," said Rick. "I'm just having a fun time. It's Friday night. It's not like you don't go out partying with Greg all the time."

"What's that supposed to mean?" asked Aaron.

"Nothing," said Rick, raising his voice louder. "I mean you go out all the time with Greg and party it up, getting messed up. It's Friday night, and I want to have some fun too."

"All right, I get it," said Aaron. He did not want this escalating any further. "I'm going to bum a cigarette out front." Turning to Tim, he asked, "Want to join or stay here?"

"I'll stay," said Tim. He was looking around the room again. Aaron wondered if he was cruising for someone better. He had been acting a little distant all night, distracted. He brushed it off.

"Suit yourself," said Aaron, snatching up his coat from the hook under the bar. "I'll be right back."

Greg was serving a couple of women close by and overheard, unbeknownst to Rick, what he was saying about him and Aaron spending so much time together. He reached under the bar and pulled out a surprise for Rick that he had been saving.

"Hey, boyfriend," said Greg. "Remember I told you I had something for you when you came in?"

Rick looked over to Greg, who was holding a foam stick that was about two feet long and had *Absolut Sorbet* written on the side. He flicked a switch on the bottom, and from inside its core, it started flashing very bright fluoro-orange.

Rick's face lit up, and he smiled.

"Oh baby," he said. "I love it. You know me so well."

"A liquor rep came around this week and was giving these out," said Greg. "I immediately thought of you."

"You're the best," said Rick.

Out on Ninth Avenue, several people smoked cigarettes. It was the middle of December and too cold for the front doors of the Saloon to be open. Through the glass, the bar looked warm. A smart-looking group of women with short hair and collared shirts were smiling and laughing inside. Aaron turned back to the street. Leaning up against a telephone booth across the narrow sidewalk and wearing a black leather jacket was the bodybuilder. In the light of the streetlamp and in full view, Aaron decided that he was a good-looking man, dark, virile. His face was scruffy but his head closely buzzed. He was smoking a cigarette, looking down at his phone.

"Got an extra one of those by chance?" asked Aaron.

The bodybuilder looked up, taking a second to realize who it was.

"Actually," he said, "I bummed this one." He slipped his phone inside his jacket pocket, holding Aaron's gaze.

"Oh, right," said Aaron.

"But you can share mine," he said, holding the lit cigarette for Aaron to take. "What's your name, by the way?

He took a pull of the cigarette. "Aaron," he said, exhaling. "What's yours?"

"Hank."

⚊⚊

Back indoors, Rick and Tim sat with Aaron's empty seat between them. They both had fresh bottles of beer, and a third one was waiting for Aaron. Tim thought that Rick's fluoro-orange foam tube blinking incessantly on his lap looked like a homing beacon on a life preserver from a plane crash. He also thought Rick looked disheveled, like something had happened. Should he ask him if he was okay? He wasn't even sure Rick would register the question.

Greg collected empty glasses from the bar, sent them through a small dishwasher, and wiped down the mahogany top with a dry towel before taking drink orders from the Saloon's thirsty patrons once more. He could not remember the last Friday night that was as this busy as this night, though in fairness, he had not worked a Friday in a while. He couldn't figure if it was Layde drawing in the crowd, or if it was just New York getting more crowded, swelling to new proportions. Either way, he felt charged by it. And tonight's cash tips wouldn't hurt either.

In the bathroom, Layde readied herself for her second number of the evening. While she was adjusting her wig—this one straight, high-volume, and black with deep purple highlights—a knock came at the door.

"Sean, honey, is that you?" asked Layde.

"It's me," replied Sean, and she unhooked the latch.

"You were on fire in that last number," said Sean. "Did I do okay with the light?"

Sean was one of the regular weekend bartenders at the Saloon. Although Layde did not perform there regularly, or even often, she did stop in, and he was her go-to bartender. He was dark, handsome, and had the most beautiful set of pearly white teeth Layde had ever seen, making it her goal to get a smile out of him as much as possible, which was never too difficult.

"You were sensational, Sean," said Layde. Sean smiled as she touched up her lips with a dark pencil.

"Can I mic you up?" asked Sean.

"Ready when you are," answered Layde, concentrating on her makeup.

Sean pulled a small plastic box with a wire attached from his pocket and handed it to Layde. She tucked it into the waistband of her undergarment, pulling the wire with the tiny microphone up around her front and to the top of her gown so that it clipped, virtually unseen, onto her collar below her chin.

"Would you mind?" said Layde turning her back to Sean to zip up her gown. It was long, black, and made of a shiny pleather-like material. There was a second open piece, a red, textured V that held her faux boobs tightly in place and went straight down narrowly, nearly to her navel, exposing a hint of her flat stomach.

Layde looked at herself in the mirror. She pulled a large, black, plastic bow from her bag of drag tricks and fastened it to one side of her wig, as if she were a Christmas gift. Her eyes were dark and smoky, her lips full and glossy. She took a deep breath, centered her head, lowered her chin, lifted her gaze, and, in her most seductive voice, spoke.

"Everybody wants Layde Licious."

"Hell yeah," said Sean. He looked her up and down, smiled, and then ran out the door.

The music playing in the Saloon stopped. People continued talking loudly, drinking, laughing. The bar was still packed, with even more people having joined the revelry since Layde's song ended.

Then, from overhead, at the fullest volume the Saloon's sound system could handle, a beat with a distinctly New York disco-funk melody washed over the crowd, electric guitars, violins, and a synthetic keyboard contributing to the bass.

Layde appeared, taking the stage from the darkness, her whole body moving to the music. This time, Sean stopped serving drinks, moved to the back end of the bar, and sat on it, dangling one leg over either side. He was mesmerized, taking position. He turned on his oversized handheld flashlight, illuminating Layde with a residual hue revealing a huge grin across his face.

It was Chaka Khan's 1978 classic, but just the music, no words. Layde wasn't lip-syncing this one. She was mic'ed.

On perfect pitch and with strength in her voice that traveled to the front of the Saloon and filled the space, arresting people's attention, she sang.

I'm every woman, it's all in me.
Anything you want done, baby.

Whereas in Layde's last number, the audience was reverent to start, and ended whooping and whistling, this time—especially in front of the stage and around the covered pool table—people danced. It was as if the music was moving through the crowd, lifting them up, and freeing their limbs.

Layde danced too while she sang, her shoulders rolling, elbows back, torso swaying, fingers snapping. She took half a step forward, swaying her hips to the beat. She hummed between the words and verses, giving her rendition a weight and fullness.

Tim was seated on a stool next to where Sean sat straddling the bar, rocking back and forth. He was also moving in his seat, looking up occasionally at Sean, then back to Layde. To his left, Aaron's seat was still empty, with Rick standing and dancing in back of it. Rick's head was down, and he was stepping his left foot a full step out and then back in again—all with genuine enthusiasm, but not aligning very closely to the beat.

Greg danced behind the bar as he served, moving with fancy footwork across the full length of the space. It was the only place open enough and free from shoulder-to-shoulder people to really get a good boogie on, and he was not wasting it.

I'm every woman, it's all in me.
I can read your thoughts right now.
Every one from A to Z.

Then Layde stepped off the stage and danced into the crowd. She worked her way up, past the pool table, hands in front of her, palms outward, opening and closing as she swayed and sang. Sean followed her with his spotlight. She moved up past Tim, winking at him, smiling. He blushed and looked up at Sean, who was also smiling. She danced in front of Rick, who was still staring down at his feet. With one finger placed delicately under his chin, she lifted his face until he was looking straight into her eyes, inches from her. He looked glazed over, drunk, but happy. She sang at him, in him, through him.

Layde continued along the bar to the large group of women by the front windows who were spinning each other, managing a halfway decent hustle in the tight space, swimming one hand down to the left and then up to the right.

Sean sat on the bar and lifted his arms high in the air, holding the light so as to maintain a direct line of sight to Layde. The beam picked up a sparkle in her dark, long, wavy hair, her purple highlights appearing deep red. Her gown glistened, reflecting back patches of white light. At the exact moment of the half-step-up key change, not missing a beat, Layde pushed through the front door into the cold December night, bringing her act to the sidewalk in front of the Ninth Avenue Saloon.

I'm every woman. I'm every woman.

Layde was dancing and singing in front of the window, facing back inside the bar. From outside, she could barely make out the music from within, but the song was still playing loud enough in her head that she was able to sing, maintaining the beat and pitch. Inside the Saloon, her voice could be heard perfectly, as if she were still there, the microphone attached to her lapel staying firmly in place, picking up and projecting her words throughout the space, filling it wholly.

Tim rose to his feet and then kneeled on his stool to see over everyone's heads. He was almost eye level with Sean and his light. He started to lose his balance while leaning forward to see outside and had to steady himself by placing his hand on Sean's leg now hanging over the patron's side of the bar. Sean felt warm to Tim's touch, his jeans taut. Sean looked at Tim and smiled. Tim blushed, but it went unnoticed in the dim lighting. He straightened up, swiveling to the right a tad on the stool. They both refocused on the show outside, where Layde was singing just a few feet next to Aaron.

Outside, from behind Layde, a few people who were smoking on the sidewalk stepped several feet back, moving, flanking her from behind. Pedestrians passed, many looking confused, others dancing before moving out of sight, and still some, so engaged in their own worlds and conversations, walked swiftly by as if nothing was happening—as if it were just another string of chaos in the fabric of New York City.

Aaron was swaying and staring up at Layde, the cigarette he was sharing with Hank expired, Hank having left, he said, to join his buddy at Pasha.

Layde stepped backward with each repeating line, her arms opened wide, her voice climbing higher and stronger.

I'm every woman. I'm every woman.

And she took another step back, and another. Glancing over her shoulder, she stepped off the curb, then backed into the middle of Ninth Avenue, on pitch and beat. Taxis, trucks, and cars slowed and pulled around her, several beeping. She was belting the refrain, singing not only to the Ninth Avenue Saloon twenty feet in front of her, but also pivoting toward Uptown and Downtown, her head held high, the muscles of her neck tight. She was singing to all of Hell's Kitchen, all of Midtown, all of New York.

The crowd inside went wild, many rushing out to the sidewalk, most crowding the Saloon's front window. People danced, discoed, whooped, and hollered. Passersby were no longer bystanders, but part of her show too.

With the final refrain, she reached up and out, closing her hands into tight fists as she and the music, at exactly the same moment, came to a hard stop. Everyone applauded—inside the bar, on the sidewalk out front, strangers across the street, even passengers in cars that slowed to a crawl.

Layde held her head still and high, heaving, the brisk air digging into her lungs. For several moments, she was frozen in place. Then, slowly looking around, coming to fully realize the song was over, her love and anger subsiding, she lowered her head and walked through the crowd back into the Ninth Avenue Saloon.

The blast of the horns from the taxis, trucks, and cars subsided. Traffic down Ninth Avenue resumed. Strangers walking past the Saloon that night continued on their way. The city returned to its normal ebb and flow, having paused, if just briefly, for Layde Licious.

CHAPTER NINE

Hank played poker with a regular group every couple of weeks in the furnished basement of a pizza shop in South Slope, Brooklyn. For the past four months, he had been sleeping on his friend Jack's couch in Washington Heights. Jack worked for the MTA as a subway driver, and most of his shifts were overnight, so, especially given their opposite schedules, he was more than happy to take his old Vermont buddy Hank in as a temporary roommate. Hank occasionally threw him a couple hundred bucks, though Jack noticed that Hank made fewer contributions over time. But Jack didn't mind the company so much either, so he didn't make an issue of it.

The poker group was made up mostly of union guys who worked with Jack. They liked to play Texas hold 'em, but usually warmed up first by taking turns playing dealer's choice. While they played regularly and treated the activity as recreational, the group was firm with the rules once there was money down on the table. Players rarely lost more than a few hundred dollars, though on more than one occasion, someone walked away with nearly a grand.

Hank shuffled a deck of cards a half-dozen times. He learned the method, the riffle shuffle, from his late grandfather when he was a kid. It involved splitting the deck in two and then bending the shorter ends of each half gently back into the other. By arching the center several inches high, the cards fanned into themselves, creating a neat, single stack. Hank liked shuffling this way because the cards made a light flicking sound at the end, and because it reminded him of his grandfather, whom he remembered fondly and thought about often.

"All right," said Hank. "Let's do this. Five-card draw. Red deuces and the suicide king are wild. Five-dollar ante."

One by one, each member of the circle tossed a chip into the center of the table.

To Hank's left, wearing a baseball cap with the Spartans logo, sat Jack, Hank's grade-school friend from Burlington, Vermont. To Jack's left were two guys he worked with, Diego and Luis. They were cousins who grew up and lived in the Bronx. Diego sported a round face and thin mustache. Luis had thick, curly hair and tattoo sleeves up both arms. Diego and Luis were considered subway veterans, having ridden the tunnels for nearly two decades. They drove lettered lines, which were older trains on a somewhat antiquated system. Jack, by comparison, drove the numbered trains, which were newer, cleaner, and required less manual control. To the left of Diego and Luis sat Gio, whose father owned the pizza shop and the rest of the building above the restaurant. Gio lived in one of the apartments above, his father living in the other. Gio was a husky man who liked to smoke clove cigarettes and drink whiskey. To Gio's left sat the sixth person at the table, Gio's older brother Rocco. Rocco started the group several years back, though there were mostly different players then. He was a bus driver in Queens, where he lived with his wife and three children. Like his brother Gio, Rocco liked to smoke clove cigarettes, but his wife hated it. So he only did so when he played poker, especially when he wasn't doing well.

Hank went around the table dealing one card face down to each person until everyone had five. The players picked up their cards, some arranging them neatly so they could figure out their best hand.

"Jack, you'll lead the bet when you're ready," said Hank.

"All right, well, we only get two shots at this, so ten dollars," said Jack. He was holding a pair of tens. He tossed in two chips.

One by one, the rest of the players put in their chips. First Diego. Then Luis. Then Gio.

"I fold," said Rocco. "Another great start." He took a clove from his brother's pack on the table and lit it.

Hank's hand was weak. He had no pairs, nothing even close to a run, and held all four suits. But he did have an ace, which meant that he was allowed to trade in four cards instead of the usual maximum of three. He tossed his two chips into the center.

"Okay, Jack, how many cards do you want?" asked Hank.

"Three," said Jack.

"Diego?" asked Hank.

"Three," answered Diego pursing his lips and touching his moustache with his index finger.

"Luis?" asked Hank.

"Three," answered Luis.

"Gio?" asked Hank.

"Two, please," answered Gio, smiling and taking a sip from a large rocks glass full of ice and whiskey.

"And dealer has an ace, so I'll take four," said Hank, swapping out four cards and replacing them with new ones, holding onto the ace. His heart raced for a nanosecond as he looked at his cards, realizing his best hand was three of a kind, three aces. He had his original ace, plus another he was just dealt and the suicide king.

"Final bet," said Hank. "You'll lead when you're ready."

Jack looked at his cards, then at the pot, then back at his cards.

"Fifteen," said Jack throwing three chips in the center.

"I fold," said Diego.

"Me too," said Luis.

"I'm in," said Gio, throwing three chips into the pot.

"I'm in for fifteen," said Hank. "And I'll raise you twenty." He placed seven chips in a stack in front of him near the center.

"Really, Hank?" asked Jack. "It's the first hand."

"Whatever, dude," said Hank. "Let's just play."

Jack shook his head and put the additional four chips into the pot in order to stay in.

"Too rich for my blood," said Gio. "I'm out." He put his cards face down on the table.

"All right, Hank, what do you got?" asked Jack.

"Three aces," he responded. "Two natural aces and a wild." He put his cards down on the table so everyone could see.

"I've got four tens," said Jack. "Three natural and one red deuce." He placed his cards face up. "Looks like I win."

"Frig," said Hank, pounding a fist on the table.

Jack reached in with both hands and pulled the chips toward his pile. He just won one hundred and sixty-five dollars, fifty of which was Hank's.

"That money is mine," said Hank. "I'm getting that back."

Hank and Jack were longtime friends, the pair having grown up together in the small city of Burlington, Vermont. Jack was familiar with Hank's temper and usually laughed it off. Hank cracked a beer from a mini fridge nearby, settled himself back down, and shook off the first round, vowing to himself to play smarter.

In their younger days, Hank and Jack were inseparable, often getting into trouble. Burlington was small by any city's standard, with fewer than fifty thousand residents, but it was the biggest city in Vermont. Although there were a couple of strong industries, the town felt, to locals, to be divided in two.

There was a thriving medical research community attached to the university. It housed ten thousand doctors, scientists, and academics. And there was a factory, which manufactured restaurant equipment, including their largest-selling product, commercial-grade ovens. It employed fewer than three thousand workers.

Both Hank's and Jack's fathers worked at the factory, as did many of their friends' fathers. Burlington's other big claim to fame economically was that in 1978, Ben Cohen and Jerry Greenfield opened an ice cream shop in an old gas station that eventually birthed the national chain Ben & Jerry's. Hank's father hated that shop because he said it was full of crunchy hippies who smoked pot and didn't know the meaning of hard work. As kids, Hank was never allowed to go there, even for special occasions. But his grandfather would occasionally take him on the sly.

Being located on Lake Champlain and less than forty miles from the Canadian border, Burlington also felt frigid most of the year, rarely reaching eighty degrees on the hottest days of summer. When he was young, Hank hated the cold, especially in the early mornings when he waited on his corner for the school bus. But then, in his teenage years, Hank—along with Jack—discovered snowboarding. Twenty miles east of Burlington was Stowe

Mountain Resort, and although Hank never once went as a kid, when he was fourteen, Jack's parents invited him there for the day to celebrate Jack's birthday. Hank could not convince his father to allow him to go, but then Jack's father called Hank's father to give him peace of mind of parental supervision, and it was all on. Hank had to promise his father he would find an after-school job to pay him back for the price of the lift ticket and equipment rental.

Hank became obsessed with snowboarding. A group of guys who graduated from Hank's high school a few years earlier started a company from someone's garage engineering snowboards. What began as a hobby turned into a profitable business. The company started producing other snowboard equipment, renting a small industrial space on the outskirts of town and employing up to twenty part-time workers during their busy season. Hank and Jack were two of these workers, and when they started, they were the youngest on staff. Hank was relieved not to be working anywhere close to the factory where his father worked. Jack was just happy for all the extra perks that came along with the job.

On Saturdays, the owners of the company piled any of the staff who wanted to go—along with some close friends—into a minivan they owned. They drove to Stowe to snowboard. In exchange for premium, Stowe-branded rental equipment sold at cost, each year the company was given a dozen season passes. In addition to the snowboarding trips, Hank and Jack were allowed to make and keep their own snowboards, which Hank stored at their shop.

It was during these high school years when Hank finally started feeling good, and found some happiness. He wasn't doing great in school, but in addition to his new job and hobby, he was hanging out with Jack nearly every day. The two were always good friends, but then, for a period of about two years, the pair became inseparable. In the summers, when they didn't snowboard, they rode bikes, snuck beers, and fished on the lake.

In their junior year, Jack got a girlfriend. At first the three would hang out as a group. But inevitably, during late-night movies or after drinking, Jack and his girlfriend would start making out, and Hank would be left watching. Hank wanted to hook up too—his buddy looking like he was having the time of his life. Once Jack even described getting to third base as better than shredding the pow, which was what they called snowboarding. That hurt Hank, but he blew it off and found other ways to occupy his time. Instead of hanging out with Jack as much, Hank turned his energy to smoking weed and lifting weights in his basement.

Then, the day before his eighteenth birthday, Hank's grandfather passed. Hank was a senior in high school and was just two months away from graduation at the time. With funeral bills piling up, his father was as short tempered as ever, and his mother had become a drone—rarely even speaking except for an occasional inanity. Hank's grades weren't good enough to get into the local university, and he was terrible in sciences and math. So even though college wasn't an option, he decided he was going to leave Burlington once and for all, on the night of his graduation. But it wound up taking him another eight years.

Days before graduation, Hank's father lost three fingers in a press at the factory, and Hank needed to start working full time to help support himself and his parents. He wanted to work for the snowboarding company, but they didn't have full-time employees other than the founders. The oven factory, though small, was unionized, and in addition to benefits, workers earned twelve dollars an hour from day one. Hank capitulated to his father's tirades and took a job there. Jack went off to a state college seventy miles south. Before he left, Jack told Hank that he overheard his father say to his mother that he thought Hank's father stuck his hand into the machine on purpose. For weeks he had been rambling on at a local bar off of Main Street about cashing in on his union dues and receiving disability. A lot of people overheard it. After the accident, a blood test at the hospital revealed there was alcohol in his father's system, so the paychecks never came.

"I'm going all in," said Diego. He counted his remaining chips, which came to fifty dollars. His cousin Luis to his left gave a loud whistle and leaned back in his chair.

The group was almost into its third hour of a Texas hold 'em tournament. Luis had already gone all in unsuccessfully. He resigned himself to eating his losses, the hundred-dollar buy in.

"I'll match," said Gio. From the size of Gio's pile of chips, it looked as if he was having a good night. But he bought in a second time in the first hour, so he actually had two hundred dollars on the table. He considered this an investment toward his ultimate win, though with the cards he was getting, his doubts were starting to trump his ego. He took a sip from a rocks glass half filled with watered-down whiskey from the residue of melted ice and rested a lit, mostly smoked clove cigarette in an ashtray.

Almost immediately, Rocco picked up the clove and pulled a drag.

"I should have been out of this long ago," said Rocco. "I'm all in too." He too, like his brother, bought in a second a time.

"I'll match," said Hank.

"Me too," said Jack.

Hank and Jack were doing fairly well that night. The blessing of playing with the same group of people was that over time, their tells became apparent. Hank noticed that Rocco lit or smoked one of his brother's cloves nearly every time he was dealt a weak hand, but still planned to stay in. Diego, across from him, would rub his right arm, where he was progressively taking on more and more tattoos—a full dragon embedded within a sea of tiger lilies. Jack didn't have a tell as far as Hank could see.

"Well, everyone," said Hank. "It's now or never."

Diego turned over his cards, revealing a flush.

Gio shook his head, flipping his cards to reveal a pair of sixes with a third six in the flop. "Damn, that's me," he said, taking the lit clove back from his brother.

Hank flipped over two hearts, a three and a queen. "Flush," he said. "Queen high."

Jack took off his cap, scratched his head. Then he flipped over the cards in his hole to also reveal two hearts, a seven and a nine. "You've got it, buddy," he said.

Hank smiled from ear to ear. This was his fourth win in the tournament so far. He had this theory that with six people playing at the table, he needed to win at least one out of every six hands to stay ahead in the game. He caught himself smiling and looked down. Then he reached his arm around Jack and gave his shoulder a few quick squeezes.

"So I guess that just leaves you and me," said Hank. He pulled his arm back from Jack and collected all the chips from the center of the table.

"Let's close this out," said Jack.

The pair played several more hands, neither having a strong enough hand to go all in. Between the two of them, they held the entire group's share. With both Gio and Rocco having bought in a second time, tonight's bounty was hefty at eight hundred dollars. That was pretty high, considering they most often played with only five people, and second buy-ins tended to be more the exception than the rule.

From their first few rounds of dealer's choice poker, which mostly consisted of five-card draw, acey deucey, and seven card—generally with as many wilds as the group could think up—Hank was up about two hundred dollars. This meant that if he won, he realized, he would be walking away with a full grand, a feat he had yet to achieve in the months he had played with this group.

Jack was not revealing much. He was pounding back beers and consoling himself by assuming that at least if Hank won this tournament, which was feeling more and more possible with each hand dealt, he should see a kickback of at least a couple of hundred dollars to put toward rent.

Having lived in New York for nearly a decade, moving to the city right after dropping out of Castleton State College in his junior year, Jack managed to make a decent life for himself. Like Hank, the last thing on the face of the planet he wanted was to do factory work like his father. Although he tried hard in school to pass all his classes—especially in the beginning—ultimately he became distracted by girls and booze and wound up partying more than studying. After it became clear that he did not have it in him to finish, he went to New York. Taking over a rent-controlled apartment in Washington Heights and finding a bartending job in the neighborhood, he put his name in for a city job at the MTA. The waiting list was over three years at that stage, but Jack was determined not to go back to Vermont, and so he bided his time.

Hank moved in with him over four months ago, though by the sounds of it, thought Jack, he had been couch hopping in one version or another for close to a year in the city. Jack tried to convince Hank to put his name down on the waiting list for a city job, and although he said he did, Jack had his doubts. Hank held odd jobs—mostly handyman and construction work, on and off. He spent most of his free time at the gym. Jack realized that his buddy needed a longer-term plan but also figured it was not up to him to nag him. Hank had, after all, a pretty rough upbringing with a jerk of a father and got stuck looking after his parents after high school for longer than any reasonable person would have considered bearable. Hank's father often went into tirades. To say that a side effect of losing part of his hand was losing part of his mind would be unfair. Hank's father was nasty before the accident, if you could even call it an accident. But the medication and frustration at his failed scheme not going the way he planned made him even angrier. Jack knew some of what happened with Hank's father, but not everything.

Hank's father would often explode at the dinner table to the slightest contrary thing Hank said. He'd hold him on the floor in the middle of their kitchen, arms pinned, each of Hank's wrists under his father's knees, screaming inches from his face, berating him, calling Hank useless and lazy, degrading him for being so ungrateful. In the later years, Hank probably could have taken him. But with his father, no matter how many weights he lifted or how big his muscles got, he felt weak, like a small child. There was another reason why Hank bore the treatment. His father occasionally exploded on his mother in this way, and Hank found if he directed the anger toward himself, his mother would be spared. He thought often, more than he wanted, about his father and how he acted, replaying those moments over and over in his head, trying to understand them, fantasizing about how they could have been different, how Hank could have been different, how he could have done something more.

Hank downed the last of his beer. He and Jack looked at the cards on the table and in their hands, both considering the inevitable. Jack flinched first.

"I'm all in," said Jack.

Without missing a beat, Hank responded. "Me too."

Neither man made eye contact with the other. The other players at the table stopped side conversations in anticipation of the final hand.

"I call," said Hank.

There were two pairs showing on the table, kings and sevens. This meant that either player could potentially have a very strong hand. Jack flipped over his cards to reveal a king and a four.

"Full house, kings high," he said.

Hank paused. Then he flipped over his cards to reveal two sevens. "Four of a kind," he said.

The group erupted in adulation. It was very rare to have such a strong hand with no wilds, but it happened on occasion, and tonight looked like it was Hank's night.

"Bam," said Hank. "Game."

"Well played, buddy," said Jack, taking a final swig of his beer.

Diego and Luis stood up immediately, Diego stretching his arms wide.

"We've got morning shifts," said Diego.

"And no chips to cash in," said Luis.

"Right," said Gio. "Let's call it a night."

"Mind if I bum one of those cloves, Gio?" asked Hank.

Gio looked in his pack. "Last one," he said. "But it's all yours."

"Are you sure?" asked Hank.

"You bet," said Gio. "You must have an angel sitting on your shoulder, bambino. This night is your night."

Gio held his last clove cigarette out to Hank and glanced over at Rocco, who looked back, then away and down, shaking his head slightly. Then Gio picked up his lighter, holding the open flame out for Hank, who leaned in, lighting the clove, not noticing the look the brothers exchanged.

"Stellar," said Hank.

CHAPTER TEN

G reg and Rick liked to host dinner parties at their apartment. They lived in a newer-construction building just west of Tenth Avenue and managed to score a great deal on the rent.

When their building went up five years ago, in order for the development company to be issued grants and low-interest loans from the city, they needed to agree to reserve a dozen below-market-rate, one-bedroom units for what the city classified as medium-income tenants. With rental vacancies being generally less than 1 percent of Manhattan at any given time, getting lucky enough to win the lottery for one of these places in the first pass was tough. Getting lucky enough to get picked when some poor fool gave up or vacated one later down the line was near impossible. But Rick was taking the lead on finding them a place, and he was determined to work the system.

Rick called the building's rental office. A sharp-tongued agent told him that although an apartment recently became vacant as a result of the passing of an elderly woman, there was a very long list of potential residents already in the pool, though he was welcome to have his name added. After close examination of the building's website, he was able to find the official policy of the management company's lottery system as published in accordance with the law. It turned out that people who put their name in the lottery needed to actively renew their standing in writing every twelve months. Because the rental agent didn't know this until Rick pointed it out, and because no apartments had become vacant since the first tenants had originally moved in, the place was theirs. Rick sat in her office explaining all of this and was not budging under any circumstances until she conceded. Unless she was able to produce renewal letters from their waiting list, he was not letting her off the hook. He even threatened to contact the Housing Authority, Mayor's Office, Human Rights Campaign, and media. Why not? This could be discrimination, he figured.

"And that, Nikki," said Greg, "is the story of how my wonderful boyfriend, Rick, found this apartment."

"New Yorkers always have a bloody story about how they found their apartments," said Nikki. "Fortunately for me, there was this lovely old queen of a flight attendant who retired to Mexico and let me sublet from him. His name is still on the lease."

"That sounds about right," said Aaron. "And you are probably paying half of what I am. Mine started out only rent stabilized. Your place is still rent controlled, right?

"Ah yes," answered Nikki. "It is. The tradeoff is that the owner of the building won't touch my place. I have to get repairs taken care of and paid for on my own. You know I haven't had a properly working heater in two years. When it's cold outside, it's positively tepid in there at best."

"Well, for the five hundred dollars and change a month you are saving in rent, you can probably afford to buy one," said Aaron.

Aaron was feeling increasingly agitated with Nikki ever since Tim called yesterday to cancel going to Rick and Greg's dinner party that night. It was not her fault, of course, and she even agreed to attend as Aaron's last-minute plus one instead, but he could not help thinking there was something she knew that she wasn't sharing. On the walk over from their building, he avoided the topic completely. But now, with each passing drink, his curiosity was starting to fester.

Greg, Linda, Nikki, and Aaron sat around a glass table that was set for five, one seat empty for Rick, who could be seen in the kitchen through a window nook close by, prepping the first course. The group had been there just an hour so far, but they were already opening a third bottle of wine, prompting Rick to speed up the starter. He didn't want his guests getting too tipsy too quickly.

"Well, I for one had a very uninteresting time looking when I bought," said Linda. "Aside from having Rick come to about half the places I saw, which made it more entertaining."

"We must have looked at ten apartments," said Rick from the kitchen.

"I love where I wound up, but if there was one thing I learned, it was that no matter where you live, you have to be willing to sacrifice something—light, closet space, something."

"Right, honey," said Rick from the kitchen. "And you sacrificed what, having a partial view of Central Park from your balcony instead of an unobstructed one?"

"Really, Rick, you make me sound like such a snob," said Linda. "It's no secret that I had help on the deposit from my parents. Even at my salary, I couldn't have done it without them."

Rick came around from the kitchen, setting plates with salad in front of each person. While Greg loved to host dinner parties, Rick was in charge of the cooking. After years of entertaining together, they had learned their strong points. Greg had a tendency to get distracted with the entertaining part, putting off the actual cooking part, which resulted in several meals during those early days of hosting not getting started until close to midnight—long after the stomachs of their guests, and Rick's, had imploded in a fire of alcohol.

"What do we have here?" asked Nikki.

"It's a goat cheese salad with organic arugula and a balsamic reduction in a parmesan cheese bowl," said Rick. "Bon appétit."

After three more bottles of wine, a tuna tartare course, and shrimp and steak kabobs over saffron rice, Rick said he had something to tell everyone. Greg looked over curiously, as he had no idea what it could be.

"Remember Layde's performance at the Saloon last Friday night?" he asked. He was looking to Greg and Aaron, who were nodding. "Well, I don't. That wasn't just because I was blitzed, which I was. It was because I got blitzed after being laid off." He was slurring a tad.

Aaron was replaying that night in his head. Tim at the bar, afraid of being called out by Layde. Rick coming in drunk and Aaron needing to get away. And then that man on the street with the huge chest and arms, Hank. They had shared that cigarette.

"Ah, baby, why didn't you tell me?" asked Greg.

"I thought I could fix it," said Rick. "New talent hasn't been coming in for a while. They didn't need as big a support team as before. Our function was absorbed by another department."

"That's terrible, Rick," said Aaron. "This city, New York, and tight places. But you know how to bounce back. It'll be okay."

"Of course, Rick," said Linda. "We can figure it out. With the people in this room alone, we probably have tons of contacts looking for someone qualified like you."

"I didn't mean to bring the party down," said Rick. "It's just been weighing on my mind. And we had this planned before it happened."

"Baby, it's not like you're dying," said Greg. "It's going to be okay. We are going to get through this."

"I know," said Rick. "You are the best. I'm so lucky to have you." Rick reached over and put his hand on Greg's knee.

"All right, but seriously," said Rick. "I'm not dying. And we need to have some fun tonight. Let's take a break for a hot second, clear the table. Then maybe we can sit in the living room and play a board game. You guys relax."

"I'm in for sure," said Nikki. "I might pop down for a quick ciggie first."

"I'll come with you," said Aaron.

The pair grabbed their coats, leaving Rick, Greg, and Linda inside.

⊁⊱⊰⊁

As Nikki and Aaron stepped outside the building, they were blasted with a cold wintery wind coming straight off the Hudson River. In the few hours they were inside Greg and Rick's apartment, the temperature dropped and the December night took hold. They immediately banked a sharp left, ducking into a large garage doorway from the commercial building next door, which successfully shielded them, mostly.

New York had enjoyed a mild and warm autumn—the trees that lined the streets and filled Central Park having turned from green to yellow, orange, and red. But the pleasant air had seemed to give way suddenly. In the week since Layde's performance at the Saloon, the nights had changed from crisp to cold and the trees from brown to bare. It felt to Aaron like the season had shed itself, leaving a void in its place.

Nikki took a cigarette from a pack, lit it, and handed it to Aaron. She lit another for herself. They smoked in silence for a full minute before Nikki finally spoke.

"Bummer about Rick losing his job," she said. She was shivering, legs held tightly together, arms scrunched close to her sides.

"Yeah, definitely," said Aaron. "I feel like they should be all right. I think he was doing well for himself before, and I'm sure Greg does fine."

"It certainly helps being in a relationship in a situation like that," said Nikki. "For the support, dual incomes, and whatnot."

"Yeah, it's the whatnot part that's really nice," said Aaron. He could not hold back any longer. He had wanted to ask about Tim all night. He knew he and Nikki must have spoken.

Over the past month or so, Aaron's relationship with Tim had been like a rocket ship. That first night they hooked up after Nikki's party was full of physical heat, the two talking, drinking, and spending most of their time hanging out in their boxer briefs, or even less. They were so comfortable with each other physically and emotionally—or so it seemed. That was followed by several happy hours and a few dinners. Aaron had previously gotten into the habit of checking in with Greg before each weekend to see if he wanted to go out. Since Tim entered the picture, he had spent every Saturday night with him. Tim seemed to be comfortable with the pace of the relationship, thought Aaron. But then at Layde's performance at the Saloon, Aaron conceded to himself that Tim seemed distracted, distant—especially after he gave him that one-month anniversary gift. It was meant to be tongue in cheek, just something kind. It was not an engagement ring or keys to his apartment.

"Tim hates me, doesn't he," Aaron finally blurted out. "I'm coming on too strong and smothering him."

Nikki smiled, almost laughing. "Don't be daft," she said. "Tim likes you a lot. It's obvious."

"So why does it feel like he is pulling back?" asked Aaron. "Why didn't he want to come tonight? That excuse of not feeling up to it was pretty weak. We saw him two nights ago and he was fine."

"I don't know, Aaron," said Nikki. She took a drag of her cigarette, exhaling slowly. "Maybe you should be asking him."

Nikki had lived across the hall from Aaron for over two years. While both lost count of how many times they had partied together at one of their apartments or in the communal backyard of their building, they ran in different circles. Aaron hung out with guys in the neighborhood mostly, guys like Greg who liked to frequent late-night bars and clubs where women didn't always feel welcome. Nikki spent the bulk of her time travelling for work. When she wasn't travelling, she preferred calling a couple of girlfriends and popping open a bottle of wine. Because much of her time involved working in and among the public, on her downtime, she liked being in someone's home. From the moment Nikki met Tim, she had considered him one of the gals. They met at a happy hour through a coworker of a coworker but decided almost instantly they were destined to be friends. At times, Nikki felt like a big sister to Tim, coaching him through his family dramas and financial anxieties. The two saw each other nearly every time she was back in town, though over the last month or so, while he was seeing Aaron, they saw each other less. Nikki didn't mind much. Tim seemed happy, and she had plenty of other friends to help polish off a bottle of wine when she was in town.

"I haven't dated much since my ex," said Aaron. "And that was a long time ago. I was trying not to get too serious with anyone."

"It's hard in New York," said Nikki. "Half of you boys are more interested in partying than anything serious, and the other half are all baggage."

"Yeah, I know," said Aaron. "It's like all these people come to New York for all these reasons, everyone looking for something, or having some expectation about what it's going to be like."

"But we are no spring chickens anymore, Aaron. I stopped looking a while ago."

"Speak for yourself, girl," said Aaron with a smile. "I have a flatter stomach and a bigger chest than I did when I was thirty."

"You are such a daddy," said Nikki, leaning over and poking Aaron's pec gently with two fingers. "You've got bigger boobs than I do."

"I do not have boobs, thank you very much," said Aaron, feigning hurt. "They are my man pecs."

The pair was more relaxed now, their cigarettes finished, the wind having momentarily settled, giving them reprieve from the nearly icy bite in the air.

From outside the apartment door, Aaron and Nikki could hear the dance version of Robyn's "Dream On." Aaron knew immediately that it was Greg who put this on and turned it up. He often played it while they were pre-gaming before they went out. It was one of his favorites.

When they opened the door, they found Greg and Rick dancing as if they were in the middle of a crowded club, grinding up on one another, coffee table pushed to one side. Linda's heels were off, and she was up, dancing in the middle of the sofa, go-going.

As she swayed her hips from side to side, she pushed down on the ends of her little black dress, her head forward and her dirty-blond hair falling into her face.

Neither Aaron nor Nikki missed a beat, immediately dancing to the center of the room. Within moments, they too were straddling each other. Aaron looked over and spotted Rick, one hand in the air. Aaron always thought of dancing, especially at bars and clubs, as a form of celebration. At times when everything was good, he partied, celebrating life, the big wins and the small ones. When things were bad, really bad, he didn't feel he had a right to be at a bar or club on a dance floor, drinking. He often thought of that when he saw nutty Hollywood stars with massive drug addictions who were clearly spiraling out of control, publically melting down before everyone's eyes, being shot by paparazzi stumbling or being escorted from clubs late night. They had no business being there. What were they celebrating, a coke or meth addiction? But Rick's dancing was different. He had lots to celebrate despite losing his job—his health, a great apartment in the best city on earth, friends who cared a lot, and an amazing boyfriend.

Aaron watched Greg as he danced around Rick, the center of his world, trying to make him smile, laugh. Greg was flinging back his head like some sort of cracked-out puppet, moving his arms as if they were on strings being controlled by a mad puppet master. Rick, for his part, looked quizzical, feigning confusion about his oddball boyfriend, who he knew was trying to cheer him up.

Aaron missed that. He missed having a boyfriend to pick him up when he fell down. He never minded being the strong one in the relationship too, shrugging off his boyfriend's bad days or sour moods when they came.

There was nothing really wrong, per se, with Aaron's ex. Their lives were just going in different directions, or at least that's what Aaron told himself. They met when they were in their late twenties and moved in together too quickly. They grew complacent, comfortable. They had fun times, traveled, drank with friends, furnished an apartment. But the years ticked by, and they worked more than played and, in the end, did not really have much to show for it—not that Aaron thought there should have been some prize at the end, necessarily. Kids maybe? A mortgage? He never really bought into that suburban paradigm like his parents. But when he was older, he thought about it. While Aaron and his ex ran out of passion, as couples who are together long term sometimes do, it was times like this one, when life dished out something cruel, that he could usually still count on him. Aaron liked being there for someone as much as having someone there for him.

That's probably why Aaron grew attached to Tim so quickly. He saw a guy down on his luck needing a hand. It also didn't hurt that he looked cute too, and the sex was so fun. Aaron snapped himself out of his own thoughts, laughed, shook his head, and decided he was probably reading too much into the Tim situation. Maybe Tim was feeling under the weather and needed a night in to unwind, without him. Everybody needed a night off, right?

CHAPTER ELEVEN

New Year's Eve fell on a Thursday, which meant that most people were given a three-day weekend. Manhattan's thumping corporate heart was due to ease to a slow, gentle beat. Yet many of Manhattan's residents had something different in mind.

Greg made sure the bar would be covered well in advance and had been looking for the right party for weeks. Some people were lukewarm about New Year's as a holiday and night out, saying expectations were too high and all the places they wanted to go—and could easily get into every other night of the year—were crazy packed with lines around the block. But that was why Greg believed in coming up with a strategy.

Carefully laying the seeds with Rick and the others at their dinner party two weeks prior, he discovered a few key bits of information that helped his plan come together. First, Linda was attending some swanky party with Allen at one of his boss's apartments in Gramercy Park. Therefore, she would need just the right pre-party before she shipped off to rub elbows with the Wall Street goons and drink their two-trillion-dollar bottles of champagne. With Rick's stressful work year culminating with him losing his job, he needed comp tickets—or at least Greg needed Rick to believe they were comp tickets—and an open bar to alleviate any guilt from having a big night out. Greg hated lying to his boyfriend, but he figured in this case, it was to cheer him up and get him out of the apartment for his own good. So it was justifiable.

His buddy Aaron he wanted to flat out impress—blow his socks off really. The pair had been partying around town for months at the usual bars with decent dance floors and resident DJs spinning solid pop mixes—nothing to shake a stick at, even by New York standards. But Greg needed something big, a great space, maybe a theme. That is when it clicked one quiet Wednesday night when he was bartending, flipping through one of the local free party rags. Why hadn't he considered it before?

The Empire Toy Party was a multiplex mega event that happened once a year in New York—sometimes over New Year's Eve—and periodically traveled to other cities as well. It was multifloored with a world-renowned headline DJ, and it was known for being a totally interactive and sensory assaulting, music-and-dance extravaganza. In addition to being a fun night out, it also promoted a good cause, since every attendee was asked to bring a toy to leave in giant bins by the doors that were later donated to children's charities. This time around, the Empire Toy Party was being held at the Thunder Room along the river in the West Village, which was located next to a huge empty lot. The promoters annexed the lot, erecting a massive circus tent with—in addition to a fourth dance floor to complement the three others inside the complex—rows of boardwalk attractions and even a jack-in-the-box-themed Tilt-A-Whirl ride.

"Tell me again," Rick was asking, "how did you manage to get VIP tickets to this?"

"I told you," answered Greg. "Layde's drag daughter's boy-friend, Danny, works for an agency that markets those electronic blue cigarette thingies, which is one of the sponsors of the party tonight. Layde was asked by Danny's agency to host some reception party next month in Milwaukee that's also run by the Empire Toy promoters and sponsored by the electronic blue cigarette thingies. I think it's a part two or second version of tonight. She got four tickets but couldn't go because she's doing this other gig, so she gave them to us."

"She just gave them to us," said Rick.

"Yeah," said Greg. Rick was asking a lot of questions, he thought.

"And she's going next month to Milwaukee?" said Rick.

Greg let out a heavy breath. "Yes, babe," he said. "Milwaukee." Greg did not even know exactly where Milwaukee was or if they had drag-hosted events there, let alone a burgeoning electronic blue cigarette thingy market. "What does it matter where we got the tickets anyhow?" he said trying to change the topic.

"It's just that they are VIP, and they don't say comp on them," said Rick. "They say they cost three hundred dollars each on the ticket."

Rick was standing in his robe in the kitchen, drinking a beer from the bottle, having just gotten out of the shower. It was almost eight o'clock, and they were due to meet Aaron and Tim for a quick drink before they went over to the party. Linda said she was going to try to make it before she met up with Allen but wasn't sure she would have time.

Coming up from behind Rick, kissing him on the neck and slipping his hand into his robe, Greg said, "Babe, we're going to have a freaking superb time tonight, mark my words. This is the biggest Empire Toy Party they've thrown to date."

Rick had to admit he was excited too. Even though he went on and on about not liking New Year's Eve because of the crowds, now that it was here, and they had VIP access, he was looking forward to it. Plus, after the rough few weeks he'd had, which included trying to network into a job right before the holiday break, he knew he could use a really sexy night out.

Tim was excited to be going to an actual Empire Toy Party. If it wasn't for Aaron's invite, he was planning to bum around Hell's Kitchen bars, thinking maybe he'd bump into someone he knew. He was familiar with the toy parties from long before he moved to New York, when he was struggling to hold down a job, go to school, and support his mother, sister, and nephew. He would flip through photos online, wondering how all these people lived—what their lives were like. Did they always go to big parties? Only go to big parties? Snap into existence any time there was a party, only to disappear into the ether shortly after the photo was taken?

In Aaron's kitchen, Tim was opening two beers. He called over to the main room of the studio, where Aaron was fumbling around in his closet, trying on different shirts that to Tim looked only marginally different from one another.

"Thanks so much for inviting me tonight," said Tim. "What does this VIP status entail?"

"Of course," answered Aaron. "Who else would I invite? Anywho, I don't really know. I'm sure there is an open bar, and a private section, maybe a balcony or something? Dancers?"

"I've never been to the Thunder Room," said Tim.

"Me neither," said Aaron. "Though judging by what's on the website, and what the promoters are saying, they completely transformed the place."

"And Layde coming through with comp tickets," said Tim. "That's really something."

Aaron pushed his head deeper into the closet so that Tim could not see him through the small pass-through that separated the kitchen from the main room.

"Yeah, pretty lucky," said Aaron.

Aaron decided to perpetuate the same manufactured story that Greg spun. He knew that Tim was just starting to get on his feet. So as not to jeopardize him declining or backing out because of financial reasons, he decided to buy Tim's ticket.

It was not that Aaron was well off, he thought. Poking his head around his closet, he was looking for the right something, turning over piles of T-shirts, digging to the back, hoping to find a hidden gem. He managed to keep himself debt free in recent years, paying his bills—more or less—as soon as they were due. And although he was in a sound and stable position, like many New Yorkers he lived generally paycheck to paycheck. His current full-time corporate events job contributed to a retirement fund, but it was the first time in his life that he'd had one, so there was not much there. Still, Aaron maintained a philosophy that a person either made ends meet, no matter what it took, to stay in Manhattan, or failed and left. The worst kind of defeat would be to have to leave the city and, in a worst-case scenario, move to somewhere like Jersey City or Long Island. So when it came to hustling—metaphorically of course—to make ends meet, he secretly prided himself on being creative with how he got by. If ever Aaron started to fall behind financially, he would pick up one-off catering shifts from his old employer, who was happy to have him. He also went through phases of selling online anything he had in his apartment that he had not touched in a year, such as old books, DVDs, and even random appliances, such as a popcorn maker he somehow inherited from his breakup. When finances ever looked particularly bleak, he would rent his apartment to visitors or tourists. Fortunately, since his place was so centrally located, just three blocks west of Times Square, there was rarely a problem finding people to stay for a few days or a week. At these times he crashed with friends or cashed in some vacation time and hopped on a train south to his parents in Virginia.

But tonight was Aaron's night to splurge and let down his hair. He was having so much fun with Tim, and he wanted to continue the ride.

"What are you looking for anyhow?" asked Tim.

"I don't know. I need something…," he said trailing off, pulling out a shoebox from the back, and setting it between them.

Tim took a swig of his beer, and Aaron did the same. This was their modest pre-pre-party—a couple of beers, some local radio playing, and about twenty minutes of good, old-fashioned primping before the main event. Their spirits were high with anticipation of the night ahead.

"Ah, here we are," said Aaron. "I've had this stupid shoebox forever. It has all this random stuff, bits and pieces left over from a Halloween, beanies and baseball caps, workout gloves, Mardi Gras beads. Hmmm...What about this?" He pulled out a thick leather armband about two inches wide that he bought on a whim when he was on vacation in San Francisco with his ex.

Tim laughed. "So you're a leather daddy now?"

"You know," said Aaron, smiling, "I've never minded a little slap and tickle."

Aaron was wearing a dark gray pair of snug Diesel jeans with his favorite black and blue, package-accentuating briefs underneath. His short-sleeve, black button-down shirt—unbuttoned to almost the middle of his chest—was tight enough to show off his newly more defined torso, but loose enough that it fell comfortably over his midriff. He snapped the leather band on his left arm between his triceps and bicep, accentuating the black leather in his belt and high-top basketball sneakers. Aaron looked at himself in the mirror and thought he looked the right amount of naughty and nice—just what he needed for this party.

"Very manly," said Tim. "I, for one, will be sticking with this," referring to his slim, untucked, deep red button-down shirt and black-and-white checkered bow tie. "It is New Year's, after all."

"Naturally," said Aaron. "I think we look great together." Aaron leaned over the room-separating window frame to kiss Tim.

"Slow down, mister," said Tim. "It's bad luck to kiss anyone before midnight."

"That's crazy. You just made that up. This isn't our wedding night." With that Aaron reached his hand behind Tim's neck and pulled him closer, giving the outside of Tim's closed lips a quick lick.

"Gross," said Tim. "You're such a dog."

"Woof."

The apartment on the north side of Gramercy Park that Richard, one of Allen's bosses, owned had a balcony that stretched around two sides of the building with a spectacular view in the far distance of One World Trade Center, which was lit inside by large, white construction bulbs between bare floors. The balcony had several large trees on it in giant pots. There were tiles on the floor that looked to Linda to be terra-cotta, probably better suited for a kitchen or bathroom somewhere in the Southwest than the East Side of Manhattan. Several small, round, iron tables were covered in thick, white tablecloths, and tea candles floated atop water vases. A canvas awning offered some shelter above, and all around were propane heat lamps, making the space warm and usable despite the nearly freezing temperature outside that evening.

Linda stood under a heat lamp wrapped in a long, white, faux fur coat with a wide cotton collar that she pulled up around her neck. She had spent the last ten minutes talking with a large man named Charlie, who was one of Allen's older colleagues. He was going on and on about skiing in the Alps, a topic she had no knowledge of and couldn't care less about.

"It's for that reason that when my wife, Gertrude, told me she wanted to sell the property in Berne, I told her over her dead body," Charlie said, laughing as if he just told himself the funniest joke.

"Puff pastry, ma'am?" asked a waiter with some kind of Eastern European accent. He was wearing a white overcoat and black bow tie. He balanced a small silver tray in one hand, presenting a neat pyramid of round pastries.

"Thank you," she said, taking one. "What's inside?"

"Salmon pate blended with Beluga," said the waiter.

"Of course," said Linda, taking two. Looking upward to Charlie, who was eyeing her pastries, she said, "I thought we'd be eating dinner before we came, but I guess we were running later than expected."

"I always just gratify myself on these things anyhow and hope for the best," said Charlie, filling his left hand with as many puffs as his giant mitt could hold. He immediately started popping them into his mouth with his other as if they were pieces of popcorn. The waiter looked down at the pyramid. It was in ruins.

"And is Gertrude here tonight?" asked Linda, wanting to say something to stop the man from eating, lest he choked he was gobbling them down so quickly.

"She's probably off somewhere with Richard's wife," he said. "Those two are as thick as thieves. Probably won't see them until next year." He chuckled so sharply at this idea that a piece of salmon Beluga pastry fell from the side of his mouth, stopping short on his chin, where he absentmindedly wiped it away with the back of his tuxedo sleeve.

"Speaking of which," said Linda, "what time do you have?"

He punched out his right fist and bent his elbow, making a show of revealing an enormous gold watch, and squinted at it.

"I can't read this damn thing," he said. "It's too dark. Here, you try."

Linda leaned in, gently angling his wrist closer to the light from the heat lamp.

"It's ten after eleven," she said.

Charlie let out a humph.

Linda had been standing out there for about fifteen minutes with good old Charlie. Allen told her he was going in to get the three of them drinks, but she was starting to wonder where he was. She was not nearly drunk enough to continue engaging in conversation with Charlie. She wanted to see Rick and the boys before she went out. They were supposed to have a pre-party cocktail somewhere, but then Allen kept bringing the time forward of when they were going to meet and then pushing it back again. By the time he arrived in a black car and they had to make their way down the West Side and over to Gramercy—circumnavigating all the street closures for the Times Square ball drop—she realized the pre-drinks were not going to happen and had to make her apologies.

"Escargot with aged blue cheese?" asked another white-coated waiter, also with some sort of Russian-esque accent.

"If you'll excuse me for a moment," said Linda, "I'm going to see what's holding up Allen with those drinks." And before Charlie had a moment to speak, she dashed inside.

Linda and Allen were more or less an item now, thought Linda. They were more of an item in the sense that they slept together every time they hung out, which was about twice a week since they met almost two months ago. They were less of an item in the sense that sometimes that was all that they did when they got together, and it was always at Linda's apartment—not once did they go to his. In fact, Linda realized that she had not stepped one foot inside of Allen's apartment in all the time she had known him. The closest she ever came was when they stopped by his place on their way up to hers so he could get a clean shirt for work the next day, but she stayed in the cab with the meter running. Truth be told, she did not care all that much. Whatever this relationship was, it was fun and easy, and fairly low risk—which is why Linda was surprised when Allen asked her if she wanted to attend this New Year's Eve party with him. He said that he wanted a gorgeous woman on his arm to ring in the new year, and that it was a spectacular apartment and it would be a fun night. He also promised that if it wasn't, they could leave any time after midnight.

Inside the apartment, there were about fifty or so people milling around. Linda handed her coat to someone on staff, who hung it on a rack nearby. In one corner of the room, there was a three-piece jazz band with a singer. A busty middle-aged brunette stood in front of a baby grand piano next to a fellow with a string bass and another with an alto sax. They were playing a rather lively, modern version of Duke Ellington's "Take the A Train." On the other side of the room, a dining room table had been pushed against a wall to make space for a dance floor, where about a dozen or so couples were in various states of swaying and spinning. Atop the table, giant vases were pouring out hydrangeas, illuminated by equally massive candelabras, both seeming to be battling for light and space. More waiters circled in white coats among drunken men in tuxedos who looked young, but were just a few years past their prime. They were accompanied by thin women, many of whose plastic faces looked as recently purchased as the gowns they wore.

The bar was off the kitchen up a short flight of stairs on the far end of a room. After scanning the revelers in search of Allen, Linda worked her way through the crowd and then up the stairs. She should have known that the room with the bar would be full. A table on one side when she immediately entered had a champagne pyramid with two white-coated men carefully guarding it—keeping it balanced and safe from tuxedoed elbows, handing out and replacing glasses as needed. She took one, downed it, handed the glass back to the waiter, and then took another.

On the other side of the room by the bar, Allen was chatting up a woman who appeared to be at least fifteen years her senior and twenty years his. She was wearing a red gown with a slit that ran up one thigh practically to her waist. Had she been wearing any underwear, surely it would have been showing, thought Linda. Around her neck hung a thin, dark, mink stole, and both her hair and heels were high, making her exactly eye level with Allen, who was relatively tall at just over six feet.

Linda smiled and sauntered over. Even from ten feet back, as soon as the crowd parted and she could see a direct line to the pair, she could tell two things. First, they were both completely coked up. And second, Allen had a raging stiffie running down one leg of his dress pants.

"Linda, doll, there you are," Allen said, oblivious but still attractive in his absent-minded kind of way. "This is Richard's wife, Julia, and Charlie's wife, Gertrude." Linda had not even noticed Gertrude standing there looking mousy and bored at best, next to the red-dressed Julia monster.

"Pleasure to meet you both," said Linda.

"This is Julia's apartment. Isn't it fantastic," said Allen. "She was just telling us how she had to have the entire place redone when they moved in. It was right after the towers fell. The balcony doors had been left open for three days because the previous owners opened the place up to air it out. Then one of them was out of town and the other got stuck in New Jersey. It was before they opened the tunnels or were allowing people to get back on the island. So the whole place was covered in soot, and they didn't know if it was asbestos or what."

Linda looked at Allen, and then to Julia in red, and then to meek Gertrude. Julia seemed to be on whatever snow-capped mountain Allen was standing on top of—having just heard what was presumably the last ten minutes of her talking condensed down and played back in triple time, and she was engrossed. Gertrude appeared to be both confused and frozen into place, her only movement being her eyes, which were squinted and darting from Allen to Julia to Linda—in a loop.

Without missing a beat, Linda said, "Look, that sounds fab, Allen. It's got to be twenty to midnight."

Then Linda turned to Julia. "You have a lovely home, of course, but can I have some of what he's having?" Linda could count on one hand how many times she had tried coke in her forty-plus years, but she figured she might as well make lemonade out of lemons.

Julia's eye widened, and one hand outstretched to Linda's. She said, "Darling, of course, welcome to the party. It's going to be a very profitable new year."

Linda looked down and saw that one of Julia's oversized rings was now flipped open, revealing a large well of white powder. How could I have missed that, thought Linda.

"You are a very gracious host," said Linda, bending slightly as if she were going to kiss Julia's ring extended toward her.

The taxi managed to get a block and a half from the Thunder Room, which even from that distance radiated a fierce energy. When Aaron and Tim met Greg and Rick on the corner of Forty-Fifth and Eleventh, everyone was skeptical they would even be able to get a cab. It was nearly ten o'clock at night on Midtown's busiest night of the year. However, they were lucky. Within a short time, they managed to get a car and drive the thirty blocks south until they came to a sudden, dead standstill.

"We'll get out here," said Aaron, shouting to the front where Tim sat in the passenger's seat.

"Good move," said Tim.

The group quickly collected some cash, gave it to the driver, and worked their way down the street along with several others who looked to be on the same trajectory, given that nearly everyone in sight was carrying some sort of children's toy. Aaron carried a teddy bear tucked under his arm, and peeking from Tim's jacket was a stuffed yellow duck—presumably held close to him on the inside so as to keep the duck warm. Greg held a plastic sack with a whole platoon of green soldiers piled up and peering from the inside, and Rick clutched a pocketbook-sized army tank. Others on the street were carrying books, balls, blocks, dolls, fire trucks, and one couple, each holding one end high above their heads, was escorting a large wooden rocking horse to the party. Aaron looked at them, shaking his head. "Overachievers," he said.

After the group navigated the crowded street, waited in a long line to get in, passed the muster of two bouncers scanning IDs, handed over their tickets to a collector, tossed their toys into a donation bin, endured another line for the coat check, and finally regrouped in the foyer of the club just outside a second set of doors from which they could hear the thumping of speakers from the other side, everyone was more than ready to make a beeline to a bar.

"I'm surprised everyone remembered to bring a gift," commented Tim, standing to one side to let revelers pass.

From behind him, flanking the door, an overweight drag queen dressed as a Raggedy Ann doll answered in a deep, desperate voice, "It's for the tattered children, won't someone please think of the tattered children." Tim turned around slightly in acknowledgment, noting that the lollipop she vigorously licked was the size of his entire head, but half the size of hers given her enormous wig.

Behind her, Tim spotted a canvas step and repeat covered in Empire Toy Party logos, which was two popped jack-in-the-boxes crossing over each other. In front of it was a red rectangular carpet, black umbrella light, and a cute blond photographer with a camera set on a tripod. People were lining up for photos.

"Come on, guys," said Tim. "Let's get one taken before we go in."

"Really?" asked Rick. "Can't we do that later?"

Greg looked over to Aaron, who said, "Yeah, let's do it now. Better to take one before we drink and look all messy."

Tim was excited to finally be one of those guys at the party that he saw in photos from club websites. He could already see in his head himself standing in front of the camera, posing with a sexy kind of flirty pout that he had practiced in the mirror a couple of hundred times over the years, the cute blond photographer snapping shot after shot like it was a private photo shoot.

But when they got up there, it became quickly apparent that they were taking a group shot. Greg stood in the middle throwing one arm over Rick's shoulder and the other over Aaron's. Tim stood squeezed in next to Aaron on the end of the foursome. He didn't get his solo shots but figured at least he was standing with a pretty sexy group of men, even if they were a little on the older side—Aaron with his huge chest and leather armband, tall Greg with his broad shoulders and tank top, and Rick, with his dark eyes, wearing a fleshy fluoro-blue mesh tee.

Finally, in the main room of the club, everyone was ready to party and explore the scene. From where they stood, they saw a huge, busy dance floor in front of them, flanked on either side with what looked like giant silver metal urns, each at least ten feet tall. In the back center was a stage and DJ booth. Directly above them was a glass-enclosed balcony.

"Let's head up there," said Greg, pointing to a set of stairs with a bouncer guarding it. "That's the VIP area."

They were each given a plastic wristband so the bouncer at the bottom of the stairs didn't need to check their tickets each time. Also, they could now take full advantage of the open bar, though Aaron, Greg, and Rick had other plans.

The VIP section was as crowded as the main dance floor down below. A different DJ spun there, his music decidedly more techno and less pop. Two go-go boys were posted at the corners of a U-shaped bar, and several Adonis-like bartenders stood behind, serving.

"Check out the countdown clock above the DJ down there," said Rick.

Everyone had drinks and was standing around a cocktail table, watching the green laser light show below.

"Forty-seven minutes until the new year," said Tim.

"I don't think I'm ready for it," said Rick.

"Me neither," said Tim.

"I think this year was better than the next one is going to be," said Rick. "At least the first 95 percent of this year."

"It's definitely ending with a bang," said Tim.

Aaron leaned in and gave Tim a quick peck on the lips. Tim wasn't expecting it and pulled back.

"Is everything okay?" asked Aaron.

"Yeah," answered Tim. "I just wasn't…"

"What?"

"Look, this is a great night. I'm really excited to be here. I like you a lot. It's just that…"

"What is it?"

"It's nothing. I think I'm going to find a bathroom."

"Okay," said Aaron. "Do you want me to come with you?"

"No," said Tim. "I'll be fine. Are you guys taking pills tonight?"

Aaron looked to Greg and Rick. "We're still deciding," he said.

Looking to the dance floor below, Tim asked, "You wouldn't happen to have an extra one, would you? I can pay for it."

After a moment, Rick spoke. "Look, I'm not really sure I'm in the best place to take a full one anyhow. Why don't we split mine, Tim? We can each take half. If we want another, I'm sure we can rally one up."

"You've tried it before, right?" asked Aaron.

"Oh yeah, definitely," answered Tim. "A bunch of times. It was mostly with work friends back on Long Island, usually at someone's house."

"Why don't we make this the meeting point," said Aaron. "You guys split your pill. Greg and I will take ours too. You can go to the bathroom, and we'll meet back here to hit the dance floor downstairs in twenty minutes. We'll probably be just about ready to get our dance groove on by then."

Everyone nodded. Rick bit off half his pill and gave the other half to Tim, who swallowed it eagerly, polishing off his vodka soda and immediately dashing off to the bathrooms.

<hr />

Ten. Nine. Eight.

Everyone at Richard and Julia's Gramercy apartment were gathered in the living room, many looking toward the busty brunette singer in front of the baby grand piano mouthing the countdown, others looking to the wall that opened up to her right, revealing an enormous, ultrathin flat-screen television with live coverage of the ball falling in Times Square.

Seven. Six. Five.

Allen managed to extract himself with Linda from Julia and Gertrude at the bar, practically bum-rushing Linda through the crowd of his Wall Street comrades. He was determined that when the ball fell, it would be just the two of them. With all of the coke that Julia plied him with, the shots of Patron he did with his buddies when he first saddled up to the bar, and the pre-party at the Metropolitan Club earlier that night with his boss Richard, Allen was already feeling queasy. But he was no lightweight, and it was only midnight, or about to be.

Four. Three.

Allen pushed open the door to the balcony, pulling Linda out with him. No one else was there, but the noise from inside of everyone cheering and counting down was deafening. He shut the door behind him with his foot, leaving them successfully deposited into the cool, faintly heated outside air. He pulled his jacket off and tossed it around Linda's bare shoulders.

Two. One.

Through the glass windows and closed door, Allen and Linda heard the crowd inside erupt with cheers. It sounded like the whole neighborhood and city beyond were celebrating with them. Fireworks boomed in the distance, echoing off the apartment buildings around them. Linda laughed and looked across the skyline, the World Trade Center blurry in the far distance. Allen stood in front of her, facing her, his jacket off, holding her with one hand on each of her shoulders. Then he turned her chin so that she faced him and leaned in, kissing her deep and long, her mouth feeling soft, her tongue tasting sweet from the champagne.

Allen's head cleared for a moment as "Auld Lang Syne" seemed to seep into his brain, past the glass windows and door, through the noisy crowd, from the jazz band and mouth of the busty brunette inside.

Looking into Linda's eyes, he said, "Happy New Year, Linda."

She replied, "Happy New Year, Allen."

The doors opened and people started to pile out into the night—happy, loud, forgetting for a few moments all their troubles, sincerely optimistic for the year ahead.

Hours passed in what felt like minutes. At least half of the party left—off to go home or to other parties, opening up the balcony, bar, and dining-room-turned-dance-floor for the remaining revelers. Linda and Allen danced. Richard and Julia danced. Charlie and Gertrude danced. Everyone danced with each other, and a small tray with a mountain of powder was passed around.

The staff, now with half the amount of people than were jammed in before, was free to cater to everyone's every whim—which included continuously pouring champagne, lighting people's cigarettes and cigars, and even rubbing the feet of one bosomy, drunk woman who was sitting on the bar holding court to a small crowd of men—her high heels in one hand and a drink spilling from the other.

Allen's mind was racing, one thought always two steps behind the next one. He would see the face of someone that he wanted to talk to, but just as he opened his mouth, he would find that he was midconversation with another.

"If everyone in this room, right now, right this second, pooled all of their money," he was saying, "we could buy a politician. I mean really buy a politician. I'm not talking about some stupid lobbyist or blue-plate special at some stupid fund raiser—or even a night in the freaking Lincoln bedroom. I'm talking about having some fat, ugly douche up in Congress sit on my…" Three guys standing around Allen were laughing, eating up his rant. He felt good—maybe better than he had felt in his entire life, he realized.

Someone handed him a shot of Patron tequila, then another to chase back the first.

Then he was suddenly on the balcony, and a buddy he recognized from the Metropolitan Club had another guy on his shoulders. They were trying to reach the balcony on the floor above to get something. The guy on the top managed to grab a hold of it. Was it a sheet? A woman's dress? His buddy from the club was laughing, and then everyone was down on the tiled floor, laughing harder.

"What?" Allen asked. He was staring at Linda. He could see her mouth moving, but there were no words coming out. Then the volume in the room came on full blast in his head and he could hear everything again.

"Do you want to go soon?" she asked, this time slowing each word down, emphasizing them.

But before he could respond, he was at the bar again. He was rubbing a girl's feet. She was sitting on the bar. This time it was the busty brunette who sang earlier. Then he was kissing her, or rather she was kissing him, pushing up against him, pulling him in, while Julia and Gertrude laughed. He was letting her kiss him. She tasted so good. He cupped her breasts. They were firm and full.

Then Allen knew. He just somehow knew. Linda was gone. That was right. She left the party an hour ago. Someone told him she was leaving. Maybe she did? He was free, he thought. He was on his own again. It was okay, he thought. And to the delight of Julia, Gertrude, and the busty brunette, Allen lowered his face to between the brunette's breasts spilling out of her gown and did the best job he could motorboating them.

⟫⟪

Ten. Nine. Eight.

Everyone at the Thunder Room gathered on the main dance floor and the VIP balcony above for the final countdown to the new year. And nearly everyone that was attending the Empire Toy Party that night arrived at the club in time for midnight. The club was packed—partygoers in various states of chemical and alcohol-infused partying all shoulder to shoulder, chest to back, facing the countdown clock above the stage.

Seven. Six. Five.

The laser lights were off and the DJ stood tall, facing the crowd. Behind him was a giant screen projecting the ball falling in Times Square nearby. He shouted the numbers at the crowd with a fist clenched high in the air. The crowd shouted them with him, back at him. Everyone was at full volume.

Four. Three.

Tim never came back from the bathroom. Aaron waited at the table near the window overlooking the main floor in the VIP section until ten minutes to midnight. Then he told Greg and Rick that he didn't mind if they went down to the main floor without him. He and Tim could meet them when he returned, which would be, of course, any minute. They picked a backup spot and time in case they missed each other.

Two. One.

The ceiling opened and thousands of red and yellow circus-themed balloons fell onto the crowd. Aaron yelled "Happy New Year" along with everyone else. He was giving Tim the benefit of the doubt. This mega club had multiple dance floors, bathrooms, and that huge outside space. Maybe with everyone piling into the main room, he got clogged up somewhere. Surely now that people were leaving the main floor in exploration of the other spaces, he would surface, wrap his arms around Aaron, give him a big smooch, and wish him Happy New Year.

Aaron planned to meet Greg and Rick at one in the morning in the center of the outdoor tent, which—from the photos of the space on the website—was a massive beam painted like a barber's poll and exactly in between a Tilt-A-Whirl and dance floor.

The music was back in full force, and everyone around Aaron in the VIP section seemed happy. He realized that he was starting to come up. He was also starting to wiggle, which meant it was time to dance. The place was full of handsome men in various states of dressed and undressed. Some had black bow ties, tuxedo jackets, and no shirt underneath. Others wore tank tops or T-shirts. A couple of drag queens were handing out Jell-O shots, and a severely toned go-go man gyrating on the bar was covered in silver glitter.

That go-go guy in the silver glitter, Aaron thought to himself, who was he? Then he saw him lean down to a beefy body-builder type, and it clicked. He was that Pasha dancer from the Ninth Avenue Saloon, the one with all the attitude. And that bodybuilder talking to him was Hank, who he had met on the street between Layde's drag numbers.

Aaron scanned the bar for the hundredth time and then gave up his prime real estate at the high-top table in front of the glass overlooking the main dance floor. He started moving over to the dancer and muscle duo—still staying within plain sight of the table less than twenty feet away should anyone come looking for him. He figured he'd waste a few minutes on the dance floor to wait and see if Tim came back. If Tim didn't show, he could make a quick circuit of the VIP area and main floor before meeting the boys in the big tent outside. Besides, he felt very ready to dance and needed a distraction.

"Hey, fun party," said Aaron to Hank, who was now standing back from his friend, nearly on the periphery of the dance floor.

Hank looked at him for a moment, squinting, pressing his lips together, pushing them out. "Hey, man! Yeah, sweet party." He pulled a bottle of water from his back pocket and took a swig.

"We met outside the Ninth Avenue Saloon a couple of weeks ago," said Aaron. "We shared a cigarette." The music was loud around them, the bass getting stronger.

"Right, right," he said. "I remember." He was moving to the music. He smiled. "I'm Hank."

"Aaron."

Hank reached out and put his hand gently on Aaron's chest, some of his fingers touching his bare skin where his shirt was open. Hank repeated back the name slowly, "Aaron."

The two stood there like this for a moment. Aaron's whole torso felt hot. His palms were sweaty. He wiped them on his jeans and then placed one hand over Hank's, his fingers tapping to the beat over Hank's hand still resting on his chest. Then he spoke.

"Happy New Year, Hank."

"Happy New Year, Aaron."

Without realizing it, the two were on the dance floor, everyone moving as a crowd. The DJ's set was heating up, and the bass from the speakers was coming through the floor now. Aaron felt great. Funny, he didn't think this would have been Hank's scene, but maybe it was. Or maybe his dancer friend invited him. In any case, he thought Hank looked comfortable, and he was clearly having a good time. Then Hank looked down at the floor and really dialed up his dance moves. Aaron had to admit that it was really nice having someone he knew close by after standing on his own waiting for Tim for so long. Tim. Aaron checked the time and saw that it was almost one in the morning.

"Hey, Hank," shouted Aaron over the music. "I've got to run to meet some friends in the tent. Do you want to come?"

Hank looked like he was flying, his face glistening, his eyes large. He was fixated on a drag queen nearby, a wiry Thai number in a short, sequined cocktail dress and what had to be stilettos that were at least ten inches high. She smiled back at him.

"Maybe in a while," said Hank. "After this song."

Aaron laughed to himself. "Got it. Okay, see you," he said. As he turned toward the stairs and started to walk away, Hank shouted after him.

"See you, Aaron."

Aaron looked back. Hank was standing there, biting his lip. He held Aaron's gaze for a moment and then turned back to the drag queen.

⊱⊰

Aaron walked through the VIP crowd, down a flight of stairs, passing the bouncer. The music on the main floor was at full throttle, and everyone was loving the energy. From the giant metal urns stationed on either side of the dance floor, periodically flames shot up, illuminating everyone's faces, washing over them in an orange glow. Aaron had never seen a dance party like this, one with such elaborate special effects. It was no wonder, he thought, that the tickets were three hundred bucks each. Well, that was for the VIP access that his friends didn't seem to be using, especially his date, who was there for all of two seconds.

Despite Tim still not surfacing, Aaron couldn't help absorbing the infectious positive vibes of the people around him. He loved the music that was flowing through him. Dancing his way across the floor to the back exit, moving between people, between the fire effects, he was reminded of all the years he missed not partying like this at big clubs.

Aaron did not come out of the closet until after he moved to New York. Back in Virginia, where he grew up and went to college, his parents were Republicans. They were not the conservative, fearmongering brand that hated everyone unless he or she was white and had kids. They were the kind that believed in live and let live, smaller government, and individual responsibility to support oneself, rather than depending on social welfare programs year after year, generation after generation. Regardless of their specific ideology, though, they were Republican, and so was their circle of friends. And Aaron grew up in a home where liberals, liberal ideologies, and Democrats were only ever mentioned if it was to poke fun at them.

Once college was over, Aaron knew he was going to come out to his parents and the rest of the world. Up until that point, he had a vague sense deep inside that he was different from most of the other guys in his life. But he pushed it way down, far down, to a place where it was barely accessible. Arriving in New York in the midnineties, he spent most of his nights working to make ends meet. When he did go out, he tended to hang around the then energetic East Village bar scene. His upbringing was more than just conservative. It was wholesome. While he felt at odds with some parts of himself, he felt loved and secure within his family. His family was an important part of his life, and his parents instilled in him strong ideals. This was probably why he shied away from most illicit drugs in those early days—except for pot. But a lot of kids smoked pot growing up in his upper-middle-class suburban neighborhood.

Having successfully passed through hundreds of warm, gyrating bodies, at least half of whom were shirtless, Aaron found himself out the back of the club and standing in a giant circus tent that looked like it could have been taking up half an entire city block. He was in a major thoroughfare, tons of people moving to and fro, some holding hands, others hanging on each other in groups, many with drinks in hand and many without. Everyone seemed to be enjoying the cooler air—though it was clearly heated enough, as some guys were still shirtless even here. He saw the giant pole in the center and worked his way to it, passing a boardwalk game where people squirted water into the mouths of clowns, blowing up balloons. One mischievous contestant squirted his friend, who promptly fired back. There was also Skee-Ball, launch the rubber frog onto a moving lily pad with a hammer, and a spinning wheel with a bunch of numbers and card suits. There was a large bin at the end of the aisle where it looked like people could donate what they won, presumably if they didn't want to carry it around. Though he saw one group of young guys carrying a stuffed snake that was at least eight feet long, and it didn't look like they had any plans of depositing it.

Then Aaron spotted Greg and Rick.

"Hey, buddy!" shouted Greg. He looked excited and was practically bouncing. "Isn't this party outrageous?"

"Did you check out the basement yet?" asked Rick. "There is some kind of fun room with a pit full of plastic balls."

"Haven't seen it," said Aaron. "Ran into a friend in the VIP room, though. Did you see the flames on the main dance floor?"

"Totally," said Greg. "Come on, let's dance." To one side of the pole was a crowded, dark dance floor with neon strobe lights spinning everywhere. The DJ booth was a large custom-made tower that stood in the middle of the dance floor high above everyone. The DJ inside was bopping his head and holding one side of his headphones to his right ear.

"I haven't seen Tim," said Aaron. "I looked around for him, but no sign. Do you think we should be worried?"

Greg and Rick looked at each other. Then Greg said, "I'm sure he's fine and having a good time somewhere."

"But what if something happened to him?" asked Aaron. "We can't just abandon him."

"Aaron," said Greg. "I don't know how to tell you this, but we saw Tim with someone else."

Aaron felt like the wind was knocked out of him. "What do you mean?" he asked. "Who? Where?"

"It doesn't matter," said Greg. "Let's just enjoy ourselves. Don't let it kill the whole night."

"Just tell me," said Aaron, looking to Rick and then back to Greg. "What did you guys see? Are you sure it was him?"

"Yeah," said Rick. "We're sure. Greg talked to him."

"Aaron," said Greg, "we saw Tim in the bathroom with some guy. It was pretty obvious what they were doing. This guy's hand looked like it wasn't where it was supposed to be. Tim saw us and pulled away. I'm sorry, buddy."

"Greg told him he was messed up and to go home," said Rick.

Aaron shook his head and said, "That little turd. Maybe it was the pill."

"It wasn't the pill," said Rick. "I had the other half. It's not that strong."

"Besides," said Greg, "you said you've been having your doubts for a while. He's pretty young."

"Sort of, I know," he replied. "But if he was just going to go off and hook up with some random as soon as he got here…I just wish I hadn't spent six hundred freaking dollars on these stupid tickets."

Greg looked to Rick, who was processing what he just heard.

"Wait," said Rick, "you told me these were comp tickets from Layde."

"Baby," said Greg, "I just wanted you to have a good time to-night and not worry about the money. You've been so stressed late-ly. I'm sorry."

Aaron was looking down at the back of his hands, which were shaking. He turned them over, staring at them. He couldn't be-lieve that Tim did this to him, betrayed him, betrayed their trust. They were so good together. The sex had been so good, beyond good. They fit together and it always felt so right, so electric. But what started as something physical had quickly grown into some-thing much deeper, or so Aaron thought. How could he have been so wrong about them? Tim opened up to Aaron, told him about his family, his sister, his abusive mother growing up. Aaron confided so much in Tim, told him his fears, anxieties, doubts about life. They talked for hours on end about everything. They even made plans together, vacation plans. They talked about going away for a weekend in the summer to Fire Island and taking a drive down to visit DC. Aaron was going to introduce Tim to his parents and sister, show him around the scene, Dupont Circle, Adams Morgan, the National Mall. They talked about that a few times. What was all of that? Aaron was confused. He did pick up on Tim being a bit distant at times, but why did Tim say all those things if he wasn't interested? Aaron's head was spinning. He reached up and wiped his face. His cheeks were wet. He exhaled slowly.

"Fuck," he said aloud.

The three stood there not speaking, listening to the music around them and the chatter of the throng. Aaron used his shirt sleeve to wipe the last of his tears.

"Right," said Rick, letting out a deep sigh. "Enough. Tim is a jackass. And between the two of you, we've spent a fortune to be here tonight. It's freakin' New Year's. We're supposed to be pressing reset or something tonight. I really can't take starting this whole year off like this—with lies." He said this word specifically to Greg. "I don't know about you, but we need to shake this off and run this dance party into the ground."

Aaron laughed despite himself. Greg smiled and kissed Rick. Then he threw his arms around Rick and Aaron, placing one hand on the back of each of their necks.

"Tim is definitely a jackass. You're awesome," said Greg to Aaron. "You know that? He doesn't deserve an awesome guy like you."

Then he said loudly, finger pointed in the air, "Happy freakin' New Year!"

Aaron echoed him even louder, "Happy freakin' New Year, everyone!"

The DJ looked directly at Aaron from his stilted booth above the dance floor. The song playing was Milk Inc.'s reboot of Indeep's "Last Night a DJ Saved My Life." While continuing to bop his head, he smiled, pointed back, and raised the volume of the music up a few notches.

On the dance floor, surrounded by a hundred men, Aaron, Greg, and Rick danced like it was the end of the world. Lights swirled above them on the otherwise dark, warm floor. Aaron felt the beat coming up from below again, but this time it left straight through the top of his head. He smiled, took his opened button-down shirt completely off, and tucked it into his belt. His bare chest was full and firm and glistened a little with sweat. His thick leather armband felt tight and good against his flesh. Greg was tugging at his tank top, feeling the heat from the floor and the crowd. Rick noticed and pulled it up and off for him. Greg was sweating, and Rick pulled a bright, fluoro-yellow handkerchief from his back pocket and handed it to him. Greg thought this was amazing, folded it longways, and offered to tie it around Rick's head Rambo style. Rick laughed, shook his head a little, and then conceded, not before removing his T-shirt and tucking it into his own belt. The floor was packed and full. It felt like the entire club had worked its way outside. The dance floor was full of shirtless men now, their bodies looking tanned and toned in the fast moving disco lights.

This was the part of partying that Aaron liked most. No matter what was happening in his life or how bad he felt or things got, out on the dance floor, with music spilling though and over his skin, surrounded by friends and welcoming faces, he could put everything on pause and just be. Throughout his closeted years at college, early days in the city scraping by, and then his long, mostly dispassionate relationship with his ex, Aaron never understood why people would go to raves or circuit parties. He also thought he would be too shy to take his shirt off or let go of his inhibitions. But once he hit forty and it sunk in that he was a single man again, he decided it was then or never. He was going to change and try new things, take chances, or he would always be the same old Aaron. And he was grateful to have two good friends like Greg and Rick—whom he trusted and genuinely cared for—to help him find this newer, more improved self.

⇥⇤

"I'm standing there, on the balcony," said Linda. "And the next thing I know, this old toad named Charlie starts getting frisky with me."

"This was after the tray of narcotics was passed around?" asked Rick.

"Definitely after," responded Linda. "But I didn't really touch the stuff. I mean, Mama tried a little of the formula to make sure it was okay, but I'm hyper enough as it is. Besides, alcohol is my poison of choice, always has been, always will be."

"So what happened then?" asked Rick.

Linda, Aaron, Greg, and Rick were sitting in Aaron's main room, swapping stories from the night before. At some time between six in the morning when Aaron got home and four in the afternoon when Linda, Greg, and Rick showed up outside his door, not only did the temperature drop almost twenty degrees, but an inch of snow fell. It was so dark and gloomy outside that even in Aaron's hung-over state, he needed every light in his apartment on and the heat cranked high. His apartment felt soft, which was aided by the several candles lit in his fireplace and another—a scented one—burning on his kitchen table.

Despite the freeze outside, Linda had brought three pints of ice cream, Cherry Garcia, Chunky Monkey, and her favorite— which she was eating with a large spoon between sentences— Phish Food. There was something about the combination of marshmallows and caramel that made everything seem just a little bit better for her.

"I managed to wiggle away from that creep," said Linda. "But in the process of doing so, I slipped out of my coat, which he promptly tossed, for reasons I'll never know, successfully onto the balcony above."

"And at this stage, Allen punched the guy's lights out, right?" asked Rick.

"Oh no, Allen was too busy making out with some bimbo," said Linda. "But we'll get to that. There were these four guys watching this whole thing from the window, unbeknownst to me. They came out laughing at Charlie, who I guess was their boss or something.

Two of them got my coat back, but not before it was completely ruined. It's covered in all this black soot, which is never going to come out."

"So Allen," said Rick. "What about Allen?"

"He comes out for a second while this is all happening," said Linda. "Yes, he's out of his mind. I don't even think he saw me. He just went back inside. I wait and manage to retrieve my coat, go inside to the bar, and, lo and behold, he's sucking face with the singer from the jazz band."

"Wait, there was a jazz band at this party?" asked Rick. "I thought it was at someone's apartment."

"It was," said Linda. "It was Gramercy. It was about four of my apartments put together. Its balcony makes my balcony look like a postage stamp."

"Oh, Linda, I'm so sorry," said Rick. "He sounds like he's a real asshole." Greg stood up and walked into the kitchen.

"Well, yeah," said Linda. "It also makes me think that he almost definitely has a substance abuse problem. I'm telling you, it was night and day. One moment he's all lovey-dovey Happy New Year, and the next he's acting like the spawn of Satan."

Greg returned from the kitchen with the Chunky Monkey opened and a spoon sticking from the top. He didn't even need to say anything. He just handed it to Aaron, who immediately dug out a big hunk of walnut and banana and ate it.

"Well, if it's any consolation," said Aaron, swallowing hard, "Greg and Rick saw Tim getting felt up in the bathroom by some boy half my age." He was still gutted about losing Tim, especially the way it all went down and how he misread their relationship. But having his friends close by made him feel better, on solid ground at least.

"Guys suck," said Linda. She reached over and dug her spoon into Aaron's Chunky Monkey.

"You said it, sister," said Aaron.

"I'm completely through with them," said Linda. "I tried to keep it simple and casual, and that didn't work."

"I tried to make it all too serious," said Aaron. "And look where that got me."

"Well, I'm sorry you went through all that," said Greg, who was slouching deep into the couch, his hands in the pockets of his sweatpants. "But despite all of the drama of last night, that Empire Toy Party was pretty freaking sweet."

"We definitely sucked the most we could get out of," said Rick.

"Um, can I ask a question?" asked Aaron. "Did you guys happen to have any—say, I don't know—temporary tattoos, maybe, say, hypothetically speaking, on one of your butt cheeks, by any chance?"

"Oh my Gawd," said Rick. "I completely forgot about that until this morning when I woke up in bed and Greg was lying face down with no clothes on. We all got them."

"Well, mine is the Superman logo," said Aaron. "And it's the size of a baseball."

"Greg has Batman," said Rick.

"And what do you have?" Aaron asked Rick.

"He has Wonder Woman," answered Greg.

"I am definitely partying with you boys next year," said Linda.

CHAPTER TWELVE

Wednesday, January 6

Winter felt like it was finally settling in for good. The sidewalks of West Eighty-First Street outside of Linda's apartment were mostly maintained, shoveled, and covered in salt. But between the doorman buildings, and on the street corners where the ice melted, refroze, melted, and refroze again, what many called the deadliest of sidewalk conditions developed—black ice.

When Aaron was invited by Linda and Rick to join them for a midweek break to watch a movie, he was of a mind-set to decline. New Year's had just passed, temperatures were bottoming out in the teens, the sky was perpetually gray, and the city began descending into darkness by midafternoon, long before evening rush hour. Then they told him the movie was one of his favorites, *Hedwig and the Angry Inch.* He had practically memorized every line of that movie over the years, having watched it periodically for days nearly on a loop. He knew he needed to take his mind off of how things ended with Tim and half wondered if Linda and Rick planned the night for that reason.

Aaron was absolutely devastated about Tim. He was more broken up than he let on at the party, afterward at his apartment, and in the days since. He didn't want to bring the others down and burden them with a poor-me attitude. Even more, he was embarrassed by how upset he was feeling, given the pair was only together a couple of months, if that. Tim made Aaron feel sexy again, like he still had it, whether he intended that or not. Aaron remembered being in his twenties—late teens even—and having pull. He would walk down the street or through a room, and he held people's attention. He never considered himself hot by media standards, but he recognized that his height, build, and youth got him noticed. There was a time in his early twenties when he remembered being able to go to a bar, look around for the most attractive guy, and get him. Maybe it was just pheromones, or hormones, or maybe it was the other way around, and he was the one getting picked up. In any case, he never realized this was something not to be taken for granted. Then he was partnered with his ex, and it wasn't until after they got together that he thought something was changing. He wasn't getting noticed as much, if at all. When he was at a bar, cute guys would walk right past. And if he was standing with a group and someone was being introduced, he'd get looked over, glazed over, with someone else being everyone's focus. But this was normal, and his ego wasn't that big, he reminded himself. Aaron reminded himself that he had lots going for himself and that being sexy in New York wasn't about age, but all sorts of other traits, such as confidence, stability, and style.

Still, when Tim noticed Aaron and gave him a whole lot more than just the time of day, he felt attractive again. Then, when they started spending time together and the hooking up was so solid, he was relieved because he thought all that self-doubt had been in his head. Perhaps he had been getting noticed all along. Perhaps not.

If only it was that easy, Aaron thought. If only he had taken what happened with Tim so badly because Tim made him feel sexy. There was more, though he couldn't quite put his finger on it. Maybe the truly upsetting and unsettling part was that Aaron was doubting his instincts. How could he have been so blind as to not see Tim's true nature, or at least that he wasn't as into the relationship as Aaron was. Were there warning signs? Were there two Tims? The one inside Aaron's head and the real one? Even with what happened, somehow he still missed him, still thought about him. He wondered if somehow, maybe they could still make things right. Maybe it was the drugs, or Aaron wasn't listening enough. Moving forward, he'd have to pay more attention and look for the signals with guys. Maybe he was rusty from being outside of the dating world for so long. Or maybe the dating scene had changed since he was last single way back in the day.

Normally, this close to midnight, in the middle of the week, in the dead of winter, Aaron would have hopped into a cab to get home. But seeing how Linda's place was only a half block from the subway, and since he had made a whole slew of last-minute New Year's resolutions, including to try to save money, upon exiting her building, he pulled up his collar and headed for the C train. Greg was closing the bar that night, and Rick didn't want to be home alone, so he decided to stay a bit longer after the movie. Rick was obviously stressed and down about losing his job, though he didn't bring it up, so neither he nor Linda did either. It would seem his crew was a bit down on their luck. Some start to a new year.

The platform was nearly deserted aside from a couple of people at the north end, where he was walking. There was a young girl standing with her back against the wall and, a little closer, a built guy seated on a bench with a large duffel bag. It didn't feel as though the train had been there recently, and it also didn't feel like it was going to arrive any time soon. But whenever it did decide to eventually pull into the station, from the north end of the platform he could board the last car, which would deposit him at Times Square, closest to his preferred exit for his fastest route home. The C train was notorious for being one of the most unreliable. It barely ran overnight and on weekends. And being one of the oldest lines in the system, the cars often labored along at a slow, rocking pace. But while the underground platforms were not heated, at least they were dry and free of wind.

Aaron was drowsy, his thoughts wandering as he approached the seated guy whom he instantly recognized. He felt heat rush to his cheeks, and he smiled.

"Hey, stranger. We meet again. Have you been waiting long?" asked Aaron. Hank looked up, rubbing his eyes with one hand, yawning.

"Aaron, hey. Yeah, forever," said Hank. "What time is it?"

"Almost midnight."

Aaron sat next to Hank, leaving a seat between them. The girl against the wall looked over at them nervously. Now that Aaron was closer, he could see that she had been crying. Her face looked red and swollen. She was still some way from them, out of ear's reach. Hank looked to the girl and then back to Aaron.

"She's seen better days," said Hank.

"Haven't we all. That was a heck of a New Year's party."

"You're telling me," said Hank. His frame filled the seat, his shoulders passing over either side of the armrests. "I'm not even sure mine's over yet."

"Really? Headed somewhere?" asked Aaron, nodding toward the bag on the floor.

"Nah, not really. I was Uptown, worked late. I'm actually headed back down to my buddy's in Hell's Kitchen. Crashing there for a few nights." There was a way that Hank spoke that felt somehow familiar, as if the two had known each other longer than they had, more than just bumping into each other a couple of times around the scene. Hank was rubbing his hands together for warmth, blowing into them. They looked big and coarse.

"Sounds like the train might be coming," said Aaron.

Hank's gaze was fixed behind Aaron, over his shoulder. "Hey, you," he shouted. "Hey, don't do that!"

The young girl who had been standing against the wall was sitting on the floor with her legs dangling over the tracks. She turned, looking straight at Aaron and Hank. Then she turned back and scooted off the platform out of view, landing on the concrete next to the tracks below with a heavy thud.

Aaron and Hank were immediately on their feet.

Aaron looked down to the girl. She was sitting on one of the tracks, angled away from him, moving back and forward slowly, peering down the dark tunnel to where the small white light of the train was approaching. It was maybe two hundred feet away at most, the light growing wider and brighter with every second. Then he looked back to the subway entrance. He remembered there was no attendant at this station. Aaron shouted anyhow, even though no one was there. "Someone help, please," he yelled, his voice echoing against the cold tile walls.

Hank was already across the platform above where the girl was seated on the track. He squatted down with his hands outstretched.

"You have to give me your hands, honey," he said. "Give them to me now. I'll pull you up."

The girl didn't bother looking at him or saying anything. It sounded like she was humming. Hank could hear the train now, her humming growing in volume and changing in pitch to match it.

Aaron started to run past Hank to the where the train was going to enter the station. He was waving frantically, reaching his arms and hands over the tracks, trying desperately to get the conductor to see him.

"Aaron," yelled Hank in a deep and determined voice. "There's no time. Even if he sees you, he won't have time to stop. Get over here." And with that Hank catapulted himself onto the tracks several feet from the girl. At full height, the middle of Hank's chest was right at the platform. The train was loud and the white light bright. The conductor must have seen them, as an unearthly screeching of breaks blasted around them. Hank reached down and lifted the girl with one hand, as if she were weightless. Her eyes were huge, fixated on the train. He passed her to Aaron, who pulled her up and back, falling to the floor with her. She was on top of him. He was pushing her off to the floor beside him as the train finally came into the station.

"Hank!" he shouted. But when he looked over, where he expected to see an empty platform, Hank was rolled over on his side, cursing, breathing heavily. He cursed the girl, the train, the MTA, his face red with anger and relief, his words muffled by the easing sound of the subway car as the train came to a standstill.

━╪╌╎╾━

"It happens more than you think," the police officer said. "They're successful at least a couple of times a week. We don't even always fill out a report for the unsuccessful ones. It just so happened to be that we were on this train headed back to the Port Authority." The second officer was sitting with the girl, presumably trying to take a statement. But it didn't look like the girl was doing much talking.

The train engines were off, the doors open. Frustrated passengers leered from the cars, back toward the group, wondering what was happening. Some scowled as if to say, how selfish of you all to hold us up, or what makes you so important, we want to get going. Others trickled from the cars out of the station, resigned to walk, take a bus, or find some other means of transport.

"So what now?" asked Hank. "Can we leave, or do you need us to stick around?"

The officer looked Hank straight on. "You were lucky here. It worked out this time, but in the future, if this ever happens again, stay off the tracks. You could have gotten yourself killed."

"Excuse me," Hank said. "Lucky? In the future?"

Aaron put his hand on Hank's chest. "It's okay, he just meant…"

"I know what he meant." Hank's face went red again.

Aaron lowered his hand. "It's been a long day officer."

The second cop was escorting the girl from the platform. They had radioed for a car. They were taking her to Bellevue Hospital for evaluation.

"You're welcome," Hank shouted after her, but she was already through the turnstile and probably didn't hear him. He smacked the wall hard, palm open. That must have stung, thought Aaron. But if it did, Hank didn't show it.

CHAPTER THIRTEEN

Saturday, January 9

Aaron was determined to start the new year off on the right foot and not wind up another sad statistic. And sure, he had been burned. He opened his heart to a really cute guy, and the really cute guy stomped all over it. But ultimately, in taking stock, what had been lost? Five weeks when he could have been dating some random? A three-hundred-freaking-dollar party ticket? An afternoon in a rental car going back and forth to IKEA? Small potatoes. He was starting to feel like himself again.

Part of his New-Year-New-Aaron plan was to turn his going to the gym fairly regularly into going to the gym at least four days a week. He would work out any frustrations or negative feelings, continue on his decent, healthy track of cardio and weight lifting, and maybe even throw in a yoga class or two. After all, he was a single man in his early forties living in Manhattan. Where better to make a second home away from home than his neighborhood gym?

Today the gym was packed. Aaron worked out with Greg on occasion, but Greg only went once every week or two, so he was on his own. He noticed that every January, it was the same deal. People joined the gym with New Year's resolutions to work out more. That usually lasted a month.

Taking solace in the fact that Aaron had belonged to gyms for years, and specifically Urban Workout since he moved to Hell's Kitchen two years ago, he felt above the resolutioners, who didn't have the drive that he did, assuring himself that he would continue going.

Upping the difficulty level of a climbing machine he had been using for the past twenty minutes, Aaron surveyed the room and allowed his mind to wander. The Empire Toy Party was over a week ago, and although he finally felt his body had recuperated, he was holding onto one small shred of the party guilts.

The party guilts, as he dubbed them shortly after he started going to bars and clubs with Greg and taking the occasional recreational pill, was that period shortly after a big night when he felt a twang of guilt. Most people said it had something to do with a depletion in the brain's serotonin due to the drugs, resulting in feeling down afterward. But for Aaron, he thought of it more that he had a week's worth of feeling good in a few hours, so it was okay that he had to make up for it by feeling a bit blue. Another great thing about the gym was that working out was a great cure for getting rid of the party guilts.

Hopping off the climbing machine too quickly, Aaron's legs buckled momentarily under his weight as his thighs burned with tightness. Good, he thought. He steadied himself on a treadmill next to him, earning a nasty glare from the overzealous woman running on it, and then headed to the weight room to work his chest. Luckily, just as he entered the room, a bench opened.

Placing seventy pounds on either side, he lay on his back under the bar and took three deep breaths. Just as he was about to start his first rep, a man appeared above him.

"Save any lives today?" asked Hank. "I hear there's someone looking to jump off the roof."

Aaron turned his head back and up. From this angle, Hank looked enormous. But Aaron remembered that when the two stood eye to eye, Hank was actually more top heavy, his mass narrowing at his waist. Aaron's faced reddened. He exhaled deeply. Such a body on this one, he thought.

"You were the hero. I pretty much remember running around like a crybaby wuss."

"Here, let me spot you."

Aaron wished that he had put on heavier weights, but it was only his first rep. He would have time to redeem himself on the next one.

"I think I finally came down from New Year's," said Hank as Aaron lifted. "That subway crap was very sobering, to say the least. Man, that party. I can't stop thinking about it. I spent almost the entire night in that VIP area."

"The DJ up there was really good," said Aaron. "The open bar didn't hurt either."

In truth, Aaron had been thinking a lot about Wednesday night. But it was less about the girl and more about Hank. He was so quick to act, and strong. Aaron was wondering if he was the only guy in Hell's Kitchen to take notice of Hank. He was getting fatigued from the weights already.

"Three more," said Hank. "Two. One. You have great form, man."

They switched positions, Hank adding another hundred pounds on either side of the bar.

"That other guy at the party, the dancer," said Aaron. "Are you guys close?"

"Perry? Yeah, he gets me into clubs and stuff when he's working," said Hank. "He's a good guy. Comes off a little bitchy sometimes."

Aaron could not help laughing. Hank lifted and lowered the weights with a calm precision, making them look almost weightless.

"Well, I would kill for his abs," said Aaron.

"If you're into that sort of thing," said Hank.

"Abs?" asked Aaron.

Hank did not answer. He was starting to struggle with his last rep. Aaron helped guide the bar back into resting position. The two swapped places again. This time, Aaron took off the hundred pound weights from each side and added thirty.

"I'm actually roommates with Perry, but I'm getting out of there soon. It is not really okay anymore," said Hank. Hank was staying at Perry's place at the moment, but that was only because his good buddy Jack recently threw him out. But Aaron did not need to know about that, thought Hank.

"Why is that?" asked Aaron.

"Well, between you and me," Hank said lowering his voice, "Perry has a problem with drugs. And I'm not talking about the party kind."

"What then?" asked Aaron. "Meth or something?"

"Yeah, meth," said Hank softly. "He says he has it under control, but he came home from the club two nights ago and completely wrecked the place. He's also taken a bunch of stuff from me— money, and my dead grandfather's watch."

"That's awful," said Aaron, slowing down, his strength starting to waiver.

"Three," said Hank. "Two. One."

Aaron rested the bar back down. "Did you call the police?" asked Aaron.

"Nah," said Hank. "You see, my name is not on the lease. I was just renting the room from him, so I'd have no say in the court of law."

The two switched positions again, Hank adding a full hundred pounds to Aaron's weight again.

"But still," pushed Aaron. "Theft is theft. And your grandfather's watch."

In fact, Hank did not have a watch from his grandfather. His grandfather did have a pocket watch, but Hank didn't have it. He did not have any mementos from him. It was not that Hank wanted to lie so much, he thought. It was that sometimes it was easier than telling the truth—especially when he needed something.

Hank lay flat on his back and took the bar again.

"I've never touched the stuff," said Hank. "It's a nasty drug."

"Me neither," said Aaron. "Pot or something for the dance floor on occasion is one thing, but meth is really bad news. They say once you're addicted, there is no turning back. You're always hooked for life."

Hank lifted the weights in silence for a minute, considering how to bring the story home.

"I don't know what to do," said Hank. "I really don't even feel safe around there anymore. When he wrecked the place, turning it over—I guess he was looking for his stash or something—he pushed me against the wall. I mean, I'm a big guy, I can take it, but I would never get physical with somebody."

"Hank," said Aaron, standing over him. "You have to get out of there. That is a dangerous situation. When are you leaving?"

"I can put up with it for another week," said Hank. "I found a new place, and put down a deposit, but it's not available until the fifteenth. January is a bad month to move."

Hank brought the bar down to the resting position, lifted his legs together, and spun around. He put one leg on either side of the bench and looked up at Aaron, directly into his eyes. If this was going to work, it had to be his idea.

"I'm sorry to talk about all this stuff with you," said Hank. "It's just that I'm sort of new in town and don't really know that many people yet." I have got to make this work, thought Hank.

"Hey," said Aaron. "It's okay. I don't mind."

"I'm going to call it a day," said Hank. "I think I need to sit in the steam room awhile, sweat it out."

"Me too," said Aaron. "I'm going to stretch first, but I'll be down after."

Hank sat in the steam room, one towel wrapped tightly around his waist, another soaked with cold water and draped over his head. He and his good buddy Jack had a giant falling out after the poker game. As soon as Hank and Jack got back to Jack's place, Jack asked Hank for rent money, saying that Hank had not paid him anything in a long while and was a freeloader.

Hank, for his part, told Jack in no uncertain terms that this was not going to happen and that Jack was just a sore loser and jealous because Hank cleaned up. Then Hank met up with Perry, and the pair went on a three-day, meth-fueled bender, blowing every last red cent of the grand Hank won. When Hank finally returned to Jack's apartment looking completely cracked out of his head, Jack confronted him, saying that he knew Hank cheated because he went through his stuff as soon as he left looking for the money and found, lo and behold, in the pocket of his sweatshirt, a bunch of cards, mostly random pairs, the type of cards exactly matching the ones the group played with that night. Jack tried to throw Hank out, which led to Hank punching Jack in the face. Jack, though not as gym built as Hank, was solid and always a better fighter than Hank, even when they were kids. Jack also had the advantage of not having been awake for three days and being a strung-out wreck. Jack physically, and not lightly, removed Hank and his things from his Washington Heights apartment, depositing him down multiple flights of stairs and onto the street. Since then, Hank had been sleeping at Perry's place. The problem was that Perry was now being evicted for not paying his rent in months, so Hank was losing that place too.

The door opened and Aaron entered with just a towel around his waist. As he came in, two other guys left, leaving him and Hank sitting across from each other, alone. The steam turned on, hissing loudly from a vent overhead, the tiled room full of heat and humidity shaking out any hint of frigid air that may have lingered, having crept in all the way from the street.

Hank pushed the towel draped over his head to around the back of his neck. The cold there dissipated too, replaced with wet warmth. He looked at Aaron and then leaned back, resting his head against the wall, closing his eyes, slumping his massive arms and shoulders, the towel around his waist creeping up above his knees. He exhaled deeply.

Aaron exhaled deeply too, his body adjusting to the room's high temperature and low lighting. He finally felt rested, at ease. His chemical exhaustion as well as his anguish over Tim from the New Year's party completely faded. It was replaced by the pleasant fatigue of a heavy workout—the muscles of his legs, arms, and chest tender to his own touch. He too leaned his head back, resting it against the tiled wall, but he didn't close his eyes. Instead he looked at Hank, taking him in. He couldn't take his eyes off him.

His apartment was a studio, thought Aaron—though a decent-sized studio no doubt, especially for Hell's Kitchen. It was also a very reasonable price, and he knew he was lucky to have it. The first year he moved in, the rent was stabilized. But the landlord and rental management company had been working on improvements to the building for some time, which would soon constitute enough of an investment into the property to raise the value of the building as a whole to go above the threshold needed to destabilize the apartments. So the second year Aaron signed his lease, the price shot up almost 8 percent. But still, even with this huge increase, because he managed to get into the right neighborhood at the right time, his rent was still far below Manhattan averages. And because his place was so affordable by New York standards, he was able to keep his head above water, managing to remain relatively debt free, which was important to him. In his younger days, he maxed out a couple of credit cards, and it took years to pay them off. He always felt bad for his friends who were still carrying around buckets of student loans well into their thirties, or longer. Aaron was lucky to go to a state school in Virginia and even luckier to have parents who were able to help pay for most of the tuition.

But life was short. What was the point of having financial stability, good friends, and good fortune just to hoard it? Besides, there were plenty of people who helped Aaron along the way. Didn't he stay with friends when renting out his apartment to tourists? He would bring alcohol, shop for groceries, and even pay for a couple of dinners, but he would by and large be living rent-free. He was always insanely grateful to those friends. In exchange, he let them

lean on him too, never hesitating for a moment to help someone
run an errand, move heavy boxes, or paint a room. Hank was one
of the good ones. He literally saved that girl's life on the subway
platform. And damn, he was sexy. Aaron hadn't been able to stop
thinking about him since that night, since New Year's, since that
cigarette they shared outside of the Saloon. He had to admit, he
was even noticing guys with big builds, and they all reminded him
of Hank. He still wasn't entirely sure what his deal was, who he
was into, but the sizzle aside, Aaron could be a friend to Hank.
And isn't this how acquaintances became friends, or even something more? By someone taking a tiny leap of faith and throwing
someone else a lifeline? Hank was in a physically abusive situation,
whether he was willing to admit it or not. Even if a guy is big, getting pushed against a wall by a cracked-out tina queen—having his
stuff stolen, including personal things with sentimental value—
was abuse. Actual abuse. And it was wrong. Nobody should have to
put up with that.

"Hank," said Aaron. His heart was racing. Hank opened his
eyes and looked at Aaron. "Why don't you come stay at my place
until the fifteenth? My place is pretty small, but my couch opens
up. It's for less than a week anyhow, right? That Perry guy doesn't
sound stable."

Hank leaned forward putting one elbow on each knee.

"Really? Are you sure?" he asked. He locked eyes with Aaron.
"Man, I don't want to put you out. That's so nice of you, but I'm not
your problem. I can deal with Perry."

"The offer is there," said Aaron. "I wouldn't have made it if I
didn't mean to. You're a good guy. It's fine. I have a new kitten and

he'd love the company. You're not allergic, are you? Besides, I've had friends crash at my place with me for that long before."

Hank didn't take his eyes from Aaron the entire time he spoke. Then he reached over and placed one hand on Aaron's knee, giving it a firm squeeze. He left his hand there and said, "Man, this would really mean a lot to me. Maybe just for a night or two until I can figure this out."

CHAPTER FOURTEEN

Thursday, January 21

There were three major areas that Aaron compartmentalized when putting on a big work event: talent, technology, and tea.

The talent referred to who was going to be in the panel discussion, one-on-one interview, or presentation. As the event's director, Aaron's focus was less on programming the event and more on making sure it ran spectacularly. He had worked tediously since the start of the week to keep the host and her people happy. It was Tama Shikibu, one of the most prominent female venture capitalists in Tokyo, who had recently set up shop in New York. And although she was fairly amicable, her people weren't, requiring triple confirmation on Wi-Fi passwords, seating arrangements, and even the guest list. Normally, the event host would only need to know the time and the place to be and would be briefed on the particulars of the event once they arrived. Tama was hosting a curated selection of several digital startups in the travel space.

The technology was—early on in Aaron's career at the company—his biggest challenge. However, he quickly realized the technology staff employed by his company was highly competent, if not often denigrated. A small crew of four or five was responsible for lighting, microphones, music, video recording, presentations and a whole slew of other glitch-prone digital intricacies. The secret to getting them on board and keeping them on their A-game was acknowledging and praising their ability. It also did not hurt that Aaron usually let them drink from the open bar once the event ended while they packed up equipment. He was probably breaking a dozen insurance or policy rules by doing this, but the history of the technology side of his events since he started—knock on wood—was nearly flawless.

Tea was Aaron's way of referring to the refreshments, which was his favorite part of organizing these events. He called them that after what some bars and clubs sometimes referred to as tea parties, which were generally just late-afternoon, early evening happy hours. In this case, though, tea could refer to anything from passed hors d'oeuvres to a three-course meal, an elaborate dessert station or custom cocktail bar. Tonight's event was catered on premises by celebrity chef Yoshihiro Yohei, who set up a sushi station featuring a seven-hundred-pound bluefin tuna that he was dissecting for made-to-order rolls and sashimi. To complement this, the full open bar featured a sakitini-based cocktail menu and Asahi beer on draft. These expenses were considered inconsequential compared to the return on investment potential for one of the two hundred investors about to arrive in the room backing any of the digital startups about to present.

"Thanks for letting us come to this thing tonight," said Rick. He and Linda were standing in the back of the room, which was starting to fill up with men in suits, most of whom looked like they came directly from the office.

"Of course," said Aaron. "The more the merrier. It's a shame Greg couldn't make it because of work."

"For sure," said Rick. "He would have loved the kimono suit thingies the waiters are wearing."

"So who are all these people anyhow?" asked Linda.

"They work for or represent most of the biggest venture-capitalist firms and angel investors in the city," said Aaron. "My company wants to appear to be a market leader, having our finger on the pulse of hot, big-payoff investments. Five groups present ten minutes each, and then there is a rapid-fire question-and-answer session."

"Maybe one of these suits can give me a job," said Rick.

"Don't think I haven't thought about it," said Aaron. "A lot of these guys need people who can speak plain English. Most of these startups are run by tech geeks, and while these people may have great ideas, they rarely have the skill set to pitch to a room of investors."

"We'll definitely stick around afterward for the cocktails," said Linda. "If there is one thing I know how to do, Rick, old boy, it's work a room full of suits."

The event went off without a hitch. The first two presenters had similar ideas—location-based storytelling device apps—the idea being, more or less, that tourists could walk around the city and a map would tell them where to find other tourists or potentially famous people, and it would provide a recorded audio, which they could then listen to, of a story that took place at that spot. Another startup offered augmented reality overlays. The presentation showed a woman walking around Paris, holding up a tablet. All around the screen was the normal, modern day. But on the screen, the city she was seeing looked like it was from the nineteenth century, complete with old buildings, street signs, and monuments. A car passed by, and it was digitally translated into a horse-drawn carriage. The fourth presenter shared a platform that could tap into the local news of an area anywhere in the world in a user's native language. The last one rebooked travelers into their current hotels for lower rates automatically, even during a person's stay. It was a little unclear if people would need to physically check out and back in again and how it might work with bookings with no-refund policies, but the idea was interesting enough. All of the startups already had some sort of initial funding but were looking for the next round to bring their idea through to further research and development. All the presenters were male. Only two were actually based in New York. One was from California, one from Seattle, and another flew in that morning from Israel.

Fortunately, most of the work that went into these events was in the planning. That was especially good tonight, as Aaron was having trouble focusing. His mind kept going back to his apartment. He had worked late every night that week, not getting home until after ten. Hank started out the first couple of nights, Saturday and Sunday, sleeping on the pullout couch. Aaron knew from experience that his pullout couch was not very comfortable. When he first bought it, on a couple of occasions, he opened it and vegged out to watch movies. However, after falling asleep on it, both times he woke in much discomfort, climbing over to his bed.

When Aaron came home on Monday night late, Hank was sleeping in his bed—well, on his bed, on top of the comforter. Hank left the apartment before five in the morning that day for a construction gig in the Bronx. He said he was working with a private contractor who was gutting a house. So by ten at night, when Aaron was still not back, Hank must have lay down to rest his eyes for a while and passed out. Aaron, trying to be a laid-back and hospitable host, told him not to worry about it and that he was not ready to sleep anyway.

Hank propped himself up, and Aaron sat on the bed with a beer and his back against the headboard. The two talked for a while, the television quietly on in the background. It felt warm and easy. Hank talked about his childhood in Vermont and how he used to love snowboarding. There was this one long, tucked-away trail called Ridgeview that few people used. It was quiet and peaceful and stretched from the highest peak all the way to the base. Aaron talked about growing up in Virginia and how he always wanted a white Christmas but rarely got it. Alexandria had much rain, sleet, and ice throughout the winter, but actual snow, if any, didn't fall and stick until well into January. They must have fallen asleep there, because when Aaron half woke briefly, they were slumped over in bed, Hank breathing heavily, Aaron on his side, his beer gone. When he woke again in the morning, Hank had left for the day. It was cold, and Aaron rolled over to where Hank had been lying. It was still warm from the heat of his body, and Aaron's kitten, Mr. Boo Berry, curled up at his side. He decided he was not going to think too much about it and would instead concentrate on his work event. The next two nights, Hank slept on the pullout again, neither of them mentioning it. Still, Aaron asked Hank about the apartment hunt nearly every day.

Most of the event room was on its feet, mingling, several of the presenters surrounded by small clusters of investors, asking questions, probing. Rick and Linda both clenched martini glasses filled with cucumber-infused sake and stood near the young Israeli man, listening to him banter.

"That's why I'm not like the rest of these guys," said the Israeli. "For them, this is life or death. They have to make a connection tonight. For me? I am already something of a minor rock-star celebrity back in my country."

"Really?" asked Linda. She and Rick were standing on the periphery of the group of suits, but she couldn't help herself. "A rock star, of sorts, you say?"

The Israeli looked up and smiled at Linda. "Why, yes," he said. "I have been in the public's eye for several years. When I was a teenager I hosted a show about digital apps."

"There were digital apps when you were a teenager?" asked Linda.

This earned a chuckle from the suits, who must have been thinking the same.

"Indeed," said the Israeli. "And I can see you are a beautiful woman who is also smart. Have you been to my country? Not many people from America have, except maybe for the Jews."

"I haven't," said Linda. He was a smooth one. How old could he be, she thought? Twenty-three? Twenty-four? "I have always wanted to. Maybe next year."

"You should come," said the Israeli. "It is a beautiful country, and I can show you around. There are so many things to see and do and a lot of fun clubs where I am a VIP member. We'll get in without a wait, have bottle service. It's very normal in Israel."

"That's very kind of you, thank you," she said. "If you'll excuse us, I'll let you get back to your patrons." Linda grabbed Rick and ushered him across the room to the sushi line.

"You really let him off easy," said Rick. "That obnoxious kid was definitely hitting on you."

"Ah, small fish," said Linda. "New year and all, right? Just because I'm off the men doesn't mean I need to be a shark and eat them alive."

"You'd rather be this tuna?" Rick asked, pointing to the still enormous fish, though a huge side of it was already sliced, served, and consumed. Two sous chefs wearing black, robe-like aprons and white bandanas around their foreheads worked alongside Yoshihiro. One cleaned and the other diligently stacked the sushi on small plates.

"You two are making friends, I see," said Aaron, coming up from behind. "Do you recognize the chef? From the cooking show?"

"The reality show," said Rick. "He's one of the judges, right?"

"Yup," said Aaron. "That's him: Yoshihiro Yohei. You should have seen him arrive with this thing. It's the biggest piece of fish I think I've ever seen in my life. Guess how much that cost."

"What," asked Linda. "The fish?"

"Yup," said Aaron.

"I don't know," said Linda. "It must be high because you are asking. Three thousand dollars?"

"Try fifteen thousand," said Aaron. "Hard to believe, right? You have no idea what I had to go through to get him here. He's a super-nice guy, but he doesn't need to be doing events of this caliber. It was all about convincing him he's serving the right crowd."

The three were next in line. They nodded and each took a plate with several sushi pieces. There was also a pickle bar, with seaweed salad and tempura being continuously refreshed from a kitchen in the back.

Rick and Linda circled the room, refilling their cocktails. Aaron kept an eye on his talent, Tama Shikibu, and her entourage. She too was mingling. The technology team was already starting to pack up some of their equipment, and the rest of the night be-longed to the sushi, sake, and sponsors. It was a good event. Aaron thought what he thought most nights after an event finished. He was lucky to have work, specifically this kind of work that kept him both busy and fulfilled. It was the right amount of running around on his feet with just enough planning from behind a desk.

Rick circled back. He was standing next to Aaron. Linda was across the room talking with the Israeli kid again.

"You all right?" asked Rick. "You look a little distracted."

"Everything is great," said Aaron.

"Have you heard from Tim?" asked Rick.

"Tim?" repeated Aaron.

"Yeah, Tim," said Rick. "Cute guy, wears bow ties on occasion, missing an organ where humans have hearts. Tim."

"Of course," said Aaron. "Not since New Year's."

"Jeez, you are distracted," said Rick.

Aaron couldn't decide if he wanted to tell Rick about Hank staying with him. Better to be upfront, he thought.

"Well, it's just that, I have a friend staying with me at the moment," said Aaron.

"Oh, a friend," said Rick. "A romantic friend?"

"No, just a friend," said Aaron. "His name is Hank. He's waiting to move into an apartment next week and was stuck for a place to crash. It's all good. He's a good guy."

"Oh, right on," said Rick. "So this friend Hank is helping you keep your mind off of Tim, and it's completely platonic. Got it. You don't have to explain it to me."

"Don't be so dramatic girl," said Aaron. "Let's refill our drinks and rescue Linda before she goes home with that Israeli guy."

By the time Aaron closed the party and cabbed home, it was after midnight. He half expected to walk in to Hank in his bed again. He also half decided on his way home that if Hank was in his bed, he was so tired that he would get into it with him. But when he opened the door, his kitchen light was on, but the place was empty. Aaron undressed and crashed. In the morning, there was still no sign of Hank. His bags were there in the corner, so he hadn't left for good. Aaron thought about calling him to see if he was all right, but in the end he decided not to worry. Hank was a grown man, as was Aaron. He was probably fine.

CHAPTER FIFTEEN

Sunday, January 31

Hank woke earlier than usual that morning. He was lying on the open pullout couch in Aaron's main room, his head propped up, facing the brick wall with the fireplace and television above. To his left, Aaron slept on his bed, curled on his side under the covers, facing away from him toward the two large windows in the back of the apartment. His cat slept soundly at his feet. Though the blinds were closed, early light from the recently risen sun was finding its way between the backs of buildings and into the apartment.

The couple of weeks or so that he had stayed with Aaron were really comfortable, thought Hank. Despite his apartment being so small, Hank felt way more comfortable than he felt at Jack's, where he had the apartment nearly always to himself, or Perry's, for that matter, where they partied nearly twenty-four seven. Hank had seen Perry a couple of times since moving in with Aaron. He was hostile, seemingly angry that Hank managed to find a place to crash and land on his feet, whereas Perry was sleeping around with someone different every night, just to have a place to go. Hank didn't know how guys could do that night after night. Though in a city like New York, working in a place like Pasha, he supposed it was possible to live that way forever.

Aaron was such a genuinely nice guy and kept a good home. He had Ben & Jerry's ice cream in his freezer, three different kinds, along with a fridge stocked full of most of the basic essentials. When Hank came in last Friday night at two in the morning, having been at Pasha drinking whatever misfired drinks the bartenders occasionally gave him, he found Aaron sitting up in his sweatpants and tank top, watching *Pulp Fiction*. Hank was drunk, as was Aaron. He plopped down on the couch next to Aaron and the two watched together. It was halfway through, the scene where John Travolta dances in the diner with Marsellus's wife. That was his favorite part.

Hank loved that movie. He smiled thinking about it. While they watched, he saw there was a small pipe with pot in it on the coffee table, and when Aaron saw Hank eyeing it, he took a hit and offered it to him. They smoked for a while, and then Aaron brought out the ice cream—Cherry Garcia, Chunky Monkey, and Phish Food. Classics. Between the two of them, they polished it off, all of it, the pot, the ice cream, the movie. Aaron's couch was small, and they fell into each other on it. Hank even put his arm around Aaron. He watched him squirm a bit, adjusting himself. Hank liked that. He liked making Aaron feel good. It was an honest time, he thought—completely different than just getting blitzed and looking for more. It was a night off with company. There were a bunch of nights off at Aaron's like that.

Hank, in exchange for Aaron's kindness, tried to do nice things for him. He crashed somewhere else when he could. He was once at one of the bartender's apartments from Pasha, after a bunch of people went back there after the club closed, and he pretended to pass out on the couch once the party thinned. He knew he was too big for anyone to try to wake or move.

Another time, he went to a girl's apartment with her two guy friends. The guys wound up hooking up, and so Hank and the girl went to her bedroom. He passed out in her bed before anything could happen. Then in the morning he left early to get back to Aaron's before any of them woke. The guys were curled up together on this tiny couch. They were both so skinny, though, it didn't matter. It must have been like a king-sized bed for them. Hank smiled again. Or like when he and Aaron, both built dudes—Hank much bigger of course—slept in Aaron's normal-sized bed.

That happened a few times. Hank was usually careful to wait to be invited, though. He did this thing where he would rub his shoulder and say something about doing too many weights at the gym. He always waited until it was late and the two of them were going to bed at the same time. Aaron was so sweet. He fell for it every time. He would tell Hank to crash in his bed with him for the night, saying that he was tired and would be asleep any minute.

Hank and Aaron worked out together too, though not as much as Hank worked out. He would go most days while Aaron only went about three or four days a week. He said that it was part of his New Year's resolution—working out more. Who better than Hank to help? He had worked out nearly every day since he was a teenager.

It was the only way he could keep himself steady, level. Otherwise, he felt like he was walking around with all this excess energy. It was as if his body was made to flex. And he knew everything about it, reading every magazine lying around the gym. He knew how to work knots out of muscles. He helped guys push them out of their backs and thighs after tough lifts. He knew how to get big and stay big and how to train others.

There was a time a short while back when Hank, through another guy he was helping at the gym, got his hands on a bunch of steroids to bulk up, though they weren't the really aggressive kind. They were taken orally, so they didn't have the same bad side effects as injectables. Also, he only took them twice a week for a couple of months. That guy was really huge, even compared to Hank. He bought an extra few batches through him at the time and passed some off to a couple of guys at the gym, which helped pay for his own. It was a decent set up.

He stopped taking them and still had about forty doses left, and he thought about giving a few weeks' worth to Aaron to help him along. Sometimes, when he had worked with guys before to help them bulk up, they got excited when they saw a ton of results right away. He thought about it, what Aaron would look like if he were really big. Hank had darker features than Aaron, but their body types were similar. Judging by their bodies from the neck down, they could even be brothers. Hank would be the younger brother who worked out way more, of course.

Aaron stirred in bed, turning over on his stomach, only half under the covers. His cat rose slightly, turning to match Aaron's new position before lying down again, immediately falling back to sleep. Aaron exhaled heavily, sinking again into a deep slumber. His head still turned toward the windows, but in pulling the blanket up over his head with one arm, he exposed a leg up to the bottom edge of his underwear. Hank caught himself zoning out on Aaron's leg for a moment, thick, muscled, with short, dark, curly hair. He could hear the wind pick up outside and the radiator click on with fresh heat. Then the sun faded on the other side of the blinds, darkening the room. He smiled again, shook his head, and turned over on his side, facing away. He was hanging out at Pasha too much, he thought.

Staring into the kitchen, Hank was now facing the front entrance. That reminded him about that hot redhead from across the hall, the British one, who knocked on the door while Aaron was out yesterday afternoon. Nikki was her name. She looked surprised to see Hank there, but he said that he was Aaron's cousin from out of town and that he was staying with him for a while. He didn't know why he said that, but he did. And she didn't seem to buy it either. It was none of her business anyway. Hank could have been Aaron's cousin from out of town. Why the hell not? Nikki said her boyfriend or something was coming over and wanted to apologize. Hank asked her why her boyfriend wanted to apologize. She told him to tell Aaron she stopped by and then left all in a hissy and went back across the hallway. Stupid woman. He didn't bother telling Aaron. Aaron had been on his case about finding a place, and Hank didn't want to do anything that might make him angry, so he kept his mouth shut about the redhead.

Hank also gave back by fixing a few things around the apartment. The shower rod in the bathroom kept falling when the room steamed up. He mounted it with screws to hold it permanently in place. One of the windows didn't stay completely closed at the top because of a busted latch. He replaced it with one that worked. And the ceiling fan clicked. Aaron liked to put it on low whenever they smoked. Hank took the entire fan apart and put it back together, tightening each piece as he went along until it didn't click anymore. Aaron was so smart. He noticed these things. Well, thought Hank, he noticed the shower rod and the replaced window latch right away. But Hank had to point out the fan. They had taken a few hits; Aaron had put it on but didn't say anything. Hank was laughing so hard and kept asking if he saw it, if he noticed anything different. Aaron did not get it, but once Hank pointed it out, he got it. He smiled and definitely got it. It might have also taken Aaron a minute to figure it out because Hank had sprinkled some crystal he had stashed away, leftover, on top of the bowl. Hank did that a couple of times—made the pot high better for Aaron if he had some crystal around.

Most importantly, Hank tried to give Aaron lots of space. In addition to crashing a few times someplace else, he spent nearly every morning out too. Some mornings, a couple of days a week, he went to the gym and showered there. He also worked. There was a house this contractor guy he knew was gutting. He had worked for him on and off since getting to the city. He was called in mostly for the muscle jobs—pulling down walls, ripping out piping, bringing equipment in or out from trucks. Hank was not in a union, and the contractor always paid him in cash. Also, he threw Hank a few extra bucks on occasion because he said he needed a white guy on site who spoke English in case anyone came by asking questions about the job. The last thing he said he needed was some illegal trying to field questions from the building owner. Or worse, a nosey neighbor pissed off by the noise, or a city inspector.

When Hank wasn't working or at the gym or hanging around Pasha or with Perry, he walked through Times Square. There were tons of stores open with the heat blasting inside, Disney, M&M World, Hershey's, and Toys "R" Us. He liked the huge, colorful children's stores most. Music played, and kids ran around with their parents close by. They were always so excited, happy to be in New York, on vacation, away from home and school. Hank did not have that kind of childhood with trips to New York to buy toys when he was a kid. But he enjoyed watching it play out in front of him with strangers. But that too made him a little sad. He didn't know why.

When he exhausted options for everywhere he could think to go, he returned to Aaron's apartment. It too was warm like the stores, but always so quiet and soft. If it was empty—Aaron being at work or out with friends—he sat quietly with the lowest of lights on, if any. He would listen to the silence, just the occasional click of the heat hissing on. Everything else drifted away—the noise from tearing down walls at his construction gigs, the constant metallic clang of metal on metal at the gym, the bass at the clubs coming up through the floor invading his thoughts, and Perry's bitchy prattling on and on after they scored a bag and consumed their first few hits. Hank liked it at Aaron's. He was the happiest there that he had been in a long while. And Aaron, in turn, liked having Hank stay with him. He was sure of it.

Aaron was still sleeping with his cat curled up close against him. Hank drifted back to sleep too. They all slept deeply for several more hours. It was Sunday.

CHAPTER SIXTEEN

Wednesday, February 17

Aaron, Rick, and Linda sat at the bar of the Ninth Avenue Saloon, drinking vodka and sodas. Greg was bartending. It was happy hour, just after seven in the evening, and mostly empty inside. It was one of those blisteringly cold and prematurely dark days in February when most people went immediately home after work, ate dinner, curled up on the couch in front of the television, and went to bed early.

Aaron had come in most nights that Greg was bartending over the past few weeks. Sometimes he would stay for a couple of drinks and then head off. Other times he hung around for a few hours. Once or twice, on really slow nights, he picked up food for the two of them to eat at the bar.

"I heard from Nikki a couple of days ago," said Rick. "She said she stopped by your place again and Hank was still there. I don't mean to be all up in your business, but why hasn't he found something yet?"

"The place he was supposed to move into fell through," said Aaron. "He's been looking." Aaron was more frustrated with Hank than he was willing to share. He had been feeling funny about the whole situation for a while. He had asked Hank many times over the past five, six weeks about moving out. Hank always dodged the question, saying he almost had something but it got scooped up before he could sign, or that it was the perfect situation but the landlord wanted three months' rent upfront, and he just didn't have that. And it wouldn't have been quite so bad if Hank hadn't been getting under Aaron's skin so much. Hank helped himself to whatever was in the refrigerator. He siphoned nearly all of Aaron's spare change from a jar in the kitchen, just saying one word when asked, laundry. He never bought any toiletries but used whatever he wanted in the bathroom, soap, shampoo, toilet paper. While Hank was mostly tidy, Aaron hadn't once seen him actually cleaning anything. He also took and wore some of Aaron's clothes without asking, mostly socks and T-shirts, though a few nights ago he came home and Hank was wearing his favorite sweatshirt, the one with his college logo on it.

"You're totally sleeping with him," said Linda.

"Whatever," said Aaron. "I'm fairly certain he's into girls."

Greg rolled his eyes. He knew some of the shenanigans that were happening between the two of them, but not all.

"Fairly certain?" asked Greg. Aaron shot him a look.

"See," said Linda. "You just avoided the question. You definite-ly are. I know he saved that emo-girl from the C train and you have some sort of Superman infatuation thing going on here, but please."

"Now, now," said Rick. "If Aaron wants to keep his new boy-friend a secret from his friends, that's his prerogative. But you do realize what this guy is?"

"No, what?" asked Aaron.

"Starts with an *r*, ends in a *d*," said Rick, looking at each person in the group.

"I have no idea what you are talking about," said Aaron. He was growing more frustrated by the minute.

"Rebound," said Rick. "I'm sorry to say it, but Hank is definitely your rebound. No issues with that whatsoever, but you have to get rid of him. Whatever it is, it's not healthy."

"Is the guy even paying you rent?" asked Linda.

"He's helped out around the place," said Aaron. "And look, like I said, he's been looking. He's probably going to be out any day. You know how fast apartments are signed in New York." In truth, Hank had said he was going to give Aaron some rent money when he was paid next. But Aaron refused, telling him to keep the mon-ey to put toward his new place. It made more sense that way. The whole point of him staying with Aaron was so that he could get on his feet and find a place of his own, not help Aaron with rent. Hell, Aaron considered spotting him money just to get him out, if he thought he'd ever see it again. But even if he did think he would see it again, he was completely tapped—at least for another couple of paychecks—from the New Year's party.

"So to be clear, he's putting out and not paying you rent," said Rick. "Isn't that like, a call boy or something?"

"Or a nineteen fifties marriage," said Linda.

"Okay," said Aaron, loudly slurping his drink until it was empty. "New topic."

Aaron only told Greg about a couple of the things that happened sexually with Hank, but there were others. Aaron and Hank started going to the gym together fairly regularly. Hank was a real positive influence there, at least in the beginning. He pushed Aaron to do more reps and lift heavier weights, encouraging him by telling him how much bigger he was looking already.

The day after Aaron's big work event, the pair went for their fourth session working out together. Afterward, they went down to the steam room. There were two other guys in there who were obviously fooling around with each other. One's towel was barely draped over his lap, and they were sitting so close together their legs were practically touching. The steam room at Urban Workout, or really most gyms in Manhattan in Aaron's experience, could be pretty cruisey. There was something about lifting, the release of all those endorphins, then sitting in a warm, steamy room in nothing but a towel, muscles worn out, feeling a little lightheaded, physically spent. The two guys covered themselves when he and

Hank entered. A minute later they left. Hank was the first to say something.

"Dudes," said Hank laughing. "We're all dogs."

"Right," said Aaron. The steam was dense and the room felt charged. "Everybody has to get off, I guess."

"Man, you said it. I haven't gotten off since I've been staying with you."

"Really?" asked Aaron. His heart was pounding. He thought about Hank's hand on his chest on New Year's, Hank putting his arm around his shoulder that time while they watched a late-night movie, and how encompassing he was when they crashed together in bed, taking up so much space, his frame so huge.

"Why? Are you jerking off all the time when I'm not there or sleeping?"

"No, I mean," Aaron stopped. He was sitting across from Hank. They were sitting in the same seats, same positions as they were when Aaron first told Hank he could stay with him. Hank was leaning back, his head down, not making eye contact. Aaron saw that his hand was under the fold of his towel. Aaron held his breath for a moment. His face was flush from the steam.

"Man, that was a hard workout today."

Hank was rubbing himself under his towel. Aaron could see his hand moving slowly. Then he decided he was going to do the same, his limbs immediately shaking with nerves. Hank's chest and biceps were wet, firm, pumped. Aaron watched him. The two were silent. Hank never looked at Aaron, never made eye contact, never glanced even remotely in his direction. It wasn't that he ignored him. Aaron felt Hank was letting him watch without comment or intrusion. From then on, this became a regular part of their workouts. And Aaron liked it. He hated himself for liking it, not at first, but soon. He hated himself for getting hooked on it, craving it, thinking about it when he was at work or couldn't sleep.

Aaron told Greg about that first time the day after it happened, omitting a bunch of details. He didn't tell him about any of the other times since, or how much he still thought about it despite truly wanting him out.

⊱⊰

"Okay," said Linda. "Let's talk about how Rick has an interview with someone in my office on Friday."

"What?" asked Greg. "Really? That's great. Why didn't you tell me, baby?"

"Thanks, Linda," said Rick. "You're really on point tonight. I don't know. I wasn't keeping it a secret. I didn't want to jinx it or get too nervous."

"So what's the role?" asked Aaron.

Linda jumped in, saying, "Well, the area I work in is sales, but on the other side of the building, there's this huge content department with a couple of studios. They create a lot of sponsored content. Basically the job is running the studio—bringing everything together once it's sold. Scripts, shooting, editing."

"Right, video project manager," said Rick. "Part of it involves working with talent who come in to do endorsements, but the main part of it is really organizing whole shoots. It sounds perfect. It's kind of a half a step from what I was doing at the record label."

"That's great," said Greg.

"Way to go," said Aaron. "It sounds exciting."

Greg poured the three another round.

"But before I forget," said Rick, steering the conversation away from himself, "I would like to discuss a certain Israeli man who one of us—I don't want to say who—might have recently been on a date with. Hint: It's nobody here who's currently living with a man."

"What?" asked Aaron looking at Linda with surprise. "That kid with the startup from my event?"

"Yup," said Rick.

"Oh, poo," said Linda. "You are all allowed to think what you will, but I lasted nearly two months on my man diet."

"Six weeks at best, Lindy," said Rick. "It's not even March yet."

"People aren't meant to keep their New Year's resolutions," said Linda. "It's unnatural. Beside, a girl's got to eat."

"Chicken," finished Rick.

"Hardy har," said Linda. "So we had drinks…and maybe made out a little…in the bathroom…of a restaurant."

"Slllllll-ut," shouted Rick.

"He's a nice guy," tried Linda. "Besides, it's not like I'm just letting him stay at my apartment in exchange for sex." She looked at Aaron.

"Really?" asked Aaron. "Are we doing this again?"

Linda turned to Rick, put her hand up to block her mouth as if she were whispering a secret, but instead said loudly, "He's so sensitive."

"For the record, we are not sleeping together," said Aaron.

Once the words escaped his mouth, Aaron realized what he said was not actually true. He and Hank were sleeping in Aaron's bed most nights. What started as a random night here and there, when they were too tired, lazy, or wasted to open the couch—whatever excuse was thought up and agreed upon—ended up becoming a nightly norm. They slept right up against each other and even sometimes got off together in bed, late at night, while they were both pretending to be asleep. Aaron told Greg about him and Hank occasionally sharing a bed to sleep, but made it sound rare, leaving out the part about them getting off.

Those late nights in bed when it happened, though, it wasn't like the steam room; it was more intimate, under the covers. Aaron couldn't decide if it was what he thought it might be, something real, or if it was something else, something just primeval. He and Hank never talked about those late-night carry-ons or did anything like that at home when there wasn't that pretense of being asleep.

It all felt so constructed, silly, childish even. But, like the steam room, he was hooked, and he wanted it to continue. He didn't want to be the one to bring those physical moments to an end.

There was one big incident that Aaron did not share anything about with Greg. That past weekend, Aaron and Greg went out, just the two of them. They barhopped in Hell's Kitchen, hitting five places for one drink at each. Then they talked about going back to Aaron's place to smoke, but decided to hit one more bar first.

Aaron and Greg exploded into the Ritz, drinking, dancing, chatting with anyone and everyone. They moved from the first floor, where the music was deep R&B, to the second, where it was more pop. The guys there that night were so cute, Aaron remembered. Everyone was flirting with everyone—bumping into each other, grinding on one another. The air was thick and felt electric. They were both feeling hot and having fun, but Greg didn't eat much for dinner and the booze was clearly getting the better of him.

"Come on, Aaron," said Greg. "Let's go back to your place. I want to smoke."

"It's just that I don't know if Hank is there," said Aaron. "You know what? Screw it. It's my place. Let's just go."

"Attaboy!"

They left the bar, stopping on the corner to pick up a six-pack. Once in his building, Aaron fumbled with his keys loudly, clumsily, even though he was trying his hardest to be as quiet as possible. Greg was singing something indecipherable at full volume, his voice bouncing through the hall, up the stairs, probably waking his neighbors.

"Did you hear what that DJ was playing?" asked Greg. "Was that the new Rihanna song?"

Slowly Aaron opened the door, not entirely sure what to expect, but as Greg pushed forward and they poured into the apartment, he quickly realized it was empty. He breathed a sigh of relief, but Greg was too distracted to notice. Greg was making a beeline to the radio. Within minutes he was sitting on Aaron's couch, hitting a small bowl. Aaron opened two bottles of beer and handed one to Greg. Then he took a hit himself.

"So what's it like having this muscle guy in your apartment all the time?"

"Yeah, it can actually be pretty hot," said Aaron. He set the bowl down, turned on a couple of dim lights, and switched the ceiling fan on low. Then he lit the candles in the fireplace. It took nearly a whole book of matches to get three candles lit, his mind reeling from the booze and smoke.

"Did you ever ask him about that conversation I overheard at the gym?"

"About selling and using...muscle enhancers?" asked Aaron. "Yeah, it wasn't as hard-core as you think." Aaron kicked off his shoes and slid back into the couch.

"What was it?" asked Greg. His eyes were half closed, and he was moving his head a little to the music. It was, by coincidence, the exact Rihanna song he was trying to remember. "This bitch is everywhere."

"Some liquid-vitamin supplement, I think," said Aaron. "Athletes training for the Olympics use it. Hank's been working out since he was a teenager. He knows a lot about it. I tried some too. It's fine." Aaron took two more hits, slowly exhaling.

"Having your own life-sized action figure aside," said Greg, "the guy is a bit creepy, right? Drugs. No place of his own. Questionable sexual preferences. You have to get rid of him."

"He's going soon," said Aaron, talking lower. "I already spoke with him a couple of times about it."

"All right, all right," said Greg. "I don't mean to bring it up again. Just be careful is all."

At that moment, the door opened. It was Hank. Aaron wondered for a half second if Hank had heard any of that conversation from the hallway. But the music was loud. Then he forgot about it and couldn't remember what they were talking about anyhow.

Greg stood. "Hank, man, speak of the devil," he said. "What have you been up to?"

Hank tried to say something, stopped, and then responded, "Out with friends." He was grinning widely. He was sauced. He tore off his coat, dropping it to the floor. Underneath, he had on a tight, white T-shirt tucked into his jeans. His shirt was so thin that Greg could clearly see the definition of Hank's chest, pecks and nipples.

"Greg, right?" asked Hank, holding his hand out to shake. Greg looked up from Hank's chest, making eye contact and immediately feeling his face redden.

"And I'm out," said Greg. "That's my cue to get home to my husband."

"So you can bang him?" asked Hank.

Greg burst out laughing, falling forward, grabbing the edge of the table to steady himself.

"Oh my," said Greg. "I think I'm high."

"I need to sit down," said Hank slowly.

"Later, boys," said Greg. "Have fun." He picked up his coat from the back of a chair in the kitchen and left, the door slamming hard behind him.

Hank fell heavily into the middle of the couch, sandwiching Aaron against one side. Before Aaron could shift, Hank's head fell back, then forward, and then he picked up and took a swig of Greg's unfinished beer.

Aaron zoned out on him, watching him from this close proximity—his defined arms and big hands. Then he tried to focus on the candles in the fireplace. All he could feel was warmth radiating off Hank.

Hank put his hand on Aaron's leg and rubbed it up and down slowly, confidently. Aaron lost his breath for a moment and his mind swam.

"You know I'd let you fuck me," said Hank.

"What'd you say?" asked Aaron.

"What?" answered Hank.

Hank shifted over, giving Aaron more room. Then he turned his massive body so that one knee rested on the edge of the cushion, his face buried in his arm resting on the back of the sofa.

"Fuck me," he said undoing his belt with his free hand.

Aaron's brain shut off, and his body ran on autopilot, defaulting to movements that were guttural, mechanical, familiar. It was over quickly.

Aaron guessed that Greg probably knew what happened that night. Then again, Greg was so wasted, maybe he didn't put it all together. What little Aaron did remember of being on top of Hank—however brief and fleeting that memory was—he was certain of one thing: that was definitely not Hank's first time.

⇥⇤

"Well, boys, it's almost nine," said Linda. "I need to get home and out of these heels before I turn into a pumpkin."

"Yeah, and once happy hour ends," said Aaron, glancing at Greg, "I hear this place is a rip-off."

"Right, but I hear the bartender is pretty hot," said Rick.

"You boys need one more for the road?" asked Greg.

"Nah," said Rick. "I'm going to head home and get something inside my stomach besides vodka."

"Me too," said Aaron.

Rick stood and steadied himself, putting on his scarf and jacket.

Greg leaned over and said to Aaron, "Hey, if you need anything, day or night, just call. Okay?"

Aaron nodded and said quietly, "Thanks." Then he turned to Rick. "Come on, old boy, you can walk me to my door on your way home."

"Yes, mister," said Rick. Then, turning back to the bar, he said, "Bye, baby, I'll be up."

Rick, Linda, and Aaron left the Saloon. On the sidewalk, Linda leaned in close to Aaron and spoke softly. "All joking aside, you're important to us. Be careful. You can always crash at my place too."

"Thanks, Linda," said Aaron. "I'll be okay. And I know we didn't talk directly about him, but as for Allen, he's a jerk, no doubt. But he clearly has a substance problem."

"I know, I know," interrupted Linda. "He's got to get past that one himself. I can't take that kind of behavior from him, or anyone."

"Of course," said Aaron. "If he does reach out to you again, I'd put it out there. I've known people in the past with problems. Sometimes they just need someone to say it to them."

"Right," she said. "There is something more there with him. It's hard to know whether he's worth a second chance. My mind says no, but when he's not on all that stuff, all helter-skelter..."

"You're the most important person in this equation," said Aaron. "Of that much, I'm certain." He wrapped his arms around her and held her firmly to his chest.

Linda gently pulled back and smiled, her eyes moist partly from the chill and partly from the conversation. She gave Aaron a peck on the cheek, then Rick. "I'm walking to Eighth to get a cab," she said resolutely. "See both you handsome boys soon."

"Later, Lindy," said Rick.

"Later," said Aaron.

It was cold and the wind strong. Rick was shivering. He looped his arm through Aaron's, and the two walked west.

Rick turned to Aaron and said, "You're such a sap." Aaron smiled and tightened his arm, pulling Rick in a little closer.

CHAPTER SEVENTEEN

Friday, March 5

R ick's new job, he quickly learned, came with perks—more
perks than his last. Because it was an agency, and he managed the content creation side of the business, he worked with
clients and high-profile celebrities for product endorsements. His
new boss, wanting to welcome Rick to the company, didn't think
twice about passing him free concert tickets. One of his reps had
bought a whole block of seats months before to use for VIP clients.
These were the last of them.

Rick, Greg, and Aaron walked through the entrance of
Madison Square Garden with purpose. They strategically cabbed
it, arriving early enough to catch the opening act and buy a couple beers before the main show began. Their seats, they realized
after getting there, were only twenty rows back from the right
of the stage. All three had been to concerts at the Garden, but
none had seats as good as these. Fortunately, they were prepped,

dressed, and ready for the inevitability of being so close to the performer that surely they would be called out, made eye contact with, or hopefully danced on, should the diva traverse the fourth wall of the stage.

Suddenly, everything went dark except for one white beam shining straight up from the front center of the stage. The venue shook with cheers, eighteen thousand people simultaneously rising to their feet in anticipation of her arrival.

From the speakers, her voice boomed.

"Hello, New York! It's great to be back in my hometown and the best city on earth! Welcome to my show!"

The floor of the stage opened. White smoke augmented by bright lights beamed everywhere. Then a figure appeared.

"It's Gaga time, monsters!"

The crowd went wild. Lady Gaga was reflective, wearing what looked like a one-piece bathing suit made out of disco-ball mirrors with two huge cylindrical cones cupping her chest. Her hair was platinum blond, and her lipstick, a deep red.

Rah-rah-ah-ah-ah-ah. Rama-ramama-ah.

Aaron leaned over Greg, shouting to Rick on the other side.

"You are a freaking god! These tickets are insane."

Greg shouted at the stage. "Woo! Woo! We love you, Gaga."

Rick whistled and clapped, thrusting one hand in the air, trying to catch her attention.

The show was full of tight-bodied dancers, a dozen outfit changes—each more outrageous than the last—wired acrobats, an assault of lights, and a battering of sounds. She performed her most popular numbers and a bunch of songs from her newest album. Although the audience had chairs, no one sat, everyone opting instead to stand, dance, or just move to the beat. After about an hour and a half of Rick, Greg, and Aaron cheering and singing along with the crowd, their voices and legs were starting to wear. That's when Gaga changed her tone.

A white grand piano rolled out to the center of the stage. Three spotlights from far above lit the keys. The rest of the stage fell dark. The audience dropped into a trance, all of Madison Square Garden quieting from a roar to a whisper as Gaga unfastened her cape, letting it fall heavily to the floor. Underneath she was wearing a thin, dark bodysuit. She sat at the piano.

Gaga sang in perfect concert with the chords that flowed through her fingers to the deepest recesses of the venue. These songs were slower, more soulful.

First she sang "Again Again," improvising in the middle and end, smashing her elbows and heels into the keys. The audience was mesmerized. Every touch of every key rang out uninterrupted by her fans.

Rick watched her fingers lift and fall to the keys as if this were her second nature—her playing and singing as comfortable to her as breathing.

When you're 'round, I lose myself inside your mouth
You've got brown eyes like no one else, baby, make it to me

Rick was moved by the music and thought about Greg and how lucky he was to have him. They had been together nearly fourteen years. They saw each other through ups and downs, though mostly ups. They evolved together from young men to grown men. Throughout it all, somehow they managed to still be completely into each other. They met while in line at a coffee shop. They both had boyfriends at the time—neither of them particularly serious. But when they were introduced to each other, standing there with their respective partners, who were acquaintances, Rick and Greg felt an energy between them—both smiling, having a hard time containing themselves, overwhelmed by their instant connection. They played it down, brushing it off. But it wasn't long before the two reached out to each other, meeting and acknowledging what they both felt so completely. Sometimes the starts of relationships don't happen as cleanly and neatly as they do in stories, thought Rick. But from that unconventional beginning, they built a strong relationship. This past time that Rick was laid off was his second—and hopefully last—since they got together. Each time, Greg knew exactly what to say to help Rick get through it. The ups were easy and often. The downs, like Rick getting laid off, were what convinced him that they would be together for many years to come, and probably the rest of their lives.

Rick looked over to Greg as Gaga was starting her next song. Greg's face was washed in light and delight. It was an acoustic-piano version of "Poker Face"—sporadic chords struck between sung lines marking her path through the number.

I wanna roll with him a hard pair we will be
A little gambling is fun when you're with me

Greg was a fan of Gaga from her early days, feeling a minuscule sense of pride since the Saloon was one of the first bars to start playing her music regularly. At the Saloon, he wore multiple hats. Bartending was one. He was also manager, bouncer and disc jockey, among other things—his mixing consisting mostly of building playlists on his downtime. He remembered the way people came alive when this song first came on.

The Saloon didn't have a dance floor per se. The space next to the pool table in the back acted as one in a zealous pinch. But when Gaga came over the speakers, the entire bar erupted into one big dance floor. It never failed, regardless of how early it was or how many people were there. When Gaga's first album came out, dance pop was in a depression. There wasn't much on the radio or in the bars in terms of a fresh sound. She reenergized the scene, and Greg loved her for it. It was during those days that he came to accept—reluctantly at first, but then with gratitude—that hospitality, bartending, and managing, specifically at the Ninth Avenue Saloon, was his career. It was also then that he sat down with the owners, having been a bartender there for a few years, to have a serious conversation about taking on more responsibility and having more investment in overseeing and growing the business. They welcomed the conversation, especially after hearing Greg's ideas for promoting the space, turning it into something more with event-themed nights to attract new patrons in typically slow times. Fortunately, with Hell's Kitchen also exploding with growth and gentrification, his ideas were successful, and he graduated to becoming the Saloon's full-time general manager.

For the most part, the Saloon was a fun place to work. But it wasn't until more recently—when he was staffed at capacity and was in a strong enough position that he could start passing on weekend shifts—that life was becoming both fun and fulfilling. That coincided with his friendship with Aaron finding its footing. Aaron became more than just a party friend. He was helping Greg grow as a person. Other than Rick, Greg didn't have many close friends on the inside circle. He had lots of people to hang out with and tons of acquaintances, but for the first time in years, with Aaron, he had an actual best friend, outside of Rick. Aaron was someone objective who genuinely cared, listened, and offered sound advice. But he also knew when to forget about life's challenges and have a truly good time. That's what real friends are for too, thought Greg—knowing when a distraction is as important as lending an ear—and he was thrilled that Rick liked Aaron as much as Greg thought he would.

Greg looked over at Aaron, whose eyes were closed momentarily as he took in the music. From less than fifty feet in front of them, Gaga pushed the piano bench behind her with one foot and stood, transitioning to her next number, "No Floods."

No matter lightning or thunder, buckets of rainwater, you can't flood this town
In a world unknown, you've gotta hold your own, and you can't stop me

Aaron felt more alive than he had felt in years. It was as if his mind were deteriorating for decades, age allowing a shadow to slowly eclipse it, so gradually that he didn't even notice it happening. The years he spent working, surviving in the city, always seemed to drag. But in that moment, at the concert with Greg and Rick, something shifted. It was as if all of that droning on and on, working and worrying, passed in an instant—leaving him with a sense of clarity as if he awoke from a dull dream.

Regardless of what had happened in the past with his love life, career, or friends, this exact moment was his. He owned it, earned it, and loved it. He thought about this distinct feeling that was so strong. It was as if his true nature as a person was handed to him as a stiff leather jacket in his youth. And as the years toiled on, the jacket grew heavier and heavier until one day, that day, he was able to take the jacket off for just a moment and shake it out. And when he put it back on, instead of it feeling heavy or burdensome, it formed perfectly to his body. All those years of discomfort and insecurity were erased, replaced by armor—his armor—molded to him by his own experiences.

Aaron had worked hard and with integrity to build a career that was finally finding footing. He had shed the passionless complacency of his near decade-long relationship. He had developed a group of friends who were his peers, whom he loved and trusted. His mind was alert, body in shape, and spirit strong. Then he thought about his home, acknowledging to himself for the first time that it was in fact under siege by a foreign entity that had taken something from him, his independence. He adored his apartment and the freedom it represented. It was time for Hank to go, once and for all. No more excuses.

CHAPTER EIGHTEEN

Saturday, March 6

Aaron woke to Mr. Boo Berry's paw on his face. As soon as he opened his eyes, Boo was at full purr. Stretching one leg outward, the still-small kitten immediately seized the opportunity to nuzzle deeper into the warmth of the bed. He rose, arched his back, turned, and then plopped himself down stomach up in the crux of Aaron's arm, pushing both front paws in the air. Aaron watched with amusement. Then he looked over to the empty couch and then to the corner of the room, where Hank's things laid strewn over a chair, across an end table, and on the floor below. Hank must have slept someplace else last night.

Before Aaron could indulge in his apartment being empty—but for himself and Boo—by drifting back to sleep, he was jarred by a key entering the bottom lock of his front door. It turned right, releasing the deadbolt. Keys jingled in the hallway. Then another slid into the top lock. Aaron sat up. Boo jumped from the bed. The second deadbolt released, and Hank entered.

"You're up," said Hank. "I didn't mean to wake you."

"I'm up," said Aaron as he scooted from bed and rose to his feet. He was in underwear and nothing else. He pulled sweatpants from his dresser and put them on along with a T-shirt.

"Do you want coffee?" asked Aaron, walking into the kitchen where Hank stood. "We need to talk."

Hank's eyes were red with deep bags under them.

"About what?" asked Hank.

"You know what."

"I just walked in the door, man, and already with this," said Hank. "This isn't a good time. I'm tired. I need to crash out. It's been a long night."

Hank was looking over to the couch in the next room. He was fully dressed and wearing boots. Even slouched over with his head low, he was taller than Aaron, who was barefoot and blocking his way.

Aaron put his hand flat on Hank's chest. Hank looked up.

"It's never a good time, Hank. I get it," said Aaron. "But we've been through this. You've got to go. It's enough already. I need my place back, today. I need my life back."

Hank's eyes opened wide. He looked down to where Aaron's hand was on him.

"You've got to give me another day or two, man," said Hank. "It's not my fault that last place fell through. I've got nowhere to go."

"It's always a day or two with you, Hank," responded Aaron quickly, speaking louder, wanting to drive home this point. He felt like he wasn't getting through. He was determined to get through this time. "You've been saying that for the past two months. This has to stop. You need to get your stuff and get out."

The two stood in silence for a moment, looking at each other, considering the other, considering themselves.

"No," said Hank finally, matching Aaron's volume and seeming suddenly more sober, speaking slower, clearer. "I'm not going anywhere. You need to get used to it." As he said this, he jabbed two fingers hard into Aaron's chest, pushing him back a few inches.

Aaron's heart was racing, adrenaline pushing through his veins. He tried to keep his voice from shaking. "I'll call the police. How about that?"

"Sure you will," said Hank, the tips of his fingers still on Aaron. "What? You want to fuck me every night?" He ran his fingers down and tugged hard at the waistband of Aaron's sweatpants, pulling him closer.

"Are you serious? Do you think this will buy you more time?" asked Aaron, pushing Hank's hand away. "That's messed up. You're messed up. You can't even admit who you are."

Hank was breathing heavily, his head still spinning from the night before. "I'm not like you," he said. "You're disgusting. What you do with guys is disgusting."

"Screw you, Hank," Aaron shot back. "You're a homo. Own it, don't own it, I don't care. Either way, I want you out."

"Who do you think you are?" asked Hank. "You don't own me. I'll fuck you up so bad you won't be able to walk for a week."

"Jesus, this conversation is over," said Aaron. He went to push past Hank, to grab his phone on the counter behind him, to call for backup—Greg, the police, somebody. Hank saw what he was going for, blocked him, reached over, and pulled a large knife from the butcher's block on the counter. He held it between himself and Aaron, the point inches from Aaron's throat.

"I own you," said Hank. "You're my bitch."

"Please," said Aaron. "You're high. And you're a muscle mary. Who are you kidding? You're trash, Hank. You're just a trashy mary." Aaron's adrenaline turned to anger. Who did this guy think he was? Invading his home, invading his life? Threatening him with a knife?

"Fuck you, faggot," shouted Hank.

Without thinking, Aaron gathered saliva from the back of his throat to the front of his mouth, pushed his chin forward, and spit in Hank's face.

Hank was no longer standing in Aaron's kitchen, Aaron's apartment. He was eighteen years old again and standing in the doorway of his childhood home's kitchen, watching his father tower over his mother on the floor as he berated her.

"You stupid, stupid woman," he yelled at her, his right hand bandaged so heavily that his entire arm seemed to extend into a white-linen stump. "What were you thinking? You're so useless."

His mother took verbal assaults and the occasional backhanded slap over the years. But this was the first time that his father had kicked her. Hank was often on the receiving end of such treatment, but he never saw his mother down on the floor.

"Where did you think you were going?" he yelled at her, saliva from his words spraying from his mouth onto her. He had been back from the hospital less than a week and needed help with everything. Hank and his mother were feeding him, cleaning him, and even wiping him after he went to the bathroom.

"Pop, don't!" screamed Hank from the doorway. His shoulders—even after working out for just a couple of years—took up the width of the frame. His father looked up, his face red. He locked eyes with Hank.

"Stay out of this, mary," he said. "You should have never been born. I know what you are. Don't you go defending this trash. You better man up or get out."

Hank froze. His father knew. He watched his father kick his mother over and over as she curled up on her side in a ball. He couldn't move an inch. He felt completely paralyzed—not knowing what to do. Should he try to overtake his father? A lifetime of trying always resulted in failure. Should he accept his offer to go forever as he had always planned? Hank couldn't leave his mother there alone. He couldn't help her. He couldn't leave her. He wished his grandfather were still alive. He wished his grandfather were there to tell him what to do. But he wasn't, so Hank did nothing. He watched. Every kick felt like it was going into his side. "You're trash!" his father kept saying to her. "Just like that mary you raised, trash!"

Aaron was staring at Hank, his phlegm making its way down Hank's cheek. Hank wasn't saying anything, just standing there, perfectly still, looking so distant. Aaron suddenly felt cold, as if he had drifted to another place far away too. He thought about what he could say to bring them back. "Hank, I'm sorry. This has gotten out of hand. It's okay if you have those feelings. We can figure this…"

Hank's shoulder and arm went forward, his hand tight around the knife's handle. With the weight of his massive chest, the top half of his body came down across the flesh between Aaron's neck and shoulder, cutting a long, permanent line. Aaron stepped back, but it was too late.

The pair locked eyes. Aaron's disbelief of what happened was quickly being replaced by a sinking feeling in the pit of his stomach. With both hands, Aaron covered the wound below his throat as if trying to reach back through time to shield himself. Then he looked at his hands. They were covered in blood. Trembling, he pressed them together palm to palm and then pulled them apart. The blood felt thin and slippery. It smelled metallic. Then he looked back to Hank, whose gaze was rapidly transforming into something different, more present. Aaron thought he recognized the expression strangely as resolve.

"What have you done?" asked Aaron in disbelief. He felt weak, confused.

"You should have never been born," said Hank. He put one hand firmly on Aaron's shoulder, and with the other slashed deep across Aaron's side, releasing a second torrent of blood, this one heavier than the first. Aaron's shirt was saturated. He wriggled sideways, almost slipping. He moved a hand to his side as he tried to reach the front door, scarcely managing to scream for help before Hank dropped the knife to the floor. He pushed Aaron's head hard against the wall, covering his mouth and nose, and simultaneously grabbed Aaron's crotch tightly and twisted.

Drained from the loss of blood and oxygen and held against the wall, Aaron knew that he had virtually no leverage, and no chance. The situation became so violent, so quickly. He understood the seriousness of what happened, and what was happening. He felt disbelief—pain too—but mostly disbelief. He punched Hank's chest over and over as hard as he could, but he felt powerless. Somewhere deep inside he knew he was barely making contact. He was dizzy. Hank's massive chest felt wet. Was that blood? Was that his blood?

Aaron convulsed, his eyes growing wide, rolling to the back of his head. Then he was no longer there. His body was weightless, his muscles at ease, his mind empty.

Hank continued to hold Aaron's collapsed body against the wall, one hand over his face, the other between his legs. Minutes passed with the two locked in this position. Then he released him, allowing him to fall heavily to the floor with a thud. He took a step back. The room was dark, almost black. Hank wiped his hands on the back of his jeans. He was aware that he was shaking. He was starting to see again, his eyes adjusting, processing what was before him. The floor below glistened. Aaron lay crumpled, folded over himself, still. He wasn't breathing. He was lifeless. Hank knew he was dead. Hank knew he had killed him.

There was no turning back from this, thought Hank. He had nowhere to go. This was one of those moments in life at which everything was different. Things could never go back. Things would never be the same. This wasn't his fault. Aaron spit in his face, called him something he wasn't. He wouldn't have done that if Aaron had let him stay. He'd still be alive if he had kept his mouth shut. Aaron went too far. He shouldn't have pushed him like that. His salvia was still on his face. He wiped at it with the back of his hand. He could tell them what happened. He could explain it to the police. The police. The police wouldn't be on his side. They were in New York City. They'd never see the truth about what happened—how Aaron was making advances toward him. Aaron picked him up when he was desperate, down on his luck. Aaron took him in, fed him booze and drugs, and then made passes at him. That's not how Hank was raised. He wasn't like those people. That's what he'd tell the police. The truth. He was held captive. He was a prisoner in Aaron's apartment. He had no other choice but to defend himself. And the only way to defend himself against his captor was physically. They argued. They fought. He won. He was free. He was free from this place, free from Hell's Kitchen. Hank smiled. That's poetic justice, he thought. He was free from this hell, from New York. It was this city. It was the city of sin. He was free from it, and over it.

Hank took a deep breath, held it for a moment, and then reached over and opened the freezer. In the door was a bottle of whiskey. He unscrewed the top, took a large swig, and swallowed hard. The liquor burned his mouth, throat, and empty stomach. He set the bottle down on the shelf separating the kitchen from the main room. The kitchen floor was covered in blood. Aaron was lying in the middle of it, his head on its side. He looked shocked, or surprised, his eyes wide open, staring up at Hank. Why did you make me do that, thought Hank. You shouldn't have made me do that.

Moving through the main room, Hank pulled the comforter from the bed. He brought it to the kitchen, placed it on the floor and rolled the body onto it. Then he dragged the comforter with the body back. Hank arranged everything on the bed as best as possible to make it look like Aaron was sleeping, rolling him on his side and putting a couple of pillows by his head. There was blood everywhere, on the floor leading from the kitchen to the bed, on the bed soaking through much of the comforter, and all over Hank. His hands, shirt, and jeans were wet with it. He stood in the middle of the room thinking what to do next, reaching to the shelf for another swig of whiskey. This time it didn't burn as much. He noticed there was blood on the bottle.

Slowly undressing—boots, shirt, belt, jeans, socks, underwear—Hank left everything in a pile where he stood. Even naked, he could feel blood in his hair, on his skin, under his feet between his toes. He had to walk slowly to the bathroom, guiding himself along the wall so as not to slip, leaving finger traces in his wake. Then Hank took a very long shower with scalding hot water. He used all the remaining shampoo and body wash, lathering and rinsing until his skin was raw and red, tossing the empty bottles to the bathroom floor. When the water stopped and he pulled back the curtain, he realized everything not in the shower, everything in the entire apartment, was tainted. He placed two hand towels on the floor, stepping one foot on each. He dried himself with a larger one, putting it over his shoulders, leaving his bottom half exposed. Then he shimmied from the bathroom, using the hand towels under his feet as buffers between him and the floor. He moved like this through the kitchen to his pile of things in the corner, pausing between for a fresh mouthful of whiskey, holding the bottle with a clean tea towel.

The room had grown more pungent, making Hank feel nauseous. The whiskey was helping steady his stomach. Avoiding direct eye contact with the bed, he tried to focus on what to do next. He could run, go north, pass through his hometown, see his parents one last time, give his father a proper sendoff. He killed once. He could kill again. It was easier than he thought. His father was such an angry little man who had ruined his life, his mother's life, everyone's life he touched. He thought about him so often. He carried that around with him, always. He could end it once and for all. He could finally save his mother. Put an end to his father. Make her father, his grandfather, proud. But he couldn't go back as the same old Hank. He needed to show them the new Hank he had become—a strong, deadly man in control, calling the shots, not bowing to anyone, not apologizing for existing, but being the one who decided who lived and who died. He took another swig of whiskey, but this time to wash down a pill he had tucked away in his bag, diazepam, a muscle relaxer. He dressed, borrowing some clothes from Aaron one last time: Aaron's socks and briefs, Hank's spare jeans, Aaron's belt and T-shirt, Hank's hoodie and leather jacket, Aaron's baseball cap, Hank's gym sneakers. He felt good in clean clothes, and the pill was coming on fast.

Packing his bag, leaving his bloodied clothes, Hank thought how he really didn't need to rush—not that he could stay there with the apartment in that state, the gore, the stink. It would take days for the police to catch up, if not longer. He had plenty of time. No one even knew who he was or where he was from. No one would even know where to go looking for him. No one would realize anything even happened to Aaron for a while. They'd think he was out, on a bender, working, visiting family, on vacation.

From a black trunk on the floor of the closet, Hank fished out Aaron's passport and two hundred dollars. Hank had found the stash on his second day there, having gone through every inch of the apartment as soon as Aaron left for work, leaving him alone. He removed the driver's license from his own wallet before tossing it into the pile of bloody clothes on the floor. His driver's license he burned in the fireplace, lighting a whole book of matches ablaze at once. It mostly melted rather than burning, but he figured it was good enough to keep anyone from reading his name. The smoke was full of chemicals, which Hank welcomed. It distracted him, made him lightheaded again, masking the growing stench of the apartment.

Hank looked around one last time. The fireplace with the candles and his burned ID sat recessed into a brick wall that ran the entire length of the apartment. In the back, two large windows with closed blinds towered high above the bed with Aaron curled up under his comforter. A leather couch lined the wall opposite the fireplace. Through the doorframe that separated the main room from the kitchen—in the middle of the kitchen floor—he could see a pool of still-wet blood.

The apartment was dark, every light off. The air was sharp, stinging, almost suffocating. He drank the last of the whiskey. He slung his bag over his shoulder, walking carefully through the kitchen, around the perimeter of the room, avoiding the wet spot where Aaron fell. Aaron. He looked back one last time, shook his head, grabbed Aaron's wallet and keys from a small shelf next to the door, exited, wiped the bottoms of his sneakers on the welcome mat, and locked both deadbolts behind him.

Shortly after, Boo surfaced from under the bed. He jumped onto the comforter, sitting close to Aaron's body. It would be days before Boo realized that he was really alone.

CHAPTER NINETEEN

"How's Greg holding up?" asked Linda. She herself felt sick, a little weak and slow. There was a lump in the back of her throat, and no matter how many times she swallowed, it remained.

"Not that great. He's still a complete mess," answered Rick. He rubbed his arm where Aaron squeezed, pulling him closer on their walk home from the bar not long ago. He called Aaron a sap for getting all mushy with Linda. They laughed, ribbing each other, running high on happy hour fumes before dinner.

Linda was sitting on her couch with her legs crossed and a giant, knitted blanket draped across her shoulders. An oversized mug of hot tea and brandy rested on her knee.

"I can imagine. I called him again this morning, but I wasn't sure how much he'd want to talk about it."

Rick was standing several feet from the window, looking across the barren treetops of Central Park. It was still afternoon, but already dark. The only light in Linda's apartment was coming from the kitchen, and it reflected the room back against itself, obstructing the view.

"He wanted to go to work today," he said, starting to tear up again. "This was his first day back. He said he needed to do something else, think about something else. Poor baby. He was very shaken up. Poor Aaron. I still can't believe this happened."

"It sounds like it was pretty messy?"

"It was."

"So nobody would have found him if it weren't for Greg?" asked Linda.

"Aaron didn't show up to work for a few days," said Rick. "They must have called, maybe even reached out to his emergency contact. I don't really know. I wonder if they would have eventually sent someone to his apartment."

"I'm sure they would have," said Linda. "If one of my coworkers or direct reports was a no-show for days, I would have—especially if it was out of character."

"Greg started getting worried on Monday," he said. "They talked about hanging out Sunday for post-brunch drinks. Aaron wasn't answering any of his texts. He figured his phone was dead or he was busy."

Linda took one last gulp from her mug, swallowing hard. Much of the brandy had settled on the bottom, and her throat stung. She pushed the blanket from her shoulders, letting it fall behind, her face suddenly flush.

"And that's when he called the police?" she asked.

"That's when he went over," said Rick. "He buzzed, tried Nikki's apartment too, but she was working. Then he tried all of the buzzers. Someone let him in. He banged on Aaron's door. He banged and banged. He said he knew something was wrong. And Hank…" He paused.

"Hank?"

"He said he had a bad feeling about Hank. He had been saying so for days—weeks even—that he felt like something was off with him."

"We all did."

"At the door, Greg said he thought he could hear Aaron's cat meowing on the other side."

"That poor animal."

"I know," said Rick. "Greg went to the backyard of the building. Aaron once forgot his keys and Greg helped him climb through his back window. But that was in the fall. The window was open. They just had to jimmy the screen. This time it was locked and the blinds closed. He climbed on a chair and looked in through a crack. He saw the place was a disaster. That's when he called 911. When the police came, they broke a window and went in. It turned out being a lot worse than he initially thought."

"It must have been awful. Has someone been in touch with his family?"

"The NYPD spoke with his parents. I think he has a younger sister. Hank was trouble from the start."

"We tried to talk to Aaron," said Linda. "He's just such a...was such a...trusting guy." Tears were stinging her eyes. She breathed in deeply. "This could have happened to any of us."

"I don't know," said Rick. "I wouldn't have let some nutcase live in my apartment for weeks and weeks on end rent free. This is crazy. This whole thing is crazy." He moved to the couch, sat next to Linda, and put his hand on her back.

"Rick, I know this isn't the right time," said Linda. "But I have something to tell you. I've been talking to Allen again. He's on his way over. I just called him."

"What? Now? Why? After everything he did to you? After everything that just happened? No, absolutely not. I'm not watching another one of my friends self-destruct with a loser."

"You don't understand. He's changed. He's in Narcotics Anonymous. He's been going to meetings."

"Really, Linda? What possessed you to even get in touch with him?"

"After New Year's, he called me. He must have left me ten messages apologizing. He said he was getting counseling and going through the steps. He's taken a leave of absence from work."

"Unreal. So another jobless druggy is stealing one of my friends," Rick said, standing again, shaking his head.

"There's more," she said. "When you called on Monday and told me what was going on, Allen was here. Of course he saw how upset I was. He made a few calls. He's pretty well connected. His firm keeps all sorts of people on retainer. They were always ready to clean up a mess, which must have happened pretty often considering how those guys carried on. He learned some things about Hank."

"What about him?"

"According to Allen's guy who works with the police, Hank has a rap sheet, but nothing really violent. He's been arrested for trespassing, destruction of property, disorderly conduct, a bunch of drug charges—possession, intent to distribute, I think. I guess nothing stuck? It also seems he's been scraping by living in the city for a while without a steady place to live."

"None of that surprises me. We should have seen this coming. We should have done something instead of just joking about it." Rick was pacing. He stopped, looking out the window at Linda's reflection. Then he caught his own reflection, saw himself staring back, saw how tired his eyes looked.

"About Allen, we're not together or anything. I'm not the kind of person to forgive someone for acting like that much of a jerk to me. If he weren't in a program, I wouldn't be talking to him. I think he knows things were out of control. We're just talking. He's been good to me these last few days."

"Be careful, Linda," said Rick. "I don't think I can take any more of this."

⇒⊣⊢⇐

The Ninth Avenue Saloon was busier than usual considering the deep freeze outside. It was after happy hour, but before the late-night rush. This was generally a down time for Greg, who would restock, clean glasses, and give the place a once over. However, tonight, it seemed every callboy and his potential john was out on the town. He welcomed the distraction.

Several days had passed since he watched the NYPD break into Aaron's apartment. Since then, a shaky, anxious jitter took up what felt like permanent residence in his chest. He could still hear the glass cracking when one of the police officers smashed the window with the back of his Mag flashlight—shards falling partly inward and partly down to the concrete outside where, ten feet away, he stood watching.

"Two vodka sodas."

Greg looked up to a familiar face. Where was this guy from? He was tall, lanky, and he looked a bit disheveled. The gym? Hank. He knew Hank. He was sitting here that night with him. It was the night of Layde's show. He sometimes forgot names, but never a face.

"Hey, you know Hank?" asked Greg. "You know what he did."

"I don't know what you're talking about," Perry responded. "Hank, yeah, I mean, I knew him. I haven't seen that prick in months."

An older man standing near Perry stepped closer.

Steady there, thought Greg. He needed to keep it together. This was his first night back at work, and he needed to keep his composure.

"Hank murdered a close friend of mine," said Greg.

"What?" asked Perry. "Murdered? You mean that guy over on West Forty-Sixth? I heard about that. Everyone's talking about it. That was Hank? Are you sure?"

"Yeah, well, you'll be happy to know that they caught him. Not the sharpest tool in the shed."

"You're saying that Hank killed someone? That he's the guy that from the West Forty-Sixth Street murder? And that they caught him?"

"Am I stuttering? Yeah, wasn't he your friend? Haven't I seen you in here with him?" asked Greg.

"He's not my friend. I don't have anything to do with him," said Perry, glancing to the older man at his side.

"It's a little late for that," said Greg. "I've seen you guys together. More than once, in fact."

The older man placed one hand on Perry's shoulder. "They caught that guy already?" he asked. "Thank Gawd."

Greg ignored him and continued talking right to Perry. "After he killed my friend, he used his credit card to pay for a black car cab service all the way to Vermont," said Greg. "The NYPD caught him within two days."

"Jesus, he must have had a death wish or been flying high," said Perry, half under his breath. "The last time I saw him, he was pretty out of it. I let him hang around a couple of times, but then he just lingered. I couldn't get rid of the guy. I had to tell him I got evicted—that I moved."

"You need to talk to the police," said Greg. "Tell them what you're telling me."

"No way, man," said Perry. "I'm not talking to the police."

"This is too much, Perry," said the older man. "I don't need it that bad. I'm out." He slipped into his jacket and was out the door before Perry could respond.

Perry turned to Greg. "You just cost me a trick. I want a free drink."

"You've got to be kidding me," said Greg. But he realized Perry was never going to talk to the police. He was going to disappear into the ether like all the rest of them. He thought about calling the cops right then and there. But if his story was true, he wasn't exactly an accomplice. If anything, he was another victim of Hank's—another guy he took advantage of. That's if his story checked out. Judging by this guy's appearance and occupation, that was a big if.

"Fine, I'll fix you a drink on the house," he continued. "So you're Perry and you used to hang out with Hank. I'm Greg." As he said this, he scooped ice into a glass and started pouring vodka into it. This saved him from shaking Perry's hand. It also saved him from reaching across the bar and punching him.

Perry looked dubious, but then sat down. "Well, that's more like it," he said.

"When was the last time you saw him?" asked Greg.

"I don't know," responded Perry. "Four weeks ago, maybe six."

"Were you guys hooking up?" asked Greg. He set the drink in front of him. Perry took a big sip.

"No," he lied, coughing sharply. The drink was straight vodka on the rocks. "He used to come into the club and mooch drinks off the bartenders. I used to dance at Pasha."

"Did he do hard drugs?" asked Greg.

"No, I mean, what are you a cop or something?" he asked. "What does that matter anyway? It's not going to bring your friend back."

"Just answer the question," responded Greg. Perry's words stung deep. It wasn't going to bring Aaron back, but he wanted to know some truth about the real Hank and how this could have happened. He was searching for answers, even if he didn't have the right questions.

"I don't know, man," said Perry. "I guess he smoked pot. Maybe he did some coke. How should I know?"

"Meth? Heroin?"

"Jesus. Sometimes meth. Ecstasy too. Any pills, really. He liked to get high. Who doesn't?" With this he downed the drink, the glass still filled to the brim with ice, not yet having had a chance to melt. Before Perry could look up and refocus, Greg placed another full one in front of him.

"Fine," said Perry. He took a sip. "But it's my turn to ask some questions. What was he doing in Vermont?"

"His parents lived there. I guess he was going home."

"Why do you think he did it?"

Greg shook his head. "I don't know, Perry," he said. "I just don't know."

⟞⟊⟝

After New Year's, Tim finally, fully unpacked. The last of his bags and boxes were emptied. His dresser from IKEA was built and filled. He even hung a giant chalkboard over his bed, drawing on it a bright graffiti design of his name. He felt terrible about how things ended with Aaron and attempted to get in touch several times to apologize. But Aaron wouldn't return his calls, and his messages were met with silence. Days passed, and then weeks. He realized that it was time to move on—time to regroup and get his life together. He didn't force himself through school, battle debt, and leave his family behind to move to the city to fail. Slowly he started to feel everything was getting back on track—his apartment, his job. Then he received a call from Nikki, and everything changed.

Nikki and Tim sat on his bed with Mr. Boo Berry lying between them. The small gray-bluish kitten was finally asleep. Nikki had brought Boo over hours before. Boo was going to stay at his apartment, and she was due to fly again that night. The day of the murder, she was out of town. When she returned, Aaron's door was open. A cop was standing outside. Behind him, she could see more police and the building's superintendent. She asked what happened. She was so taken aback that a police officer had to unlock her door for her and help her inside. Once she calmed down, another joined and asked her a lot of questions. She told them about Hank—about how he was staying there, and how she went over a couple of times to see Aaron but could never get past him. He seemed to have taken up residence on their front stoop too. He was always there smoking. He was a creep and made her feel uncomfortable. As she spoke with them, the moments she saw and took away from inside Aaron's apartment kept coming back to her—huge dark circles of dried blood on the floor, blood everywhere, everything topsy-turvy. Aaron always kept his place so neat, so welcoming. And there was an odor. Even being next door, she imagined she was still breathing it in. Was it rotten eggs? Soil? She couldn't get the sight out of her head. She couldn't get that smell out of her nostrils.

"Are you sure it's okay if I look after him?" asked Tim.

"Of course," responded Nikki. "Aaron's parents were glad that I was looking after him initially, and we've been in contact. They said they were happy for me to find him a good home. They have enough to deal with right now. And his mother said that keeping Boo herself would be too much to bear right now. I also spoke with Greg and Rick. What happened is in the past. They knew things weren't right romantically between you guys. It's rubbish how it ended, but everything is different now."

"I'll give Boo a good home."

"Of course you will, love. Of course you will. I don't know how I can stay in that flat. I feel so rattled."

"It's horrible," said Tim. "You said the police caught him. Hank?"

"He was hiding in some kind of snowboard shop—at least that's what it used to be. Greg said it was mostly vacant, but there was a sofa or studio off the back. He was there for days, apparently. Burlington, Vermont. That was the place. Then he called his parents. The NYPD had already been in contact with local police."

"I wish we had the death penalty in New York," said Tim.

"Life in prison sounds worse. He didn't put up a fight when he was arrested."

"He must have known the police were going to catch him."

"I would think so, but who knows?" said Nikki. "He's obviously not right in the head." Boo stretched his front paws, flickered his ears, and then fell back asleep. The pair stared down at him, Nikki's eyes full of tears.

"This poor kitten," said Tim. "I can't believe he was alone in there all that time."

"It's just the worst."

"So his parents told the cops where Hank was staying?"

"Wouldn't you if your son did something like that?"

"I've never been with someone who died," said Tim. "It's a really weird feeling. It wasn't all bad, not by a long shot. Who knows?

Maybe it would have worked out between us. Maybe if I wasn't such a turd, he wouldn't have taken Hank in." He was crying again.

"Don't think too much about that, love," said Nikki. She edged herself from the bed and stood. Looking into a mirror above the dresser, she ran the tips of her fingers through her bangs. Then she took out a small compact and applied powder and eyeliner to her face. "In a way, I'm glad I have to fly tonight. I'm not looking forward to returning to that apartment."

"Call me as soon as you get back," said Tim. "If you want, I can meet you there." He looked down at Boo. "I wouldn't want to leave this little guy alone for too long, but I'm sure he'd be okay for one night if you want me to crash on your couch."

"That's a very sweet offer," said Nikki. She turned from the mirror to face Tim. "There's something I haven't told you, something you should probably know."

"What is it?" Tim was petting Boo's tiny head carefully. He stopped and looked up.

"When Hank stole Aaron's wallet, there was a picture of you guys in it. You, Aaron, Greg, and Rick. It was from New Year's Eve. It was in one of the free rags with party photos. Aaron must have ripped it out and put it in his wallet."

"The photographer from the Empire Toy Party," said Tim. "I never thought to look. There was so much happening."

Tim felt the blood rush from his face. "So this Hank, the killer..."

"He had your picture in Aaron's wallet when he was arrested."

"That's creepy," he said. "Do you think we have anything to worry about? Do you think the police will question me?"

"Hank is being charged tomorrow in court. Then he can be sent to New York for the trial. You don't have anything to worry about. He confessed to the murder. Everyone knows he did it, and he's not trying to hide it. It's second degree, maybe identity theft too. Who knows what else they'll throw at him. It might even be considered a hate crime. He's going away for a long time. I thought you should know about the photo. There are reporters covering this, and they came to the building this morning. Only your first names were printed with the photo. I saw a copy of it from the boys. I really don't think you have anything to worry about, but thought you should know. Copies are still floating around. Someone could spot Aaron and you guys together, maybe bring it up if they know you. Or someone in the media could put it all together and run the photo, I suppose."

"How could this have happened?" asked Tim. "How could Aaron have let this guy into his life like that?"

"I guess his good nature got the better of him."

CHAPTER TWENTY

S aint Clement's Episcopal Church opened its doors in 1920 to a diverse congregation. A much smaller church by the same name farther south shuttered its doors and built the larger, more functional version after a loyal member with no children or next of kin died. The benefactor's only request was that the congregation widen its acceptance to the community so that all could be comforted by the love and forgiveness of the Lord.

The building was constructed on West Forty-Sixth Street several doors east from the place that would become—some seventy-odd years later—Aaron's last apartment. This particular section of Midtown West at the time was a densely populated, first-generation immigrant community, predominantly Irish and Puerto Rican, the bulk of both having come through Ellis Island within a couple of decades of each other. The area also housed Broadway actors, producers, directors, stagehands, musicians, and scores of others needed to put on big shows several blocks away in New York's growing Theater District. When the old congregation hit the streets and knocked on doors with a welcoming message to their new church, they succeeded in collecting a much more diverse group than they had been.

Saint Clement's was built from local clay bricks that quickly turned from a bright orange to a warm tawny. Five narrow, stained-glass windows towered above the street alongside a large red door. The windows depicted images from stories about God the Father, the birth of Christ, the crucifixion, Christ rising, and, lastly, Christ in heaven sitting atop a throne, ready to judge the living and dead. These were angled to direct focus and sunlight to an altar on the opposite wall. To the left of the altar stood the thick brass pipes of a large organ, and to its right a circular pulpit raised several steps high.

The theme of diversity continued over the years from what started as honoring the benefactor of Saint Clement's to a mantra that kept the church full. In the early days, Irish families filled the pews early on Sundays, and at noon the minister delivered to the Puerto Rican worshipers a service that was—at least in part—in Spanish. The basement evolved into a community resource, with half of it dedicated to a functioning soup kitchen. The other half was fashioned into a working black-box theater where aspiring actors and musicians practiced and performed, drawing small crowds for shows that helped fund the charities of the church.

Over the years, the brick facade took on an even darker, reddish hue, the stained glass that once shined bright gently faded, and layers of thickly coated paint amassed on the low, iron gate that protected the front entrance. But inside, away from the city's often-brash temperaments and extreme temperatures, the wood of the pews was well-oiled and the pipes of the organ well-polished. A succession of ministers and their families spent lifetimes keeping the church clean, warm, and safe. While the makeup of people in the neighborhood around Saint Clement's changed, its mission stayed the same. It was a space where everyone was welcomed to join hands and take sanctuary.

Almost six weeks had passed since Aaron's murder. His killer was extradited to New York, where he was awaiting trial, a judge ordering that he remain in custody without bail. While Aaron's family held a funeral in Virginia, his friends wanted to have a celebration of his life in New York. It would be another four months until Hank was sentenced, twenty-three years to life.

In the vestibule of the church, Greg spoke quietly with a fellow bartender from the neighborhood—a muscled pretty boy who worked at the Ritz. He was helping set up the black-box theater space in the basement for a reception after the service.

The pews were full, and a low murmur ended when Greg eventually ascended to the pulpit. He pulled at the knot of his tie with one hand and clutched tightly his notes in the other. He wasn't used to dressing up. Looking down, he saw Rick, Linda, and Allen sitting up front. Rick had his arm around Linda, who looked as though she had been crying, eyes red, cheeks swollen. Directly behind them were Nikki, Tim, and two girls with droopy eyes who looked a little stoned. Friends of Nikki's, no doubt, Greg thought, smiling to himself. Quite a motley crew.

In the back of the church, behind the last row, Perry stood alone, his head hung, his cheeks sunken, his frame thin. Perry couldn't get Hank's face out of his head. He had doubled his efforts to numb his mind since hearing the news about Hank being the murderer. He thought about visiting him in jail, trying to find out what really happened, why he did it. But knew he could never bring himself to step foot inside a prison with all those police around. He'd never go, not without being dragged in kicking and screaming. But Perry was like everyone else that was touched by Aaron and the murder. He craved answers, closure.

"People knew Aaron as a son, an older brother, a neighbor, a colleague, a friend," Greg spoke gently. "He was the first person to help in any situation. He would go out of his way to help others. When a friend lost power and water to his building last year, Aaron let him stay with him. He helped another paint her apartment. He always brought too much wine and beer to dinner parties. He even helped friends move, which in New York, where elevators are a luxury, is no small effort."

Some in the crowd laughed a little. Greg shifted his feet, wiped his brow, and looked down. He unintentionally looked at Tim, who started to cry.

"But Aaron's charity went further," said Greg. "Few people knew—actually, I don't know if anyone knew—that Aaron made a lot of small donations. He wasn't a wealthy man in the traditional sense, but he was a generous one. I discovered this early in our friendship. He once gave away an umbrella, while it was pouring, to an older woman on the street as we were walking into a bar. He said he got it free from a Red Cross donation. They didn't want his blood, but he was still determined to help. Aaron also had a blanket over the back of his couch that I noticed had a Wounded Warrior Project logo on it. When asked, he just said that his grandfather was a veteran. And I never noticed until I was helping his parents clean out his apartment..." Greg paused, looking down. He tried to smile a little before continuing. "Almost every mug in his kitchen was from a different charity: the Ronald McDonald House, Action Against Hunger, the Animal Welfare Institute. It's a small thing about Aaron that most people probably didn't know. But he really was one of the good guys. He was also my best friend, and he got a raw deal. I guess he tried to help…let in one person too many."

⏤⏃⏂⏤

Normally, the large square room in the basement with high ceilings and black walls housed bleachers, but those were stacked and stored. With the help of some neighborhood friends who had theater connections, Greg converted the space into something of a popup bar with chairs, tables, lighting, and a decent sound system. He even brought in some staff and glasses from the Saloon and purchased booze and mixers at cost through the bar's vendors.

Everyone was welcomed. Everyone was invited. Aaron's murder affected not only the people who knew him, but others in Hell's Kitchen who wondered how something like this could happen in their relatively close-knit community. People died. Murders happened every day in the city. But not the way Aaron died. And certainly not in their neighborhood like this. Or at least that's what they thought before.

Tim sat with a small contingent at a round table in one corner. He felt particularly shaken by the murder, guilty for the way things ended with Aaron. He had messed up, and he knew it. Worst of all, he never had the chance to properly apologize. His two roommates were with him. Since moving in, they had become friends and wanted to go with him for support. They were also huge fans of Mr. Boo Berry. Tim's sister came from Long Island, trying to make amends. Their mother finally moved out, and his sister wanted Tim to be in her son's life again. She conceded that her son needed better role models if he was going to break their family's cycle and make it when he was an adult. And his cool uncle who was already making it in New York City was just the guy.

Greg, Rick, and Linda sat at a table on the opposite side of the room. They were glad that Tim was there, even if they weren't going to suddenly be best friends with him. People messed up. They all shared a common history. And Tim was obviously trying to make good on something that could never really be remedied. By all accounts, he was looking after Aaron's cat very well. That too counted for something.

Music played and drinks flowed. People mingled to and from a makeshift bar. It was rumored that someone was going to perform. Three girls sat on a sofa—a leftover prop—in front of a small, flat stage. They chatted away, seeming to talk over each other. Four primped guys stood around a large plastic bucket filled with ice and beer, cracking jokes about a recent episode of "Mob Wives"—preferring, like some, to talk about anything lighter than the reason they were all there. Even Linda's father drove down from Westchester in his best Wall Street suit to be there for his only daughter. He chatted with two of her female colleagues, trying to syphon information about Allen and how they met.

Aaron's parents, Barbara and Henry, couldn't help but smile at the colorful cast of characters that came to celebrate Aaron and his life. It had been the worst few weeks of their lives, and while they would never truly get over their son's tragic demise, they had faith that they would eventually live again one breath at a time. Their daughter—Aaron's younger sister—stayed close and reminded them of something that her therapist told her. Allowing a smile or laugh when mourning and not trying to push it down or feel guilty was like coming up for air while drowning. She liked that metaphor.

From the entrance of the black box entered the lanky male shop worker from City Bitches that everyone knew—the tight one from the front window with all the puppies. He was escorting Layde Licious. She was wearing a long, black, mod dress, and her veil was weaved into a platinum, feathered wig. Layde immediately made her way over to Baxter and Carlos—two burly men who were helping her organize her number. A handsome blond man and a woman trailed from behind, already looking a little unsteady on their feet. Within minutes, Layde took the stage and was handed a microphone.

"Aaron was a member of our community, this community," said Layde. "He will be missed, but certainly not forgotten. If there is one thing that Aaron put into the world, it was love. Love for his friends. Love for his family. Love of people. It is especially difficult in the face of such tragedy to remember love and hold onto it. But if there is one thing we can be sure Aaron would want of us, it is for us to continue to try to love, before it's too late."

From speakers overhead came an instrumental version of a Donna Summer classic. Layde took a step forward into the light, inhaling deeply to fill her chest, raising her head high.

Last dance
Last chance for love

A young guy not dressed properly for the occasion, only wearing a black tank top with a huge knitted scarf, moved right to the front of the stage. His friend followed and put an arm around him. In turn, they were followed by a sort of small man-child with a slight frame. Soon others from around the room joined, moving closer to Layde, moving closer together.

Oh, oh, I need you by me
Beside me, to guide me

Closest to the stage were a group of middle-aged men in much black and some leather, smiling, swaying. Sandwiched next to them and the couch where the girls still sat were some younger guys with their mouths open in awe. Layde was beautiful and hitting a nerve. From the other side of the couch came Sean, the handsome, second barback from the Saloon. He held his hand high in the air in a fist and flashed Layde his best pearly white smile. Her tempo climbed. Everyone was moving with the music, swaying, dancing.

So let's dance, the last dance

One large man opposite the stage, turning in circles, looked to be half in drag, wearing blue pants, a giant, dark-red flannel shirt, and a red wig with locks. A nervous-looking girl with red, puffy cheeks stepped out of the way just in time to miss being trampled by him. She smiled. From behind them, a cute blond guy snapped a photo above his head of the crowd—just for posterity's sake, he thought. In the center of it, a smart woman wearing a kimono-like black dress was kissing a young guy who looked like a rock star, of sorts. Greg, Rick, and Linda stood off to one side—out of the spotlight—in a row with their arms around each other.

C'mon, baby
Last dance tonight

Layde held the last high note with unwavering strength. When it ended, the music ended, and the lights over the stage went out.

CHAPTER TWETY-ONE

O'Brien's Grill on the Hudson River—west of Hell's Kitchen—
maintained a large outdoor space with umbrellas, tables,
and chairs. It was flanked between the Circle Line, a boat-touring
company for tourists, and the *Intrepid,* an aircraft carrier turned
museum. From the outdoor-seating area, the bank of New Jersey
was visible clear across the water. Sailboats, launches, cruise ships,
and even an industrial tanker were either moored close by or moving up and down the river.

Linda arrived at just past four in the afternoon to secure a table
before Friday's after-work crowd took over. It was the first really nice
day of late spring. The air finally felt still and warm. A deep blue sky
held a few wispy, high clouds, promising a spectacular sunset. She
was ordering a pitcher of margaritas and nachos when she spotted
Greg and Rick walking toward her from behind the waitress.

"There they are," she said, standing and waving. She removed
her sunglasses to get a better look. Greg was wearing only jeans

and a T-shirt, but Rick was still in dress pants and a buttoned-down shirt, a sports jacket slung over one shoulder.

"Linda, darling," said Rick on approach.

"Boys," she replied. "Always a pleasure. So glad you could make it on such short notice. I couldn't let this day go by without getting outside for a few hours."

"I'll get this in," said the waitress.

"And three waters, please," added Rick. "Gosh, it is beautiful here. I feel like it's been forever." There was a moment of silence while Rick and Greg took in the surroundings. There was tons of foot traffic, surprisingly so since it was early in the season. Locals strolling, running, skating, and biking passed between throngs of tourists, everyone moving north or south around each other, seeming like they might collide at any moment, but somehow never doing so.

"It has been forever," echoed Greg a minute later as the margaritas arrived.

"Are you meeting up with Allen later?" asked Rick.

"Don't start," said Linda.

Greg shot Rick a look.

"What," asked Rick coyly. "I'm just asking. It's a legitimate question."

"Well, I might see him," she said. "As it happens, I haven't decided yet. You know he's a hundred days clean next week."

"NA, right?" asked Greg.

"Yes. And he's also seeing a shrink who specializes in career counseling. It turns out the high-stakes broker lifestyle and a sober one don't mix well."

"That seems pretty obvious," said Rick.

Allen and Linda reconnected as the events in March started to unfold. He was as stunned as she was at what went down. In the following weeks, he was very supportive to her and the group—more than just emotionally. Right before the service in New York, Allen helped establish a memorial trust fund that was to give scholarships to underprivileged teens. He even kicked in five figures at the start. He said it was the best way he could contribute to trying to create something positive from such a rotten situation.

After a lot of consideration, Linda decided she wanted to give Allen a chance to redeem himself. She was used to being single and not accustomed to a relationship needing work. In the wake of the recent tragedy, she was struck with the feeling that life was short and fragile. She wanted to pull people closer, not push them away. A second chance was okay, but a third wouldn't be forthcoming, she told herself. She and Allen were also talking about taking a vacation together—maybe Aruba in a month or so. It seemed they both needed to look forward to something and wanted an escape together. She thought about the two of them on a beach in the Caribbean, white sand, bright sun. They could even scuba dive.

Looking from the Hudson River, glistening from the low sun above, Linda turned to Greg. "So how do you like being an owner?" she asked.

"Well, it's not official yet," he said. "We're still drawing up the papers. But if everything goes well, we should sign soon."

"It's very exciting," said Rick. "I'm very proud of you." He reached over and squeezed Greg's knee.

Greg was in discussions about a small part of ownership of the Saloon. There were four owners already, though none of them had appetite any longer to be active in the day-to-day operations of the business. Greg was the obvious contender, as they unanimously felt they needed someone there whom they knew and trusted, someone responsible and vested. For the first year, Greg would earn almost nothing from the business. But after that year, he would hold a 10 percent share in profits on top of drawing a modest general manager's salary. And if he picked up shifts, he could take home tips too. The first year would be a struggle, but with Rick's contribution from his new job, the couple figured they could swing it.

While Rick was still relatively new to the agency, he had a growing role in the fledgling content studio that was rapidly gaining ground. He was in a great position to steer the growth of new productions. There was even talk of him co-producing the next video project with a credit. The group was finding traction in creating music videos shot at five-star hotels and Michelin-starred restaurants. B-list, indie label musicians with extensive, existing followers were being tapped to be featured in highly produced music videos at no cost to them. The sponsor was paying for their venue to be used as the location. The idea was that the sponsor received only a thank you credit, but no funding credit for the projects. And every video was to be distributed through a third party not attached to the agency. It was a new revenue stream that Rick was helping develop, and it was already showing results.

"With the way things are going at work," said Rick, "we should be in good shape for the next year or so."

"At least," said Linda. "From the sales side, several people on our team are almost solely focused this quarter on your sponsored video strategy. I'll see to it personally, if I have to, that we get at least a couple of big names on the books before the summer."

"This sounds a bit like insider politics," said Greg.

Linda laughed. "I'm game for whatever brings in sales with a hefty commission."

"I'll deliver," said Rick. "We'll make it work."

"Speaking of commission," said Greg, "at what stage do we try to make some money off of the Mr. Boo Berry franchise?"

"Those photos are so adorable," said Linda. "I'm really not a cat person, but even I couldn't resist printing one and putting it on my refrigerator."

"The one where he's sitting with the mini-guitar and the mohawk?" asked Greg. "What does it say, 'I'm naming my band Boo'?"

Linda cut in, "So that when people boo, they'll really be cheering me on."

"Funny, I haven't seen that one," said Rick. "I did appreciate the one where he's sitting in a slow cooker with 'honey' written on the outside, and it just says below, Honey Boo Berry."

"Too cute," said Linda topping up everyone's glasses with margarita from the pitcher.

"My favorite?" asked Greg. "It's the one where he's sticking his head out of an Abercrombie & Fitch shopping bag, and it looks like it's his head on a beefy guy's body."

Rick and Linda both said at the same time, "Hey, I'm Boo. How you doin'?"

The photos were Nikki's idea. She and Tim were drinking wine and hanging out in his room several weeks back. She had finished a long stretch of flights and had some time in New York to recoup before flying again. Tim wasn't very talkative. His room looked well lived in. There were clothes on the floor and several empty glasses on the nightstand. Mr. Boo Berry was trying to get his attention but wasn't very successful. Tim had this stuffed rock-and-roll teddy bear with a leather jacket and guitar on his dresser. Nikki decided then and there that Boo needed some rebranding, and Tim needed a project. Nikki cracked a window and pulled a doobie from her purse. She and Tim spent the rest of the night planning the unsuspecting kitten's meteoric rise to global fame. There would be posters, groupies—maybe even an international tour. But first, he needed a striking headshot. Later that night at his desk, Tim started playing with text around the photo. In the following days, the kitten took on a wide range of characters, each thoughtfully crafted. The cat didn't understand what was happening or why he was being dressed up and propped into various positions. But he didn't mind one bit. He loved the attention and started purring loudly every time he suspected another photo shoot was about to take place.

Greg, Rick, and Linda watched the sun set over the Hudson River while Manhattan moved and spun around them. They finished the pitcher of margaritas by the time the waitress brought the nachos, so they ordered another. There was still plenty of sun in the sky, and summer hadn't even started yet.

ACKNOWLEDGMENTS

Thank you, Marisa Laureni, Melissa Bedrick, Danny Petre, Adrienne Smith, and the team at Amazon's CreateSpace for your invaluable feedback and edits, and Art Boonklan for your brilliant cover design. You helped transform a rough manuscript into a book.

Thank you to my family, especially Peter Petrone, Paige Petrone, Judith Petrone, and, of course, my mother. Your love and support helped catapult this book into the real world.

A special thank you to my partner, Alex Brown, for your feedback, edits, love and support, and, most importantly, for your unrelenting encouragement along the way. Without you, I would have never had the grit and gumption to see this project through.

ABOUT THE AUTHOR

 Dennis Petrone currently lives in his hometown of New York City with his partner, Alex, and a small cat named Meep. He works in media as a manager and editor. He lived overseas in New Zealand for many years, where he eventually became a citizen. Before that, he studied literature and history at Colorado State University in Fort Collins. He enjoys adventure travel, reading, writing, and, above all, the transformative power of story.

51365673R00153

Made in the USA
Lexington, KY
20 April 2016